THE RUNAWAY WIVES

KAREN KING

B

Boldwood

First published in Great Britain in 2025 by Boldwood Books Ltd.

Copyright © Karen King, 2025

Cover Design by Head Design Ltd.

Cover Images: Shutterstock

The moral right of Karen King to be identified as the author of this work has been asserted in accordance with the Copyright, Designs and Patents Act 1988.

Every effort has been made to obtain the necessary permissions with reference to copyright material, both illustrative and quoted. We apologise for any omissions in this respect and will be pleased to make the appropriate acknowledgements in any future edition.

A CIP catalogue record for this book is available from the British Library.

Paperback ISBN 978-1-83617-605-3

Large Print ISBN 978-1-83617-606-0

Hardback ISBN 978-1-83617-604-6

Ebook ISBN 978-1-83617-607-7

Kindle ISBN 978-1-83617-608-4

Audio CD ISBN 978-1-83617-599-5

MP3 CD ISBN 978-1-83617-600-8

Digital audio download ISBN 978-1-83617-601-5

This book is printed on certified sustainable paper. Boldwood Books is dedicated to putting sustainability at the heart of our business. For more information please visit https://www.boldwoodbooks.com/about-us/sustainability/

Boldwood Books Ltd, 23 Bowerdean Street, London, SW6 3TN

www.boldwoodbooks.com

For all the women who've been brave enough to start all over again.
And for those who want to. You're never too old for second chances.

PROLOGUE

Sender: reservations@vistamaravilha.com
Subject: Confirmation of Booking

Dear Mr Parkins,

Attached is confirmation of your booking for our luxury villa for the week 17-24 May.

The housekeeper, Aline, will meet you at the villa with the keys at 2 p.m. on Saturday 17 May.

We trust that you will enjoy your stay at Vista Maravilha.

Best wishes,

Dinis Kaminski

1

DEE

Friday

'Has Nige mentioned your surprise birthday holiday yet?' Babs asked, taking a big bite out of her chocolate éclair. Cream oozed from the sides onto her fingers and she licked it off slowly.

Dee shook her head as she took the froth off her cappuccino with her spoon and put it in her mouth. 'He hasn't said a dicky bird. I wouldn't have known anything about if I hadn't seen the booking email come through on his phone.'

Nigel had been in the shower on Sunday, having just returned from a game of golf, leaving his phone on the kitchen table, when the email notification had pinged. As the screen lit up, Dee had automatically glanced at it, surprised to see the subject line 'Confirmation of Booking'. She'd opened the email and quickly read it, amazed and delighted to see that Nigel had booked a villa for a week in the Algarve, Portugal, for this weekend. It was her sixtieth birthday on Saturday, so he must have booked it as a surprise present for her. Goodness knows, she'd dropped enough hints about wanting to go abroad for a holiday this year, and was delighted that he had taken notice. It was uncharacteristically thoughtful of him. Usually, he took her out for a nice dinner or bought her a bottle of perfume – courtesy of his PA, she was sure – but this year he'd really pushed out the boat. Well, sixty was a big birthday, wasn't it? She'd heard Nigel coming down the stairs so quickly marked the email as unread and put the phone back on the table. She'd excitedly waited all week for him to mention it, but he hadn't said a word. He must be planning on keeping it a surprise until tomorrow morning, her actual birthday, before whisking her away immediately.

'Men, they're hopeless, aren't they? I mean it's a lovely surprise but surely he must realise that you need to buy new clothes to take? It's lucky you saw the email, so you could get some. And that you know his password.' Babs finished the last bite of her éclair and picked up the serviette to wipe her mouth, leaving a smudge of red lipstick on the white paper. She always wore red lipstick, it was the first thing she put on when she got up. She said it gave her confidence to face the day. Confidence was something Dee didn't think Babs was lacking in, she was always unapologetically herself, with a louder than life personality, chin-length blonde hair (although it was courtesy of the hairdresser now), bubbly and big-hearted. She always wore colourful clothes too. Today she was wearing coral cropped trousers with a brightly patterned top and white sandals. Dee preferred a more elegant, toned-down look and knew that, with her short, highlighted hair, crisp white cotton slacks and tailored blue and white shirt, she and Babs made an odd couple.

Nigel had told her so often enough. He disapproved of Barbara – he refused to call her Babs – because he thought she was too loud and brash, although he got on quite well with her husband, Geoff, when they occasionally went out as a foursome. It was the only subject on which Dee ignored him. She had been friends with Babs since high school and that bond remained to this day. And with Nigel working away so often, she didn't know what she'd have done without Babs to share a coffee or phone chat with over the years. She had other friends of course, but not close friends. Babs was the only one she could confide in, and she knew Babs felt the same way.

Dee looked down at the pile of carrier bags under the table by her chair, containing a couple of tankinis, three summer dresses, new sandals and a matching handbag. She had plenty of clothes, her wardrobes were bursting actually, but this was a special occasion and Nigel would expect her to be suitably dressed up. 'Nigel always uses the same password and adds a couple of letters on the end related to the subject, so in the case of his phone he adds an "N" and "P" – for Nigel's phone.'

'I bet he thinks you aren't clever enough to remember that,' Babs said.

'More than likely. Anyway, I'll put these in my suitcase ready. He's probably planning on telling me in the morning and expecting me to pack in a few minutes.'

'It's really romantic, jetting off on your actual birthday.' Babs sounded envious. 'I didn't think Nige had it in him.'

'I was surprised too,' Dee admitted. Nigel didn't usually have a romantic bone in his body, he was a very practical, unsentimental man, but then he was a solicitor so it was part of the job criteria she guessed. 'I don't know what's come over him.'

'A whole week in a villa in the sun, I envy you,' Babs said. 'It's been ages since we went away. When it was my sixtieth a couple of months ago, I didn't even get a weekend away. Although we did have a lovely family party,' she added. 'Molly and Lennon both came home for that.' Bab and Geoff's daughter, Molly, was cabin crew with Emirates and travelled to lots of exotic locations, and their son, Lennon, worked in London combining acting, with part-time bar work at a trendy nightclub. Babs was very proud of them both.

Dee still couldn't believe that Nigel had booked such a wonderful surprise for her. They had been married for thirty-five years now. However, since their children, Annabel and Hugh, had grown up and flown the nest, she and Nigel had both sort of trundled along doing their own thing. Annabel lived an hour's drive away and was busy juggling her work as a designer with looking after two-year-old, Hallie, whilst Hugh was an events manager in Edinburgh. Nigel spent most of his weekends golfing with his mates, and had even gone on a couple of golfing holidays, leaving Dee home alone. Babs had told her she should book herself holidays away, too, but Dee didn't fancy going away alone. Besides, she actually liked a few days to herself when she could do what she wanted without Nigel's constant critical comments. He had high standards and liked everything to be 'just so'. Dee liked a clean and tidy home herself, but she didn't feel the need to have the furniture gleaming so much you could see your face in it, like her husband did. Nigel could be hard work, and they'd had a few rough patches when the children were younger, but they'd come through it. Maybe – now he was older – he was starting to appreciate her more?

Or was it guilt? Was he—

She realised Babs was speaking and snapped out of her thoughts, focusing on her friend who was now spooning sugar into her coffee. She envied Babs' ability to be herself, to eat cream cakes if she wanted to, have two spoons of sugar, to not be bothered if she carried an extra pound or two. Dee had pushed the boat out and had a cappuccino and cookie today, because being with Babs always tempted her to forget the diet she was constantly on. Nigel said that Babs was too loud, too fat, too out there. But, as Dee told him, Babs had a big personality and a big heart to match. Her and Geoff would help anyone out.

'Sorry, I was miles away...'

'I could see that,' Bab said with a grin. 'Imagining yourself sunbathing at the villa in Portugal, were you?' She cocked her head to one side. 'Knowing Nige, it's very posh.'

'Well, I only saw a quick glimpse of the picture before I heard Nigel coming down, but yes, it did look rather luxurious, and there's an enormous pool.'

Babs sighed. 'What more could you want?'

'I must say I am looking forward to it. It's been quite a while since Nigel and I went away together.' Dee finished the last of her cookie and looked thoughtfully at her friend. 'Is Geoff still trying to talk you into moving to Spain?'

Babs nodded. 'He's been doing up the house ready to sell up and move, even though I keep telling him I'm not going,' she said. 'Mind, it's been great to have all the repairs and odd jobs done, I've been waiting for him to get around to them for ages.'

It had been a bone of contention between Babs and Geoff since they had both retired a few months ago. They had often gone to Spain for their holidays over the years, especially since their children had grown up and left home. Geoff had never mentioned moving over there though, not until he'd actually retired and then he'd become obsessed with the idea.

'He doesn't shut up about it. Honestly, he's driving me mental. To be honest, I thought it was all talk and he would never actually want to do it. But...' Babs leaned forward and whispered, 'I found a stack of magazines in Geoff's divan drawer this morning when I was tidying up.'

Dee screwed her nose. 'Yuck! Do they even have those magazines any more? I thought it was all on the web nowadays. Not that that's any better—'

'Not porn, you idiot. Travel brochures and houses for sale. He went to one of those *A Place in the Sun* exhibitions the other week. He wanted me to go with him but I refused. He even suggested we should go on the programme but there's no way I'm going on the telly and then being pressured into buying something I don't want.'

'Goodness. He really *is* serious then?'

Babs shrugged. 'I'm not sure, it's been like a sort of joke between us, but now Geoff's started learning Spanish. I walked into the kitchen the other day and found labels in Spanish stuck on everything. And he says *"Buenos días!"* to me every morning and *"Hasta luego!"* when I go out.' She giggled. 'He really tries to sound Spanish too!'

Dee tittered, she could imagine Geoff, with his heavy Bristolian accent, trying to speak Spanish. 'Maybe it's just a phase, and it will pass if you ignore it?'

'I was hoping so but he keeps harping on. And – get this – he wants us to live in the middle of nowhere, surrounded by olive trees and perishing goats! He said he wants to "get away from it all and live off the land". I think he's having a "later life crisis".' Babs took a mouthful of her coffee, then put the cup back down. 'Well, bugger that. I'm going to tell him that I've found the magazines tonight and put a stop to this once and for all.'

Dee was sure there was no way Geoff would persist in moving to Spain if Babs put her foot firmly down. He doted on Babs and would never do anything to upset her. There were times that Dee had wished Nigel was so considerate; he always did what he wanted when he wanted. Still, Nigel had booked this lovely surprise holiday for her birthday treat, so maybe things were improving.

'Lucky you, heading off to a luxury villa, I could do with a bit of sunshine right now. It sounds like Nige is going to spoil you rotten. And about time too!' Babs told her. 'Now, do you want your present before you go or when you come back? I've got it with me, just in case.'

'Oh well, I might as well have it now,' Dee said with a smile.

Babs reached into the shopping bag she was carrying and took out a pretty floral gift bag. 'I thought it might come in handy for your holiday,' she said, handing it to Dee. 'It's not wrapped, so you can take a peek.'

'Thank you.' Dee opened the bag and took out a beautiful turquoise silk kimono and matching flip-flops. Turquoise was her favourite colour. 'Oh, they're gorgeous! Thank you so much.' She gave Babs a big hug. She really was a good friend.

'You're very welcome. Now, make sure you enjoy your holiday.'

2

BABS

Well, Nigel had certainly pulled out the stops this year, whisking Dee off for a week in Portugal for her birthday. Good, it was about time he looked after her instead of treating her like a jumped up housekeeper and secretary, Babs thought, as she walked up the hill from the station. She had considered taking the car, Geoff was home today so wouldn't be using it, but the parking in town was terrible.

Babs was surprised to see a smartly dressed woman with a clipboard walking away from the house as she approached the drive. The woman smiled at her and continued on her way. Had she been selling something, double glazing perhaps? Their windows were actually double glazed already, although they definitely needed upgrading. Not that the woman would get any custom from them. Geoff would have soon sent her packing, he didn't approve of door-to-door sales. If he wanted to buy something he went by recommendation, he said, and always did his research. No impulse buys for him. Babs was the opposite, thinking that people had to earn a living one way or another, and she often chatted to any salesperson who knocked on the door, even offering them a cup of tea, if Geoff wasn't around to disapprove.

She opened the door and walked in. 'I'm back.' She paused, looking around in surprise. Geoff had evidently been tidying up, which was a first for him, the shoes that were usually scattered in the hall had been put away, the coat rack that was normally overflowing with various coats and jackets was almost empty and there was a vase of fresh flowers on the little table in the hall.

'Oh, hello, dear. I didn't expect you home yet,' Geoff said, walking out of the lounge, looking a little flustered. He'd changed out of the gardening clothes he'd been wearing when she'd left this morning into navy cords and a short-sleeved light blue shirt, which made him look very smart. He'd even trimmed his beard. They must be having visitors. Why hadn't he messaged to let her know? She could have got a cake or some nice biscuits.

'Dee needed to get home, Nigel is whisking her away to Portugal tomorrow as a surprise holiday for her birthday,' Babs said as she walked past him into the lounge. Her eyes widened when she saw the plumped-up cushions on the sofa, another vase of fresh flowers on the sideboard, the freshly vacuumed carpet and magazine-free coffee table.

'How can it be a surprise if she knows about it?' Geoff asked.

'She found the booking email. Anyway, what's with the cleaning blitz? Are we expecting company?'

Geoff gave her a shifty look and she saw the beads of sweat forming on his bald head. Something fishy was going on. She frowned and folded her arms across her chest. 'Geoff?' Then a thought unfurled in her head. Geoff had been acting really out of character recently. And she'd heard about men going astray when they got to a certain age. Not Geoff though, surely? But what about the young woman she'd seen leaving as she came up the hill? Could she be Geoff's fancy woman? Never one to beat about the bush, she demanded, 'Who was that woman I saw leaving?'

Geoff fidgeted, straightening one of the perfectly straight, furry cream cushions on the burgundy velour sofa.

'Geoff, what's going on?' she snapped.

'Well, you know we talked about selling up and moving to Spain?' His eyes didn't quite meet hers but there was a determined tone to his voice.

'You talked about it, I said no,' Babs reminded him.

He coughed. 'Well, I thought I'd test the waters. So I asked an estate agent to come out and value the property...'

Phew! Not his fancy woman then. But an estate agent? He'd had an estate agent valuing their house? Babs stared at him, hardly believing he had arranged this behind her back. 'You've had the house valued?' she squeaked, plonking herself down onto the sofa.

Geoff nodded. 'And guess what, she said that we could easily get over four hundred thousand for it.' Excitement crept into his voice. 'That's quite a bit more than I expected. She said houses like ours are in great demand at the moment and she expects it to sell very quickly.'

Fury burned inside her. 'How bloody dare you arrange to have someone value the house while I was out. What a sneaky thing to do! Well, you've wasted your time because we are not putting the house on the market.'

Geoff played with his shirt collar. 'I sort of already have.'

'What the hell, Geoff?' She got to her feet. 'You can't be serious!'

'Oh, come on, Babs, what harm will it do to take a look? We could fly over to Spain and see what we can get for our money?'

He paused. 'Actually, truth be told, I've already gone ahead and booked us flights over there for next weekend. There's a nice little villa on the outskirts of Alora and I've lined up appointments with estate agents to view some spectacular properties. I was going to tell you this evening. I want us to be ready to go as soon as our house sells.'

Babs could hardly believe it. How dare he?

'Look at this one.' Geoff picked up the iPad from the coffee table, swiped the screen and tapped on it, then turned to show Babs a photo of a small white house surrounded by what looked like a forest of trees. 'It's got a pool.' He swiped the screen again and up came images of a large pool with a crack running along the stones at the top. 'And there are five bedrooms.' He swiped again and Babs stared in disbelief as image after image of small, dark bedrooms came up on the screen, then a galley kitchen that looked as if there wasn't room to swing a cat, and a largish lounge, but again very dark. 'And look at all the outdoor storage. I'd be busy in that garden all day.'

'And what do you think I'd be doing while you're in the garden?'

Geoff flicked an astonished look at her. 'Sunbathing. Or swimming in the pool. You'll love it!'

'I will not love it. There's no one around for miles,' Bab said through clenched teeth.

'What about this one then?' With a couple of taps Geoff brought up a photo of a large mustard coloured villa. 'This is light and airy.' He swiped to the next photo. 'And look at those views. Aren't they amazing?'

Babs eyes almost popped out of her head. 'It's halfway up a bloody mountain, Geoff! I am not going to live halfway up a bloody mountain!'

'There are plenty of other properties. I'm sure you'll like one of them. I've booked us a few viewings each day,' Geoff told her.

Babs silently counted to ten in her head. 'What part of "I don't want to move to Spain" don't you understand?' she demanded. 'I've told you over and over.'

'But you love Spain. We've been there loads of times.'

'I enjoyed holidaying in Spain, lying on the beach and drinking a few cocktails. I don't want to uproot and live there.'

'You'd love it if you gave it a chance, all that sun, and fresh air. Imagine waking up to a view of the mountains, orange and lemon trees growing in the garden, swimming in our own pool.'

'Miles away from Molly and Lennon and everything we know. And what happens when they settle down and have kids? We won't see our precious grandchildren grow up.' Babs flopped down onto the sofa. 'I'm not going, Geoff. I'm not selling up either, so you'd better tell the estate agent that the house isn't on the market. And you can cancel all the flights and holiday villa viewings too.'

'You're being unreasonable!' Geoff told her. 'You could at least consider the idea.'

'Me? Unreasonable? That's rich coming from a man who wants to sell my home from underneath me!'

'I can't believe you're being so selfish. You know how much I've dreamed about this. We both said when we sold the shop that we were going to relax and enjoy our life now. Live our dream.'

'This is not my dream, it's yours. I've made it perfectly clear that this is not what I want to do with my life,' Babs said firmly. 'I mean it, Geoff. I'm not selling up. Not now. Not ever. So you can jolly well tell the estate agent that you've made a mistake.'

'I don't actually need your permission to sell up,' Geoff told her, tilting his chin defiantly.

Babs sprang forward and narrowed her eyes. 'What are you saying?'

'This house is in my name. You can't stop me selling it.'

As the words came out of his mouth he looked guilty and stared down at the floor, avoiding her eyes. He was ashamed of what he'd said, she realised. And so he jolly well should be. Yes, the house was in his name. He'd inherited it when his parents had died within a year of each other thirty years ago, along with the corner shop they'd owned. She and Geoff had lived in the house and worked in the shop ever since, until the shop had been compulsory purchased last year to make way for a new major road. The house and shop might have been in Geoff's name but they'd been married for thirty-seven years and she'd paid towards all the repairs the house needed, helped with the additional mortgage they'd needed to update it, and contributed to the expenses. She'd also worked unpaid in the bloody shop whilst bringing up Molly and Lennon, which hadn't been an easy feat. There were times when she'd wished she could spend more time with their children, but she'd buckled down and got on with it. She was Geoff's wife, she had stuck by his side through thick and thin, and now he was threatening to sell their home from underneath her.

'Of course I don't want to do that. I want you to come with me,' Geoff said, he had that stubborn look on his face. 'But I'm going to live in Spain. I want to enjoy the last years of my life. And if you don't want to come... well, maybe I'll go without you!'

He wouldn't do it. Not Geoff. He wouldn't sell the house and leave her homeless.

Would he?

3

DEE

When Dee pulled up at her house she saw Nigel's silver BMW in the drive. He'd come home early then, probably to pack. Butterflies of excitement fluttered in her stomach as she picked up her bags of shopping and went in. 'Nigel!'

He was in the kitchen, rummaging through his wallet. He'd obviously finished work some time ago, as he'd left this morning wearing his dark blue suit and blue and white striped shirt. He'd changed into beige slim-fit chinos, a white Ralph Lauren polo top and what looked like a new pair of brown loafers. Although Nigel was sixty-four, he had a full head of silver, expertly styled hair, and always kept himself trim and fit. He was still a handsome man, she thought admiringly. Nigel liked to look after himself, and he expected Dee to do the same. He glanced over at her. 'You've been on a bit of a shopping spree, by the look of it,' he said, looking pointedly at the bags she was carrying. 'What's the occasion?'

She giggled. 'Very funny. Pretending that you've forgotten.'

'Forgotten what?' Nigel was still rummaging through his wallet. 'Now, where did I put it?'

'What are you looking for?' Dee asked.

'My bank card— ah, here it is.'

Dee suddenly noticed his suitcase. 'Is the flight tonight?'

'Early in the morning, so I've booked a room in a hotel near the airport.'

'Gosh, you could have told me. What time do we have to leave? I'll only need half an hour or so to pack.' Thank goodness she'd bought all these new clothes today, she could simply put them straight into her case. It was already packed with the essentials.

'Pack? What do you mean?' Nigel peered through his designer spectacles at her, his slate-grey eyes puzzled. 'Where are you going?'

'With you. To Portugal. Stop teasing, I know about the surprise. I saw the booking for the villa.'

Nigel's jaw dropped open. 'You want to come?'

Dee started to feel a bit uneasy. 'Of course I want to come. You've booked it for us, haven't you? As my birthday surprise.'

The stunned look that swept across Nigel's face couldn't have been faked. 'When's your birthday?'

'Tomorrow,' Dee said slowly. 'It's my sixtieth.'

Nigel slammed his forehead with the heel of his hand. 'Sorry. I forgot! I thought it was next month.'

Dee looked at the suitcase, then at Nigel. 'So the villa isn't a birthday surprise for me...?'

'Er... no, I'm going golfing with the lads. Didn't I tell you? We managed to get a brilliant late offer.' Nigel glanced at his Rolex. 'And I have to go. Sorry, love. I'll bring you something nice back for your birthday.'

Dee stood rooted to the spot as Nigel kissed her on the forehead, grabbed his case and walked out of the house.

He was actually going on a golfing holiday to Portugal without her on her birthday!

* * *

Dee sank down onto a kitchen chair, stunned. This was typical Nigel, she should have known that he wasn't planning a surprise trip for her. She couldn't remember the last time he'd ever arranged any kind of surprise.

She was so deep in thought that it took her a few minutes to realise that her phone was ringing. It might be Nigel, apologising, maybe even telling her to come – not that she would, she didn't want to be stuck in a villa with him and his golfing buddies. To her surprise, Babs' image was flashing on the screen. She hit accept.

'Sorry, I know you're probably busy with all your holiday preparations but I had to vent, I'm fuming!'

'What's happened?'

'Geoff has put the house on the market and decided that we're going to live in Spain. That's what's happened.'

'What?'

'Yep. He booked an appointment with an estate agent while I was out today! Apparently it goes on the market Monday and he's arranged for us to fly over to Spain next weekend and view some properties so we can be ready to go as soon as it sells. Can you believe it? Without even discussing it with me! Well, he can think again! I've told him he can jolly well cancel the sale *and* the trip to Spain.'

Dee couldn't believe it herself, this seemed completely out of character. She'd always thought of Geoff as being generally considerate and caring. Other than the big bone of contention between him and Babs about how much time and money he spent on the garden, particularly in his shed, especially now they'd both retired. 'It's a wonder he doesn't move his bloody bed in there,' Babs often said, and Dee would gently point out that he might like a bit of time to himself and at least he was home. Dee often wished Nigel would spend more time at home.

'I think he's having his midlife crisis late,' Babs was saying. 'He's being selfish and inconsiderate, only thinking about what *he* wants to do with his life.'

Just like Nigel. Why did men think they could do whatever they pleased and the women would simply fit in? No wonder Babs was fuming! Though, Dee was sure Geoff wouldn't go ahead with his plans if Babs insisted that she didn't want to.

'Why don't you treat this trip away as a holiday?' Dee suggested as she helped herself to a large glass of chilled wine. 'You were saying how much you're craving sunshine, so here's your chance to get out of Bristol. And it might be nice to have a look around, some of those Spanish villas are amazing. You don't have to agree to buy one. Besides, Geoff might actually decide that he doesn't want to live over there once he's had a look around. He's probably bored now you're both retired, and looking for something to fill the time.'

'No chance! He's not looking at any villas. He's looking at sprawling farmhouses in the middle of nowhere, surrounded by olive trees and goats.' She could hear the anger in Babs' voice. 'Well, I'm not bloody doing it! I'm not upending my life and moving to another country because he's decided he wants to. And I've told him so.'

Dee couldn't imagine Babs and Geoff living in a remote place like that. They both loved company, that's why they enjoyed working in their corner shop, chatting to the customers every day. They were both really sociable. What on earth was Geoff thinking of?

'I don't blame you. And I'm sure when it comes to it, Geoff wouldn't want to live anywhere like that either,' she said. 'He probably got a bit carried away watching those programmes on TV.'

'He's like a dog with a bone, no matter what I say he goes on and on.' Babs paused. 'Sorry I didn't mean to phone and spoil your evening, I just needed someone to rant to. I bet you're having a glass of wine together and chilling out before you fly out tomorrow.' Her voice was still simmering with anger but the volume was lower now. 'What time are you leaving?'

'I'm not.'

'What? Why? Have you had a row?'

Dee gave an ironic laugh. 'Row? There wasn't even time to row. When I got home Nigel already had his suitcase packed and was out the house before I had time to draw breath.'

'What? But your surprise holiday... is he coming back for you? You're meant to be going tomorrow.'

'Well, it turns out that the surprise holiday was a golfing holiday for Nigel and his pals. He left half an hour ago, they're all staying overnight at a hotel at the airport.'

'But what about your birthday?' Babs sounded incredulous.

'Apparently, Nigel thought it was next month.'

'You mean he's gone off with his mates and left you all alone on your sixtieth birthday?' Babs said the words slowly as if she couldn't quite believe them.

'That's right.' Dee finished her wine and considered pouring another glass.

'So what are you doing right now?'

'Drinking wine. Want to join me?' she added on impulse. 'Bring a suitcase and stay over if you want. That'll show Geoff you're seriously peed off.'

'You know, I think I will. I'll be there in ten.'

* * *

Dee only had time to put another bottle of Pinot Grigio in the fridge to cool, open a packet of crackers and put them on a tray with some cheese, when Babs was at the door with a large suitcase and a taxi was reversing back down the drive.

'I've told him that I'm not coming back until he stops being an arsehole,' Babs declared as she left her suitcase in the hall then followed Dee into the lounge. 'He said I'm overreacting and hopes I've cooled down by the morning, and that we can have "a civil conversation" about this.' She dropped into the nearest chair. 'I've told him that there's no way on this earth I'll be changing my mind and agreeing to live in the back of the Spanish beyond with him.'

Dee handed her a glass of wine. Babs took a long gulp, then exhaled. 'I'm sorry, listen to me banging on when you've been left home alone for your sixtieth.' She took another gulp of wine. 'These bloody men, they don't deserve us!'

'They certainly don't.' Dee sat down on the sofa and curled her legs underneath her. 'Look, if you dig your heels in Geoff will have to listen. He can't sell the house if you don't agree.'

'The trouble is, he can.' Babs' heavily mascaraed eyes met hers. 'His parents left him the house and the shop when they died, remember? It's in his name.'

Dee stared at her in disbelief. 'You mean he's never added your name to the deeds?'

'No, and I didn't actually think about asking him to. It was his family home and I never dreamed that he would do anything like this.'

Dee digested this. 'You must have rights, surely? You're married. And you worked in the corner shop all those years.

Your money went towards the upkeep of the house,' she pointed out.

Babs nodded. 'I know, but it's Geoff's name on the deeds, not mine, so he can legally sell it without my signature. Mind, I'll make it bloody hard for him. I'll make sure no one wants to buy it. If he wants a battle, he can have one!'

This was awful, Dee thought. She couldn't believe Geoff was threatening to sell the house and move to Spain whether Babs agreed or not. And she knew Babs, the more Geoff pushed her into a corner the more she would rally against it. They could end up separating over this. And where would that leave Babs?

'What are you going to do?' Dee asked.

Babs looked at her over the rim of her wine glass. 'I'll tell you what I'm *not* going to do. I'm not going to stay at home and let him walk all over me. I'm going away for a few days. That's why I've brought a big suitcase with me.' She finished her wine. 'Why don't you come with me? That'll give Nige a shock.'

It was tempting, Dee thought. Babs was right, why should she spend her birthday week here alone while Nigel was living it up in Portugal.

'Are you serious?'

'Deadly!' Babs' eyes glinted. 'I'll tell Geoff I'm not coming back until he takes the house off the market and gives up on this ridiculous idea of living in Spain. If he can make decisions without me, then I can make them without him too.' She nodded adamantly. 'Let's find a hotel or a cottage somewhere by the sea and have ourselves a little break. I didn't think to bring my passport or we could have gone abroad and I can't be bothered to get a taxi back to the house for it now.' She frowned. 'Actually, Geoff must have needed it to book our flights.'

Dee was tempted. She didn't fancy staying here by herself while Nigel had a holiday in Portugal with his golfing buddies. It would be good to get away. A week by the sea sounded like a great idea.

'You know, I think I will.' Dee refilled both their glasses. 'Now, where shall we go?' Then she had an idea. 'How about Cornwall? I had some lovely holidays down there when the kids were young. And it's only May so there should still be some holiday cottages vacant.' She picked up her phone and opened her weather app. 'Look, it's mild and sunny at the moment. Lovely walking weather.'

'Sounds good to me.' A smile curled across Babs' lips. 'That'll show them.' She held out her glass. 'To us! The Runaway Wives.'

4

SATURDAY

The sun was shining brightly when Dee pulled open the bedroom curtains, a beautiful day to go away. It would be even sunnier in Portugal, she thought, then pushed the thought away. Today was her birthday and she wasn't going to let anything spoil it. Nigel was selfish, always had been and probably always would be. She had learnt long ago not to dwell on the unpleasant things he did, and instead concentrated on getting as much happiness as she could out of every day. She had a lot to be grateful for. She had amazing kids, a lovely home and enough money to do what she wanted. Besides, she would much rather go down to Cornwall with Babs and have a few days in a little cottage by the sea, than hang around on her own while Nigel and his friends played golf. She hadn't been on a girlie holiday for years and she was looking forward to it.

She hadn't heard a sound from the guest room next door and guessed that Babs had gone to sleep as soon as her head had hit the pillow. They'd stopped up late chatting and Babs had drunk rather a lot of wine, not that Dee blamed her after what Geoff had said, but Dee had swapped to soft drinks after two more small glasses. Babs had left their car at home so Dee would be doing the driving today and needed to keep a clear head.

She glanced at the clock, it was past ten already and she really wanted to leave before lunch. She picked up her phone from the dressing table and scanned the screen. There were a few messages. She always turned her notifications down at night, not wanting to be disturbed as she was a member of a couple of online global book groups and messages came in at all hours. Annabel and Hugh knew that if they needed her urgently it was best to phone.

She opened the messages one by one. There was one from Annabel wishing her a happy birthday and promising to take her out for lunch one of the days next week when Hallie had recovered from her cold, one from Hugh telling her a surprise was on the way, and a couple from friends. Then another message pinged in. It was from Nigel.

> Happy birthday, Dee. Sorry about the mix up. I'll make it up to you when I come back. I've put five hundred in your bank account so that you can treat yourself while I'm away. N x

That was typical of Nigel, he was generous with money but thought it could buy everything, that if he gave her enough she would forget anything he did.

She sighed, slipped her phone into her dressing gown pocket then went downstairs. She made a mug of tea and poured a glass of cold water, putting them on a small tray with some paracetamol. She had a feeling Babs would need them.

Ten minutes later she tapped on Babs' bedroom door. 'Babs! Are you awake?' she called.

Silence.

Dee put the tray she was carrying down on the hall unit, opened the door then picked the tray back up again, taking it into the room where Babs was lying in bed, her eyes closed, the back of her hand flung across her forehead. Her clothes were lying in a heap on the floor. Dee groaned, remembering countless holidays when they were younger when Babs' clothes and possessions had littered the room. It seemed that she hadn't grown out of her untidiness.

'Morning – just!' Dee said cheerily.

Babs opened her eyes a fraction. 'You look far too bright and cheerful for someone who's been downing wine half the night. Or was it only me drinking? It's all a bit of a blur.'

'This will make you feel better.' Moving Babs' phone over, Dee placed the tray on the bedside cabinet.

'Nothing will make me feel better! I feel like someone is bouncing a ball around in my head,' Babs groaned. 'Surely it's too early to get up.'

Dee surveyed her friend. She did look pale, but a bit of breakfast and a shower, and she would be fine. Thank goodness she'd talked Babs out of opening another bottle of wine last night. She handed her the glass of water and packet of painkillers. 'I thought you might need these.'

'Thanks.' Babs edged herself onto her elbows and squinted at Dee. 'Aren't you hungover?'

Dee shook her head. 'I went onto soft drinks seeing as I'd be driving today.'

'Driving?' She clapped her hand to her forehead. 'Gosh, I forgot. We booked a week away in a holiday cottage in Cornwall.' Then her eyes widened. 'And it's your birthday! Happy birthday!'

'Thank you. You do still want to go away, don't you?' Dee

asked. 'Because it's fine if you've decided against it and want to go back and talk things through with Geoff.'

They'd found a lovely little cottage in the small village of Port Telwyn in Cornwall. There'd apparently been a last-minute cancellation so they had booked it for the week. However, Dee was more than happy to go by herself if Babs had thought better of it this morning. She really hoped her best friend and Geoff would make up.

Babs nodded then groaned again. 'You bet I do. I forgot about it for a minute.' She took the glass Dee was offering her, popped two painkillers out of the blister pack, swallowed them and downed the glass of water. 'These will soon kick in and I'll be right as rain. I need to go to the loo though.' She flung back the thin duvet and raced out to the bathroom a couple of doors down.

'I'll make us scrambled eggs on toast then we can be on our way. We have to collect the keys for the cottage before five, and it's almost eleven already,' Dee shouted as she headed down the stairs. It was about a two and a half hour's drive from Bristol, but the weekend traffic was likely to be heavy.

'Give me quarter of an hour to shower and get dressed,' Babs shouted back.

Dee was putting the bread in the toaster when Babs came down, showered, dressed in bright red trousers and a red and yellow top, just over fifteen minutes later. She sniffed appreciatively. 'Oh, I love the smell of fresh coffee.'

'Me too. The scrambled eggs are in the microwave and it's about to ping,' Dee told her. 'Sit down and help yourself.'

Babs walked over to the kitchen table which was laid with a cafetière of coffee and a jug of orange juice, two mugs, two glasses, two plates and cutlery. 'Very nice, I feel like I'm in a hotel.'

The toast popped up out of the toaster at the same time the microwave pinged.

'Let me help.' Babs went over to the microwave and took out the jug of perfectly cooked scrambled egg. 'This looks delicious.'

Dee looked up from buttering the toast and smiled. 'It's the easiest and least messy way of doing it, I find.'

'True. But one minute too long and it's like rubber, and my timing isn't always so great,' Babs said. 'Want it spooned onto your plate or onto your toast?'

Dee placed a piece of buttered toast on each plate. 'On the toast, please.' She cut up the other two slices of buttered toast and put them in the toast rack then they both sat down to eat just as Babs' mobile rang.

Babs peered at the screen then pursed her lips as she dismissed the call. 'Geoff,' she replied to Dee's enquiring glance. 'Well, I'm not answering it, let him sweat for a bit.' She picked up her knife and fork and tucked into her breakfast.

Dee watched her thoughtfully. 'Maybe you should, he might be apologising.'

'So he should be!' A text pinged in and Babs looked down at the screen. 'Geoff again. No doubt begging me to come home.'

'Read it, it might be important,' Dee told her.

Babs sighed, put down her knife, swiped the screen and opened the message. A look of outrage crossed her face. 'He wants me home. Not to apologise, but because he's got the estate agent coming back this morning to take photos and do the floor plan.' She dug fiercely into her toast with her knife. 'He's got no chance.' She looked up at Dee. 'Well going away for a bit will show him that I'm serious, and give him chance to miss me. Let him see what it's like living by himself, because if he insists on moving to Spain, he'll be going alone.'

Dee nodded sympathetically. 'I must say I'm surprised at his attitude, it's very heavy-handed of him.'

'Geoff might come across as easy-going, but as you know he's got a real stubborn streak and it's got worse since he retired.' Babs jutted out her chin defiantly. 'Well, so have I. And this is one battle he isn't going to win!'

'Are you sure you have everything you need in your case? We'll be away for a week,' Dee reminded her.

Babs nodded her head. 'I've got plenty and I don't want to go back to the house, I don't want to see Geoff right now. Not after how he's treated me.' She cut another bit out of her toast and chewed it. 'Do you know what he said to me when I told him I was coming to yours last night? He said, "you're overreacting as usual".' She looked outraged. 'As if it's perfectly reasonable for him to decide to sell our home, and book flights to Spain so we can view properties, without even talking to me about it first.' She scooped up the last of her scrambled egg with her fork. 'I'll be damned if I let him get away with this. He can stew.'

Dee agreed Geoff was being very selfish. Which was totally out of character. Whereas, Nigel was always selfish and him forgetting her birthday or going off with his mates for a week was totally *in* character.

'Have you heard from Nige?' Babs asked, as if reading her mind.

'He sent me a text wishing me happy birthday and apologising. And he's transferred five hundred pounds to my bank account so I can treat myself.' Dee glanced up at the clock on the kitchen wall. 'He'll be in Portugal now, too busy enjoying himself with his golfing friends to worry about me.'

'Men! All they care about is what they want!' Babs reached for some toast from the rack. 'They don't deserve us.'

* * *

They were about to leave when Annabel video-called Dee, and little Hallie sang 'Happy Birthday', almost word perfect. Tears sprung to Dee's eyes as she listened to her adorable little granddaughter.

'Thank you, darling,' she said, blowing a kiss to Hallie who blew a kiss back.

'Is Dad taking you out to dinner?' Annabel asked.

'No, he's gone off on a golfing holiday to Portugal with his friends,' Dee said matter-of-factly. 'He booked it at the last minute.'

'What! And you let him go?' Annabel exploded.

'I couldn't really stop him, could I?' Dee replied. 'Anyway I'm off myself, you've just caught me.'

'Where are you going?' Annabel asked. 'Hallie seems much better today so we were planning on driving over tomorrow, to bring your cards and presents.'

'That's very kind of you, darling, but I've booked a cottage in Cornwall for a week. I'm going with Babs. Save the presents until I return and we'll have a get-together then.'

'If you're sure, Mum. Text me your address in Cornwall though and I can at least post your cards, they should arrive on Monday. Better a couple of days late than a week late!'

'Bless you, darling, I'll text it over in a few minutes. Now I've got to go, we're all ready to set off. I'll speak to you later.'

'Have a lovely time, Mum. You deserve it,' Annabel said. 'Dad's unbelievable sometimes.'

You can say that again, Dee thought. Although she had to admit, a big part of her was happier she was going away to Cornwall with Babs than she'd have been going to Portugal with Nigel.

5

BABS

They'd been travelling for about an hour when Babs also had a call from her daughter. 'Are you home tomorrow? I've got a stay-over and thought I'd pop in to see you.'

'No, I'm not in. I'm on my way to Cornwall with Dee for her sixtieth birthday. Your father is in though. Why don't you go and see him?'

'You're going away without Dad?' Molly sounded surprised.

'I bloody well am and I might not come back. Your dad has decided he's selling the house and going to live in Spain, whether I agree or not.'

'What? You're kidding, Mum!'

'I wish I was!'

'I'll talk to him, Mum. He's being ridiculous!'

'Good luck with that one!'

'I'll get back to you later, Mum. Don't worry, I'm sure we can sort this out,' Molly told her. 'And tell Dee Happy Birthday from me. I hope you both have a good time.'

Babs guessed that Molly would be straight on the phone to her father. Well, he'll be shocked when Molly tells him that

Babs had actually gone away. That would give him something to think about.

She looked out of the window. They were still on the M5. Her head was aching and she fidgeted in her seat. Dee seemed fine, her gaze fixed on the road ahead. Dee was like that though, calm and unflappable. Babs would be raging if Geoff had gone away with his mates on her birthday, especially a big one like sixty. 'How much longer before we get there?'

'About an hour and half. Shall we stop for a break?' Dee suggested.

Babs nodded. 'I could do with a coffee and a trip to the loo.'

Dee pulled in at the next service station and Babs went to the loo while Dee ordered the coffees. When Babs returned Dee was seated at a red plastic table for two, with two milky coffees in front of her, looking wistfully at her phone.

'What's up?' Babs pulled out the plastic chair opposite her friend.

Dee raised her eyes, she looked a bit troubled. 'I've had another message from Nigel. It's quite a lovely message, really. He's about to go on the golf course but said he's sorry again he forgot my birthday and he'll book us both a holiday together when he comes home to make up for it.' She chewed the inside of her lip. 'Perhaps he did genuinely forget.'

'That's not the point, Dee. He shouldn't forget. Sixty is a big birthday. He should have planned something special for you. And it's not the first time he's forgotten your birthday, is it?'

'He's busy—'

'And you're his wife.' Babs stirred sugar into her drink. 'Look, if Nigel can swan off to Portugal without you for a week, then what's wrong with you going on holiday too?'

'Nothing. You're right. Nigel should have remembered and

this might make sure he does in future,' Dee said, sounding stronger.

Babs bit back a sigh. She loved Dee to bits, but truth be told, she couldn't stand Nigel. He was selfish, pompous and Dee was far too good for him, even though she couldn't see it. Babs had, in fact, felt a little sorry for Dee over the years, thinking that she and Geoff had the stronger marriage. Nigel had behaved badly in the past and Dee had forgiven him, not wanting to disrupt the children's lives by having to take them out of their private schools and moving from their gorgeous home. But Babs had never forgotten.

Meanwhile, Geoff, for all his faults, had never treated Babs badly – and they'd always worked as a team. Until now. He could be single-minded, yes, but he'd never made a major decision like this before without consulting her. Ever since he'd retired though, he'd been restless. She knew he was bored, and could understand that he wanted a change but why was he so obsessed with moving to Spain? And how dare he think that she should have to go along with what he decided? Like hell she would!

She pulled herself out of her thoughts and looked over at Dee who was calmly sipping her coffee.

'We're going to make this birthday really special,' Babs said. 'Did you say you'd been to Port Telwyn before?' Dee had mentioned it when they were looking for holiday cottages to let last night; they'd been lucky to get something last minute.

'Yes, we went on day trips there a couple of times when we were holidaying in Cornwall with the kids when they were young. Beautiful place, although it could well have changed now.' She took another sip of her drink. 'Don't think you have to make a special effort, Babs, I'm fine about my birthday and looking forward to staying in the cottage for a week. Don't feel you have to stay there for the whole week either. If you want to go home anytime, then please do it.'

'Oi! Don't you want me with you? Well tough, cos I'm staying and that's that. I'm not leaving you by yourself!' Babs told her.

'I'm used to being by myself, and quite happy just to have a change of scenery.' Dee leaned over and patted Babs' hand. 'It's great to have your company, but you are not responsible for making sure I have a wonderful birthday. And you have things to sort out with Geoff. That must come first.'

'Huh! Well Geoff isn't exactly putting me first, is he?' Babs scoffed. 'Let's forget about the men and concentrate on having a good time. It's been years since we went away together.' She tittered as a memory crossed her mind. 'Do you remember that week in Kos when we were only eighteen and we hooked up with that stag party who were staying at our hotel?'

'Oh God, yes! We had some great nights clubbing with them.'

Babs chuckled. 'What about that evening they all went out dressed in tutus and left their keys in their rooms? We had to sneak them all into our room and let them sleep on the floor until the next morning when the cleaners came around and opened the door of their rooms. The cleaners' faces were a picture when these hulking guys dressed in pretty tutus strutted in.'

'As if I could forget? They were a bit wild, weren't they?' Dee laughed. 'It was such a fantastic week.'

They'd had some good times, her and Dee, Babs thought. They both went back a long way, friends since they were twelve and Dee had moved to the local high school that Babs attended. She was a bit shy but Babs had taken her under her wing and they'd been friends ever since, often going on holiday together in their late teens and early twenties. Babs and Geoff had been the first to get married. Dee had been focused on her teaching career until she was swept off her feet by smooth-talking Nigel as soon as she met him. 'I can't believe he's interested in me, he could have any girl he wanted,' she'd told Babs. That was the trouble with Dee, she didn't know her worth.

Dee never liked to argue, or cause any kind of conflict. Whereas, Babs always stood her ground, fought her corner; she wasn't going to be a pushover for anyone. She and Geoff had had their arguments over the years, but they'd always had each other's back. Once Geoff realised that Babs was serious about not moving to Spain, surely he'd drop the idea. Meanwhile, she might as well have herself a holiday with her best friend.

6

DEE

'I hope Sylvia's got it right this time,' Dee said as she followed the instructions and took the very sharp bend to the left. Sylvia was Babs' nickname for the voice of her Google Maps phone app, because she said the woman speaking sounded like one of the regular customers at the shop who was called Sylvia and always spoke with a fake posh accent. Thank goodness Dee was in her Clio and not Nigel's BMW because Babs' Google Maps had taken them along some narrow and windy roads. Not that she'd have been able to use Nigel's car as he'd taken it to the airport and left it in parking. She was getting tired now and her head was aching a little. She'd be glad to get there. It had been a long journey with a fair amount of traffic, and the satnav instructions had been constantly punctuated by texts and phone calls from Geoff urging Babs to come home.

'I'm so sorry, maybe we should use your phone for Google Maps,' Babs said. But Dee had left her phone in her handbag in the boot of the car, so in the end Babs had blocked Geoff's number. 'I'll unblock him when we get there,' she said.

Dee turned the corner into a long narrow road going down a

cobbled street lined with quaint little houses, and there at the bottom was a blue ribbon of sea. Port Telwyn.

'Oh wow!' Babs exclaimed from the passenger seat. 'That's gorgeous!'

It was spectacular. The advertisement had boasted sea views but Dee hadn't expected this. When she'd visited before all those years ago, they'd been in a hotel in a nearby town and only visited the harbour front on a short day trip.

'Continue straight for 250 yards and your destination is on the right,' Sylvia the Google Maps lady said.

'Thank goodness we're near the bottom of the hill. I wouldn't want to be walking up here every day from the beach,' Babs said. 'I don't know how you're going to park here though, the road is too narrow.'

'It said on the website that there's car parking around the back.' Dee looked out for a turning on the right. Ah, there it was, just before the row of cottages – one of which she presumed was Sunset View. She took the turning and drove past the side of the end cottage to an open patch of land at the back, noticing there were already a couple of cars parked on it. 'I think this is where we're meant to park,' she said, pulling up. 'We'll leave the car here and walk to the letting agents. They're apparently only a couple of streets away.'

'That's fine, I could do with stretching my legs,' Babs said as they both got out of the car and looked at the row of gated high walls enclosing the back gardens of the cottages. 'I wonder which one we're stopping in.'

'The name might be on the back gate.' Dee grabbed her handbag from the boot and locked the car, putting the keys in her bag before walking over to the row of gates and reading the signs on them, Babs beside her. 'Maritime Wanderer, Primrose

Cottage, Dun Roaming – that was an old classic – ah, here we are, Sunset View.'

'Hard to tell what it's like from the back with these high gates, can't wait to look inside,' Babs said. 'And to have a cuppa.'

A cuppa – or a glass of wine! – was Babs' answer to everything, although Dee had to admit she could do with a nice hot drink too.

'How about we collect the keys then walk on down to the harbour and find a nice café to have a drink in?' she suggested.

Babs nodded. 'Suits me! I can smell the sea air and I'm dying for a paddle.'

Dee felt her spirits lift as they walked down the hill to the letting agents. It was so wonderful to be here by the sea, and with Babs too.

'Thank goodness it's downhill,' Babs puffed as they turned the corner into the next street. 'Mind I don't fancy the walk back up again. I'm not as fit as I used to be.'

'Not much further now,' Dee said, glancing at the shops they passed. Davis & Co, the letting agents, was halfway down the street. What a gorgeous place to work, she thought. A few minutes down the hill and you were at the harbour.

When they walked in a tall, thin woman with a mop of dark hair looked up and smiled. 'You must be Dee and Babs? Did you get held up in the traffic?' She held out her hand. 'I'm Sylvia Davis,' she announced in an upmarket accent.

Babs caught Dee's gaze, her eyes twinkling. The woman even sounded a bit like Babs' satnav, Dee thought, suppressing a smile. 'Yes. Sorry we're late, our satnav sent us the wrong way a couple of times. We were also hoping to set out earlier but we kept being distracted.'

'It's Dee's birthday so she had lots of phone calls and messages,' Babs added.

'Ah, I thought it must be your birthday. The courier tried to deliver some flowers to the cottage but no one was there so he brought them to us. I've taken them to the cottage and stood them in water. I hope that's all right?'

'Perfect, thank you.' Could they be from Nigel, Dee wondered. He might have got the address off Annabel and sent her flowers to make up for going away.

'Well happy birthday!' Sylvia smiled. 'Now, we have some paperwork for you to sign. You're lucky, we had a last-minute cancellation on this one and it's a lovely cottage.' She indicated for them to sit at the two seats by the desk and then took a piece of paper out of the in-tray. Placing it on the desk in front of Dee she pointed to the printed page. 'If you could sign by the crosses, please.'

Dee picked up the pen offered to her and signed where Sylvia had indicated.

Sylvia handed her the keys and a business card. 'Any problems, either phone this number or come and see me. I need the keys back by noon next Saturday.'

'Thank you.' Dee put the keys in her pocket. She still couldn't believe she'd done this, and without telling Nigel either. She bet Annabel had told him though. And given him an ear bashing for going away on her birthday. That's probably why he'd sent her the flowers. If they were from him. Maybe Annabel had sent them, although she had said she'd give Dee her presents when she returned home.

Her birthday. She was sixty today.

'Enjoy your visit, and happy birthday again,' Sylvia said. 'I think you'll love the cottage, it's aptly named Sunset View because of the beautiful sunsets you can see from it.'

'It sounds perfect!' Babs said. She'd been sitting quietly up until now. 'First though, we're going down to the harbour and finding a café to have a nice cup of tea.'

'There's one right on the harbour front. It's called Moira's Café and has a delicious selection of home-made cakes and sandwiches as well as hot drinks.'

'Fab!' Babs said.

They both set off down the hill to the sea, coming out right in front of the picturesque harbour. Half a dozen fishing boats were moored, bobbing up and down on the calm sea, and out in the middle of the ocean, a jet ski zoomed past leaving a white foamy trail in its wake.

Dee drew in a deep breath. She could taste the sea air. It was so beautiful and invigorating she already didn't want to go home.

Her phone trilled in her pocket to announce an incoming call. She took it out and looked at the screen and was surprised to see that it was Nigel. He never called when he was away, he always said he didn't have time. All she got was the occasional text message. He was probably still feeling guilty about forgetting her birthday. Well, so he should. She was about to answer when the call stopped. A couple of minutes later a text pinged in.

> Annabel said you've gone away for a bit. I'm having an important document delivered to the house on Monday afternoon. Can you make sure you're back to collect it? It has to be signed for.

'Is that from Nige?' Babs asked.

Dee nodded and told her what was in the text. 'I wish he'd have told me sooner, I could have gone away Monday once the document had been delivered.'

'Don't you go feeling guilty! Nigel takes you for granted far too much. He'll have to arrange for the document to be delivered to his office. It's not your problem.'

No, it wasn't, Dee agreed. She guessed Nigel had arranged for the document to be delivered to the house because it had sensitive information in it. He did that sometimes if he was working on something confidential and wasn't in the office. She quickly messaged back that she'd gone away for a few days, and couldn't possibly drive back in time so he would have to make alternative arrangements. She'd pressed send before she realised that this was the first time she had ever refused to do anything that Nigel had asked. She had built her life around him, seeing it as her job to keep him happy. He'd be shocked at her reply.

'Well done, you're finally standing up to him,' Babs said approvingly. 'How appalling of him to expect you to drop everything for him when he can't even be bothered to remember your big birthday.'

A text came whizzing back from Nigel.

> How inconsiderate! You could have let me know you were going away. I hope you're home for when I return early on Saturday morning.

'He wants to make sure you'll be there to do his cooking, cleaning and washing,' Babs said, reading the text over Dee's shoulder. 'Don't you dare go home early to wait on him. Let's stay all day Saturday! That'll teach him.'

Dee gazed out at the ocean. Babs was right. Nigel hadn't asked where she was, how long she was intending to stay away, told her to enjoy herself, or showed any concern at all. He merely wanted to make sure was there to do what he needed and that he wasn't coming home to an empty house. Nigel hated having to fend for himself, although he was always leaving *her* to fend for herself.

And there was no mention of the bouquet of flowers. Maybe Annabel had sent them.

'You should block him for a bit, that'll teach him,' Babs said. 'Actually, I'd better unblock Geoff now or he'll be having a fit.' She felt in her pocket, took out her phone and swiped the screen. 'Wow. A dozen missed phone calls and God knows how many messages from Molly.' Then she swore.

'What it is?' Dee asked.

'Apparently Geoff's been trying to call me. The estate agent has taken the photos and they're putting the house on the market right away.'

'That's quick!' Dee said.

'Well, he can whistle, I'm not going home.' Babs followed Dee's gaze out to the sea. 'Gorgeous here, isn't it?' She turned to Dee. 'Fancy an ice cream instead of a cuppa?'

'You know, I think I will,' said Dee.

They both bought a 99 cone and sat on the wall overlooking the harbour.

'There's a lovely-looking restaurant over there, shall we book a table for tonight?' Babs asked. 'We can celebrate your birthday.'

'I'd like that.' Dee licked the soft ice cream that was dripping down the side of her cone. This birthday was completely different to any she'd had before, but she had a feeling she was going to really enjoy it.

7

'Hey, this is gorgeous!' Babs exclaimed as Dee opened the back gate to Sunset View a little later. After eating their ice creams and booking a table at the restaurant, they'd walked up to the cottage, taken their suitcases out of the car and gone in the back way.

'It is, isn't it?' Dee felt her heart lift as she looked around. The courtyard was small but pretty with lots of colourful potted plants, a wooden bench, a cute blue shed with a white seagull motif on the side and a small wooden table with two chairs, perfect for sitting and having your morning cup of tea. If the outside was so pretty, she couldn't wait to see the inside. It certainly looked promising with its granite walls, and judging by the modern white window frames it was double-glazed, probably to cater for any holidaymakers who wanted a winter break.

They wheeled their cases over the cobbled courtyard to the back door. 'Let's get these cases inside, unpack and unwind before we go to the restaurant.'

Dee took the keys Sylvia had given her out of her handbag, then unlocked the door. It was a bit stiff but a big push and it was open. They walked into a small galley kitchen with light wooden cupboards lining the walls, a slate-grey floor and dark grey work-tops. A large window across the sink helped let in the light, as did the small glass panel in the back door. And there, standing in a bowl of water in the sink was the most gorgeous bouquet of irises, freesias and lisianthus in different hues of blue, exquis-itely contrasting with white roses, Eryngium and Tanacetum. A small envelope was stuck on the outside of the cellophane.

Her heart jumped a little, wondering if they were from Nigel after all. They really were spectacular. She pulled off the enve-lope and opened it. The little card inside read:

Happy Birthday, Mum. Enjoy a well-deserved break. Love Annabel, Gareth and Hallie. Xx

'Don't tell me you were hoping they were from Nigel,' Babs said, obviously noticing Dee's disappointed face.

'I did wonder,' Dee admitted. More fool her, of course, they would be from Annabel. She was such a thoughtful daughter. She and Gareth were so busy working that they didn't get chance to visit Dee often, but they exchanged messages regu-larly and Annabel sent lots of photos of Hallie. They caught up on Facetime every weekend if they could and Hallie always shouted 'Nanna!' and blew her a kiss when she saw her on the screen. Modern life, but at least it meant she got the chance to build a relationship with her little granddaughter.

'It looks very spacious and clean,' Babs remarked, putting her suitcase by the wall. 'No table though, that could be awkward. Although there's a lot of worktop space.'

'There's a pull-up table over on that wall, and two high stools,' Dee noticed. 'It's only for a week, we'll manage fine.'

'Yeah, we don't want to be spending our time cooking anyway, we're here to enjoy ourselves. Let's explore the rest of the house,' Babs agreed.

There was an archway leading to a lounge diner. They walked through it and gazed around at the small but bright room, thanks to the double windowed aspect. A couple of beige rugs were scattered on the grey floor, a dark green chesterfield with cream velvet scatter cushions ran along the far wall, and two matching chairs filled most of the other space. A boarded white wooden staircase led up to the bedrooms, with a small light wood unit with a TV, books, magazines and knick-knacks running along the wall underneath it. A coffee table and an emerald-green velvet pouffe were the only other furniture. Thick cream drapes hung at the front bay window and at the French windows which led out into the courtyard. The white radiators on the walls were evidence that it was centrally heated. It would be cosy in the winter, Dee thought. The owners had obviously given a lot of thought about the comfort of their guests.

'This is very nice,' Babs said approvingly, going over to the bay window. 'There's a little front garden with table and chairs and some statues.'

Dee walked over to join her, gazing out at the cobbled street. 'I think we made a good choice coming here,' she said.

'Let's take a look upstairs,' Babs suggested. 'With a bit of luck one of the bedrooms will have a sea view.'

If it did, Dee decided that she would let Babs have it. Although her friend was trying to put on a brave front, she knew that this business with Geoff had really upset her. However, when they reached the top of the stairs, she saw that both bedrooms were at the back of the house, the doors were wide open and, over the rooftops, they could see the sea from the windows of both.

'You take the one you prefer,' she told Babs. 'I don't mind.'

'No, it's your birthday, *you* decide,' Babs insisted.

Both rooms were spacious with en suites and large multi-paned windows that let a lot of light in the rooms. A bright floral throw covered each double bed, and they were furnished with light wood bedroom furniture and a chair with a padded seat. They were identical apart from the colour scheme, one floral throw was turquoise – Dee's favourite colour – and the other one was coral – Babs' favourite colour. It was almost as if it was meant to be. Babs caught her eye and grinned. 'I guess it's a no-brainer which room we're each having!'

Dee suggested that they unpack, freshen up and then go for dinner, so they took their suitcases upstairs and both disappeared into their respective bedrooms. Dee walked over to the window and gazed out. She loved the sea, it always made her feel more relaxed and her problems never seemed so important. When you looked out at the wide ocean you realised that you were just an insignificant part of the whole universe and that everything passes eventually. She was going to enjoy this time away.

8

BABS

Port Telwyn was a pretty place, Babs thought as she unpacked. She was going to make the most of their week here. She and Geoff had often taken a trip to the coast for the weekend before they'd had the kids and when Molly and Lennon were little. Sometimes they'd just driven there for the day. A paddle in the sea, and ice cream, inhaling the salty sea air. Taking in the atmosphere refreshed them so much and left them feeling relaxed and ready to cope with the coming week. Geoff often said that a day at the sea was all he needed to recharge his batteries. And she'd felt the same. Maybe if Geoff was planning to live in a little Spanish village near the coast instead of in the middle of nowhere up a flipping mountain, she might feel more like going with him.

She shook her head. No, she still wouldn't. She didn't want to live abroad. She enjoyed a bit of sun, but too much of it made her feel uncomfortable, and she didn't want to up sticks and go somewhere completely alien. She'd never fancied living in another country. She'd loved their holidays in Spain but had always been happy to return home, to a familiar language, food, and sights. She couldn't understand why Geoff suddenly wanted to move there. She'd have thought he'd prefer living in Devon or Cornwall. They had talked about doing that once, years ago when the kids were little, and she'd quite fancied the idea of retiring to the coast back then. They'd never talked about living abroad though. She'd been stunned when Geoff had mentioned it a few months ago. She'd said no straight away, knowing it wasn't for her, but Geoff hadn't listened and here they were, with the house for sale and still arguing about it.

The tring of an incoming call startled her. Geoff's name popped up on the screen. Maybe he had missed her and realised how stupid he was being.

'Babs,' Geoff said as soon as she pressed answer. 'You've got to come home immediately.'

She felt a warmth of affection flood through her. He had missed her.

'The estate agent is coming back today, and I can't find the spare house keys. I need them.'

Babs knew exactly where they were but wasn't about to tell him, he obviously wanted to give them to the estate agent so they could go ahead with viewings when he was out – or away. Well she wasn't going to make selling the house easy for him! And he hadn't asked her how she was or where she was. What a cheek for him to phone up and expect her to help him sell their home when he knew she didn't want to move.

'Can you hear me, Babs? When are you coming home? Stop being a drama queen and come back. We've got things to sort out.'

'A drama queen—?' she repeated, enraged. 'What about you being a selfish prick! I'm not coming back! Not until you take the house off the market.'

There was a pause and his tone softened. 'Look, I'll compromise. We don't have to live up a mountain, if that's what you're upset about. There's some *casas hermosas* – that means lovely houses – with lots of land on flat ground.'

Here he goes again with his bloomin' Spanish! 'Geoff, I am not moving to Spain. I don't care if it's a penthouse on the coast!' She paused as she thought that one over fleetingly. Would a penthouse on the coast be quite nice? Could she imagine waking up every morning and going for a dip in the sea, walking along the beach feeling the sand between her toes…?

'The trouble with you, Babs, is that you've got stuck in a rut. You want to do the same old boring things every day. Well, I don't. I want to live my life while I can. I want new horizons. Adventures.'

Live his life while he could! Anyone would think they had one foot in the grave! 'And the trouble with you is that you're making stupid decisions that affect my life too!'

'Forget it, I'll find the bloody keys myself! You'll soon get fed up of staying at Dee's and come back. Then we can have a sensible conversation.'

'I'm not at Dee's…'

She heard Geoff catch his breath. 'Then where are you? Don't tell me you've booked into a hotel for a couple of nights?'

'Nope. I've gone away with Dee. And if you don't change your attitude, I won't be coming back!'

She ended the call and threw the phone down onto the duvet. That told him, she thought, as she went into the bathroom for a shower. She was surprised that Molly hadn't told Geoff that Babs had gone to Cornwall, maybe she was trying to keep out of it. Well, she going to enjoy this little holiday and let Geoff stew for a bit. She almost wished that she hadn't unblocked Geoff's number from her phone now. She immediately blocked him again. That would give him something else to think about.

Half an hour later, showered and changed into a bright yellow maxi dress, she went downstairs to join Dee who looked gorgeous in a pale blue floaty dress and strappy blue sandals. She looked lighter, happier, as if she wasn't at all bothered that her selfish husband had gone off on a golf trip abroad with his mates and left her alone on her sixtieth birthday. But then Dee was used to Nigel acting like this, wasn't she? Whereas Babs and Geoff had been a team and this wasn't like Geoff at all.

'You look stunning,' Babs told Dee, honestly. Dee always did dress so elegantly.

'Thanks. So do you,' Dee told her.

'All ready for your birthday dinner?'

'I certainly am.' Dee picked up her blue handbag. 'Let's go.'

As they walked down the hill to the harbour for the second time that day, and the beach came into sight again, the sea now having gone out enough to leave the boats resting on the sand, Babs felt a mix of exhilaration and sadness. She hadn't been away without Geoff in all the years they'd been married and whilst she missed him she couldn't help feeling a little excited at the thought of the carefree days ahead. For the first time in thirty-seven years she was free to do whatever she wanted with her time. She could be herself. Not Geoff's wife or Molly and Lennon's mum. She was simply Babs.

9

DEE

Thank goodness they'd reserved a table, Dee thought, as they walked into the packed restaurant. It was obviously a popular venue, even though it was still early in the holiday season. She glanced around, taking in the white-washed walls, the arched windows that looked out onto the harbour, the polished wooden tables, white serviettes, blue and white bud vases with white roses in them, and the pictures on the wall – one of a magnificent old ship bobbing on a stormy sea, another of some houses dotted about on a cliff overlooking a rugged sea, and one she recognised as St Michael's Mount. Several couples and a few families were sitting at the tables chatting and laughing, with soothing music playing in the background. She felt her spirits rise at the lively atmosphere. It wasn't the sort of restaurant Nigel would have taken her to. He preferred crystal glasses, red tablecloths, an expensive décor. Nigel always wanted to go to the best restaurants and part of her – a very big part of her – was sure it was because he wanted to give the impression he was a person of taste, someone important. More important than Dee that was, for sure. She'd always felt second best to Nigel, always been in his shadow, the last in the line, behind Annabel and Hugh.

Even her career hadn't been important, she thought wistfully. Nigel had persuaded her to give up her much-loved job as a primary school teacher as soon as Hugh was born. 'I want you to be there for our *own* children,' he'd coaxed. 'I want them to have their mother at home, happy to see them and spend time with them, not one who comes in from work frazzled. And I need someone here taking care of the home, cooking me dinner, helping me relax at the end of the day. My job is so stressful.' So she'd done as he'd asked, and she'd made a good job of being a mother, she thought, always giving the children her undivided attention.

Over the years what she wanted had become less and less important. All she'd cared about was creating a secure and happy home for her two children. And if that meant turning a blind eye to Nigel's occasional indiscretions, then so be it. As he'd pointed out to her the first time she'd discovered that he'd been *indiscreet* on a business trip away, asking: 'is it worth destroying the family, taking the children out of private school, giving up their beautiful home and holidays abroad for one mishap when he'd been feeling lonely and missing her?' He'd made it sound as if it was her fault he'd fallen into the arms of another woman, pointing out almost reproachfully that he worked so hard to give them all a wonderful lifestyle, but that he was only human and it was lonely living in a hotel room far away from home.

Whereas, Babs and Geoff had always run the shop together and spent every evening home together. They'd been inseparable. Until now. She couldn't believe that Babs had walked out, and that Geoff hadn't come after her, promising to do anything if she would come home again. They would get back together though, she was sure of that. Thirty-seven years was a lot to throw away, two years more than her and Nigel. Besides, they adored each other.

'It's pretty in here, isn't it?' Babs asked, her voice jolting Dee back to the present. 'As soon as I saw it across the harbour, I knew it was the right place to go.'

'It's very picturesque, I like it,' Dee assured her.

The waiter came over, smiled at Babs, obviously recognising her from earlier. Most people remembered Babs; she was such a bright, bubbly person. He showed them their table, pulling out a chair for first Dee then Babs.

'Can I get you both a drink?' he asked when they were seated and he'd handed them a menu each to browse, then waited for their drinks order.

'You know, I think I'm going to order a bottle of champagne. Let's celebrate in style,' Dee decided. Sod Nigel, she was going to enjoy her birthday.

'A good decision. We have a very nice bottle of house champagne,' the waiter told them. 'Give me a few minutes.' He returned with a bottle of champagne in a bucket of ice, and two glasses. He expertly uncorked the bottle, pouring some of the sparkling golden drink into two glasses, placing one in front of each of them. 'Happy birthday, madam.'

'Thank you,' Dee said with a smile. She might have known that Babs would mention it was Dee's birthday when she booked the table. She picked up the glass. It looked so inviting with its chain of pearly bubbles around the surface. She took a long sip, savouring the sweet, velvety taste.

Babs raised her glass. 'Happy sixtieth birthday, Dee.'

'Thank you.' Dee held her glass out and they both clinked cheers.

'Happy birthday, but surely it isn't really your sixtieth?'

Dee looked over at the couple sitting at the next table. The woman – slim, dark-haired with a gamine face and pixie haircut – was the one who had spoken. Her male companion, stouter and a bit older with dark hair thinning on the top, smiled at her. 'Er, yes, it is.' She felt a little embarrassed, wishing that Babs hadn't announced her age so loudly.

The couple raised their glasses. 'Well, happy birthday to you!'

'It's your birthday?' A waitress taking meals to the people at the table behind them paused to look questioningly at Dee, who could feel her cheeks flush.

'It's her sixtieth, so we're celebrating,' Babs said.

The waitress looked from one to the other. 'Ah, you are a couple—'

'No!' Dee shook her head wildly. 'No, we're friends. We're both married. Not to each other,' she added emphatically. Heavens, she loved Babs to bits, but not in that way!

'Ah, forgive me. Happy birthday. But surely not sixty?'

Dee was feeling rather flattered and embarrassed by the attention she was getting. 'I'm afraid so,' she admitted.

'Then I wish you a wonderful evening,' the waitress told her.

'Gosh, that was embarrassing,' Dee whispered to Babs.

'It was a compliment, make the most of it,' Babs said with a grin.

Babs was right, and it was nice that so many people didn't think Dee looked her age. It had been a long time since Nigel had paid her a compliment. She didn't think he even looked at her these days, except to criticise if he thought she was wearing the wrong clothes or her hair needed a trim. Not that he ever openly criticised. He merely stared at her and said, 'Are you wearing *that*?' or 'Isn't it time you booked a hair appointment?'

'Stop thinking about Nigel. We're not going to think about

the men tonight. We're going to enjoy ourselves.' Babs had thankfully lowered her voice to make this comment.

Her best friend was right. Dee was going to enjoy her birthday and push any thought of Nigel from her mind.

They both ordered steak, which was divine. Dee's was medium-rare and Babs' well-done, exactly as they each liked them, with mushrooms, pepper sauce, a generous portion of chips and salad garnish. They both topped up their glasses as they tucked into their meals, quickly devouring them, laughing as they shared previous holiday memories.

'Do you remember that time we went on holiday to Brean and I'd bought a new white bikini?' Babs giggled. 'I didn't know it was completely see-through when it got wet!'

'You certainly turned a few heads that day. I had to run over to you with a beach towel so you could cover yourself up.' Dee chuckled. She refilled their glasses. 'And what about when we both wandered out to sea not realising that the tide was going out and that gorgeous-looking lifeguard came to rescue us on his quad bike. Everyone clapped as we got off.'

They'd had such a giggle back then, when they were both young and carefree. Dee took another sip of champagne and rolled the bubbles over her tongue. She was glad she'd come away with Babs. Babs was the only person she had ever been able to truly relax with.

Suddenly, she was aware that someone was singing 'Happy Birthday'. And others were joining in. She turned around and saw the waiter heading towards her, carrying a plate containing a chocolate brownie, a lit candle inserted in the middle, the flame flickering as he walked.

Now everyone was joining in. Dee had to blink back the tears as the waiter put the makeshift 'birthday cake' in front of her and Babs told her to make a wish and blow out the candle.

She closed her eyes and impulsively wished that being sixty would bring her happiness, then blew out the candle. Everyone clapped and cheered. She smiled at them all and thanked them once the clapping and cheering had died down.

'You know, Babs, this is one of the best evenings I've ever had,' Dee said as she sipped the champagne, enjoying the glow in her throat as she swallowed the fizzy liquid. She was feeling happy and relaxed. And very glad that she'd come away with Babs rather than stopped at home by herself. What a miserable birthday that would have been.

10

BABS

Sunday

Babs had a restless night. She and Geoff had barely been away from each other before, apart from when Babs was in hospital having the children, and when Geoff had pneumonia a few years ago. They had always holidayed together. Always done everything together. It seemed strange sleeping in this big double bed by herself. She had so much wine on Friday night that she'd crashed out in Dee's guest room and slept through until Dee woke her in the morning. Last night though, despite the champagne she had barely slept a wink. She wondered if Geoff had slept any better. Surely he would be missing her?

She reached for her phone on the bedside table and checked the screen. No messages or missed calls. So Geoff wasn't missing her then.

Or he was sulking because she'd gone away with Dee, instead of running back home as he'd demanded.

She touched the screen, opening her photo gallery and scrolled through the photos, stopping to look at a photo of her and Geoff sitting outside a pub, a glass of lager in front of them both. Bozo, their old rescue dog, at their feet. It was a mild spring day and they'd gone for a walk by the river, then stopped for a pint. They'd often gone for a walk with Bozo on Sundays, when the shop wasn't open, it had been their way of unwinding, and reconnecting. They'd sit chatting to each other as they sipped their pints, talking about their week, and the week ahead. A couple of years ago, Bozo had died of old age and they had talked about getting another dog but decided that it wasn't fair as they were working in the shop all day. Bozo had been older, settled, happy to go with them and sleep in the back or wander in the small courtyard, but a new dog would have to be trained. When they'd sold the shop a few months ago, Geoff had started to get bored, restless, and Babs had suggested they get another dog, but he'd said he didn't want to be tied down. So she'd suggested he take up a hobby. Instead he'd started getting obsessed about moving to Spain – and learning Spanish. She'd thought it was all a bit of a joke at first; how wrong she'd been.

She scrolled back to more photos, stopping at the one of their wedding day that she'd shared on Facebook back in February for their anniversary. They'd been married thirty-seven years this year, first meeting at primary school then meeting up again years later when Geoff had walked into the insurance brokers she'd worked for, wanting a quote. They'd been delighted to see each other again, gone out for a meal to catch up and hit it off so well they'd started dating. They got married on Valentine's Day the following year. It was several years before Lennon came along. They were starting to fear that they would never have children, then Molly swiftly followed. They'd been happy together, until now.

Her phone buzzed. She looked at the screen. It was Lennon. 'What's going on, Mum? Molly said that Dad's being a dickhead, talking about selling up and moving to Spain. And apparently you've run away to Cornwall and blocked his calls?'

Damn, she'd forgotten that she'd blocked Geoff again! 'I haven't run away, I've come away with Dee for a week to give your dad some time to think about what he's doing.'

There was a pause. 'You are going back home though, right?'

Was she? Right now, she didn't want to be in the same town as Geoff, never mind the same house. 'It depends on whether your dad agrees to take my feelings into account or still insists on doing what only he wants.'

There was a silence whilst Lennon digested this, and probably thought how to respond. 'You're going to have to come home. Where else will you live? You don't have the money to rent a place,' he pointed out. That was Lennon, calm and matter-of-fact. Like his dad. Only Geoff wasn't being calm and matter-of-fact now, was he? He was being selfish and irrational.

She was fully aware that she couldn't stay here forever, but Geoff had to realise that she was serious about this. 'I can afford to rent for a while and I'm not coming back until your dad takes the house off the market,' she said firmly. 'So, it's him you need to speak to, not me.'

'I intend to. I'm going to phone him now, but I wanted to find out your side first. I'll talk some sense into him. I think he's having some sort of old-age crisis.' Lennon sighed. 'You need to unblock him though, Mum. How can you sort things out if you don't talk to each other?'

'I will. I only blocked him temporarily because he kept phoning and distracting Dee when we were driving down here.' And because he annoyed her when she did unblock him, she remembered. But she thought it best not to tell Lennon this.

Babs thought over the conversation when they'd ended the call. She wasn't sure if Geoff would listen to Lennon; he wasn't listening to anyone, least of all her. All he cared about was what *he* wanted to do. Was Lennon right and Geoff was having some kind of age-related crisis? There had to be some explanation why he was acting like this, it wasn't like him at all.

She chewed her lip, her mind in turmoil. She'd walked out on Friday night in a fit of pique, determined to show Geoff that he couldn't order her about, wanting to teach him a lesson so that he backed down, but now she was worried their problems ran deeper than that. Even if Geoff took the house off the market and cancelled his plans for retiring to Spain, had the damage already been done? He'd made a big decision without caring how she thought about it, how it affected her, so what did that say about their marriage? She'd thought they were solid, a partnership. Also, even if he did back down, would he still be hankering after going to Spain? Would he resent her for not letting him live his dream? Would their marriage ever be the same again?

11

DEE

Dee slept like a log and woke up feeling really refreshed. She glanced at the clock and was surprised to discover that it was only seven thirty. She got out of bed and pulled on the new kimono Babs had bought her, deciding to make a cup of tea and take it out into the garden, enjoy the fresh air and the quietness of the morning. She'd leave Babs for a while, it would do her good to rest. Dee could tell that this business with Geoff had really upset her. And she was a bit of a morning grouch Dee remembered. Easy-going, fun Babs didn't surface until she'd had her second cup of tea.

Padding down the stairs into the kitchen, Dee saw the sunlight streaming in through the back window. They'd arrived home late last night after her birthday meal at the restaurant and gone straight to bed, not bothering to close the downstairs' curtains. She filled the kettle and switched it on, then opened the French doors out into the garden. This was probably a fisherman's cottage once, but it had been updated. She was pleased to see that the owners had kept the original beams though, and hadn't gone too modern. The quaint French doors were made of small panes, like the rest of the windows in the cottage. She left them open to let in some fresh air, then went back to make a drink as the kettle was about to boil.

She'd just finished making her tea when she felt a furry body brush against her legs then heard a loud 'miaow'. Glancing down in surprise she saw a little white cat sporting a red collar with a silver disc dangling from it. 'Hello. Do you live here?' she asked as the cat jumped onto the worktop, as if it did indeed live there, and sauntered over to the milk jug, miaowing again.

'Do you want some milk?' Dee looked around for a saucer, found one in the top cupboard and put it down on the tiled floor. The cat immediately jumped off the worktop, its tail arched in a question mark as it waited patiently for Dee to fill the saucer with milk, then started drinking.

'Well, you're a pretty little thing, aren't you?' Dee said, stroking the cat softly. It must live nearby and was obviously used to coming into the cottage, but surely it couldn't belong to the owner. This was a holiday let. She guessed it must belong to one of the neighbours. Perhaps it befriended all the holiday-makers and they all fed it. Cats were a bit like that, they weren't fussy who fed them and often had a few 'owners'. She tried to check the identity disc on the cat's collar but it stepped away from her.

She took her mug out into the garden and sat down on one of the chairs. The cat jumped onto the table and lay down in front of her. A male, she noticed, as it rolled over onto its back, then onto its side, gazing at her. And it had been neutered so obviously did belong to someone. She stroked its tummy and it purred. 'You're friendly, aren't you? I wonder what your name is?' she said softly. This time the cat allowed her to look at the disc. 'Snowy. Primrose Cottage.' She remembered that name, it was one of the cottages near the end of the block. As she had guessed – a neighbour's cat.

She'd always wanted a pet, but Nigel was against it, telling her he was allergic. She was sure he wasn't though, as she'd never seen him sneeze when a dog or cat was about. He also always pointed out that there would be no one to look after the pet when they were both out. She thought a cat would be perfectly happy to curl up in its basket and sleep on the odd occasion they were both out together. She loved dogs, she'd always made a fuss of Babs' old dog, Bozo, but as well as being allergic, Nigel said they were too messy, and needed a lot of exercise. It was a shame, a pet would have been company for her when Nigel was away on all of his business trips. The house felt so quiet and empty now the children had grown up and left home. She kept busy doing a bit of volunteering and some paperwork for Nigel but she still had a lot of time on her hands.

The cat jumped onto her lap and settled himself there. Dee stroked him gently, her mind going over the last couple of days. She hadn't heard from Nigel again and doubted that she would.

She looked around the pretty courtyard with its colourful plant pots. She could live in a place like this. It felt like home. She sipped her tea slowly, enjoying the peace and quiet.

* * *

'Morning! Oh, what a cute little cat!' Babs, dressed in a bright floral dressing gown, stepped out through the open French doors a little while later.

'Isn't he just? He's from a cottage a couple of doors down. He wandered into the kitchen for some milk as soon as I opened the doors,' Dee told her. 'I did think about bringing you a drink up, but decided to leave you to wake naturally.' She tilted her head to one side and studied Babs. 'How did you sleep? You look a bit tired.'

'Not too good.' Babs pulled out a chair and sat down. 'I kept thinking about Geoff. I can't believe this has happened. I was looking forward to us both retiring, doing things together. I thought it would bring us closer but instead it's driven us apart.'

'It's just a hiccup. I'm sure you'll sort it out. You two are so good together.' Dee had often envied their close relationship. Although they bickered sometimes, they adored each other and she was sure they would sort things out soon. Meanwhile, it was lovely to have Babs' company for a while.

'I hope so,' Babs said. Then her eyes rested on the kimono Dee was wearing. 'I knew that would suit you.'

'It's perfect,' Dee replied with a smile. 'The postman has been too and Annabel's cards have arrived. I've put them on the unit.' She'd picked up the letters when she'd gone inside to make another cup of tea.

'That's great. I wish the post came that early back at home.' Babs gazed up at the blue sky. 'What a gorgeous day. How do you fancy a walk along the harbour once we've had breakfast? We could pop into that café, too.'

The cat jumped off Dee's lap and she brushed the white hairs off her kimono. 'That sounds good. I think I'll go and have a shower now.'

'Go ahead. I'm going to make myself a cuppa and enjoy the view for a few minutes.'

Dee could see that her friend was upset but decided it was best to leave her to her thoughts. As she went up to the shower, she mused over what she would do if Nigel suggested moving to Spain. Or Portugal. He did go there a lot to play golf. Would she agree? The thought would fill her with dread, she realised. To move away from her friends and their children and everything she knew. Sometimes the days seemed long when Nigel was away, as he was now, but she had lots to keep herself busy and often met up with Babs and other friends, or went over to visit Annabel and Hallie. She'd miss Babs, she was like the sister Dee had never had. It would be just Dee and Nigel, and he would probably be off playing golf every day. She guessed she could go with him, but the game bored her, and Nigel had never suggested she accompany him. It was as if she was excluded from this part of his life.

They hadn't actually got much in common. Nothing but the children – who were now grown up and had gone their own ways – to hold them together. The thought hit her with a jolt. She'd never really considered whether she was happy with Nigel before. She'd simply accepted her lot and done her best to keep the family together. It was the only family she had. Her parents had died years ago and she'd been an only child. She sat down on the edge of the bed as a sudden realisation hit her. She was sixty. She'd spent thirty-five years doing what Nigel wanted, and trying to be a good mother to Annabel and Hugh. Did she want to do that for the rest of her life? Wasn't it time to do what *she* wanted?

12

BABS

'It's breathtaking,' Babs enthused as they walked along the harbour front, past the small beach where there were already a few children playing in the sand whilst their parents chatted. Rows of shops along the front were open, selling a selection of items from souvenirs, surf equipment and clothes to confectionary and pasties. Granite-grey and white houses scattered the cliffs rising up from the harbour on the left, and a long, narrow cobbled road wound up the hill into the town.

'There's the café the estate agent told us about.' Babs pointed to a little café with a cobalt-blue square-paned bay window and wooden door. Above the door was a hanging sign with the words:

Moira's Café

written above a picture of a steaming cup. It looked very welcoming.

They crossed the road over to the café, Babs in the lead. A bell tinkled as she pushed open the door and a woman carrying a tray over to a couple sitting in the corner glanced over and smiled at them. 'Hiya. Grab a table and I'll be with you in a minute.'

'What a pretty café,' Dee said as they made their way over to an empty table in the bay window. All the tables were covered in white tablecloths, with a delicate glass bud vase with one white rose in it. Glancing over at the other tables she saw that people were drinking out of pretty china cups, not small cups, but big enough to hold a decent cup of tea or coffee, and interestingly, they were in several different patterns and colours. It was unusual, but she liked it.

'Now what can I get you both?' The woman, who looked to be in her early fifties, beamed at them. According to the name badge on her top she was called Andi. She was wearing a short-sleeved top which revealed a blue rose tattoo on her left upper arm. The colour had faded a bit so she must have had it done when she was quite a lot younger, but it was still very clear.

'The estate agent recommended this café to us, and no wonder, it's really pretty,' Dee said.

'Thanks. I think so too. I've worked here a couple of years now. Moira,' she nodded at the slightly older dark-haired woman at the till, 'is the owner. She and her husband used to run it between them but he passed away a couple of years ago.'

Babs looked over at the older woman. She had a friendly face and was joking with one of the customers.

'That must have been hard for her,' Babs said sympathetically.

'It was but as she said, running the café helps keep her busy, less time to think.' Andi smiled. 'Now what would you like, ladies? We've got a selection of home-made cakes, scones and sandwiches, and we serve tea, coffee or various herbal teas.' She handed them the menu. 'Can I get you a drink while you decide?'

Dee nodded. 'Tea for me, please.'

'And me,' Babs added.

The two friends studied the menu whilst Andi went back to get the teas. She and Moira seemed to be the only ones serving and the café was half full, even though it was only mid-morning. They must be run off their feet at lunchtime, Babs thought. She glanced at the menu.

'Is it too early for a cream scone, do you think?' Babs asked.

'We're on holiday so you can have whatever you want whenever you want,' Dee told her. 'I think I'll go for a couple of toasted crumpets though.'

When Andi came back with the teas, they gave her their order, which she wrote down on her notepad. 'It'll be a few minutes.'

'No rush,' Dee told her.

As they both sipped their drinks, glancing out of the window at the passers-by, Babs noticed how relaxed Dee looked. More relaxed than she'd seen her for a long time.

'It's nice here. I think we chose the right place for our holiday, don't you?' Dee's eyes rested on Babs then she frowned. 'Is everything all right? Have you heard from Geoff again?'

'No, but Lennon phoned me. He's going to speak to his dad today, try and talk some sense into him.'

Dee reached over and patted Babs' hand. 'It will all work out. Geoff won't sell the house and go to Spain without you. He's bluffing.'

'Well, I'm calling his bluff. Let's see who holds out the longest,' Babs replied. Her eyes lit up when she saw Andi coming towards them with their order on a tray. 'Wow, that scone looks amazing!'

'Enjoy,' Andi said taking the plate containing a large fruit scone, knife and small pots of cream and jam, and placing it in front of Babs. 'Where are you both staying?'

'Sunset View,' Dee replied as Andi placed the crumpets and butter in front of Dee.

'Ah, I know it! That row of cottages is lovely. You're near Edna, she's at Primrose Cottage, a really nice lady. I know her quite well. She often pops in for a cuppa and a chat.'

'Oh, we've met her cat, Snowy. He paid us a visit this morning,' Babs said as she sliced her scone in half and started to butter it. 'He was all over Dee.'

Andi nodded. 'He's a sweetie, and he's not one to wander far. Edna spoils him.'

They both tucked into their breakfast. Then asked for another drink to wash it down.

Andi brought some leaflets with her when she returned with their second cups of tea. 'I thought you might want to look at these, some local places of interest. There's a good bus service to them if you don't have a car.' She put the leaflets on the table.

'How kind of you, thank you.' Dee smiled at her.

They both looked through the leaflets, deciding that they fancied visiting the art gallery which showcased the work of local artists, the house where a famous writer had once lived, and the Maritime museum, as well as a trip to St Michael's Mount. There was also a guide to local cliff walks.

'Also, if you're still around, there's a big garden party at the Manor on Saturday afternoon, to raise much-needed funds for the new Artists' Studios – the money will go towards the conversion of an old warehouse into individual working spaces for local artists and craftsmen,' Andi told them as she came to collect their plates. 'There's plenty of stalls, an auction and Simon Hemingford, from *What's it Worth?* is officially opening it and giving free valuations if people want to bring their "family heirlooms".'

'Simon Hemingford! I think he's gorgeous. It's a shame we didn't know, Dee! We could have brought some things down with us. I've got this lamp that was my mother's, and I always thought it was worth something, but Geoff scoffed at the idea.' Babs finished her drink and put the cup on the saucer. 'Shall we go?'

'Yes, lets, it sounds fun,' Dee agreed. 'I could ask him about the brooch my grandmother left me, I have a photo of it on my phone.' She'd been meaning to get it valued for years.

'There's a £5 entrance fee, which goes towards the conversions,' Andi told them. 'It starts at one thirty. I'm going to pop in for a couple of hours.'

'Thanks for the tip. It sounds interesting,' Dee replied.

'You're welcome. Enjoy your holiday.'

'How about we go to the art gallery today then drive to St Michael's Mount tomorrow?' Dee suggested as Andi walked away.

'Sounds good to me,' Babs agreed. 'We can have a paddle in the sea too. Good job we're both wearing shorts.'

They strolled up the hill to the art gallery. 'I wouldn't mind coming down here again. Maybe Annabel and Gareth would like to bring Hallie down, too, she'd love it here. Although they both prefer to go abroad nowadays.'

Babs noticed that Dee didn't mention Nigel coming with her; she knew he wouldn't. She couldn't remember the last time Dee and Nigel had gone away together. He was always too busy working, although he always had time to go off on a golfing holiday with his friends. She'd never known what Dee saw in Nigel but there was no accounting for taste where love was concerned. Though it had always seemed to Babs that Nigel hadn't really loved Dee, not in the way he should, but had married her because he'd thought she was good wife material.

The art gallery was up a little side street. You would have walked past it if you hadn't known it was there. According to the sign inside the doorway, all the paintings were done by local artists. There were the inevitable beach scenes, ships on a stormy sea, and a few abstracts. Babs was standing in front of a vivid abstract painting, trying to make out what it was supposed to be, when she was interrupted by a phone call from Molly. 'Mum, you need to come home. Dad says he's got a viewer coming tomorrow!'

What? 'How dare he!' Babs said, then lowered her voice when she noticed people staring at her. 'He knows how I feel about it and he's still gone ahead and done it.'

'I've tried talking to him, Mum, but he won't listen. You've got to come home and talk some sense into him.'

Babs glanced around. Dee was mesmerised by a painting of a lighthouse at night-time, its beam of light slicing through the dark night sky, guiding a ship to safety.

'I love that one,' Dee exclaimed.

'Thank you.'

A man was standing behind them, his long silver-grey hair thick and a bit wild-looking. He was suntanned and had deep blue eyes and a small moustache. Dee's eyes widened and Babs heard her exclaim, 'Kenny Roscoe!'

13

DEE

'Dee Walton! Goodness me, it's been years!'

It had, but Dee would have recognised Kenny anywhere, especially that rich deep voice of his. Fancy bumping into him here!

Babs looked from one to the other. 'You know each other?'

'Kenny and Margot lived near Nigel and me when we were first married. They moved away though, and we lost touch,' Dee explained.

Babs indicated her phone, then the doorway and stepped outside into the street. Dee guessed that Geoff or one of her children had called. She turned her attention back to Kenny. 'Is Margot with you?' She looked around for Kenny's wife.

Kenny shook his head. 'I'm afraid she died a few years ago.'

'I'm so sorry,' Dee said softly, reaching out and briefly touching his hand in sympathy.

'Me too, but I've learnt to live with it. You have to, don't you?' He smiled at Dee. 'How about you? Is Nigel with you?'

'No, he's on a golfing holiday in Portugal.' Dee looked again at the painting. 'This really is good. Have you always been an artist?'

'I started painting in France, as a hobby, then when we came back to live in Port Telwyn – I grew up here, you know – we opened a craft shop. In the winter Margot made jewellery and I painted, in the summer we sold what we made in our shop.'

'Do you still have the shop?' Dee asked.

'No, I'm retired now and I paint as a hobby. I've a little studio in my backyard.' He stroked his beard. 'How long are you here for?'

'Only until Saturday, we got a last minute deal,' Dee told him.

'Well if you're at a loose end tonight why don't you and your friend drop into The Pirate's Head later for a drink and a chat? It would be good to catch up again.'

'That sounds great, I'm sure Babs, my friend, would enjoy it too. What time would be best?'

'We've got a meeting about raising funds for the new Artists' Studios first, but we should be finished by eight, so make it after then?'

'I'll run it by Babs, see what she thinks. If not, maybe I'll bump into you again while we're here.'

'I'm sure you will. You'll find me in Moira's most lunchtimes. That lady does a mean bacon and egg buttie.' He nodded. 'Enjoy the rest of your day and hopefully see you later.'

'Well, he's a bit of a dish, isn't he?' Babs joined her as Kenny walked away. 'He reminds me of an older David Cassidy. You had quite a thing for him, didn't you? You used to plaster your walls with pictures of him, remember?'

'And you used to be mad on Donny Osmond,' Dee replied. 'Goodness, where have those years gone?'

'It feels like it was only yesterday.' Babs fixed her eyes on

Dee. 'Now tell me more about this Kenny. Is he on holiday too? How long has it been since you last met?'

Dee thought for a moment. 'It must be at least thirty years.' She repeated her conversation with Kenny. 'It's such a shame about Margot, she was a lovely woman. So full of life, and always ready to lend a hand.' Like Babs, she thought. She could tell that Nigel had been delighted when Margot had moved away. He would have probably liked her to lose contact with Babs too, but they had been friends far too long for that. And Margot leaving brought them even closer, as Babs had moved nearby a few months later when Geoff's father died.

'Fancy meeting down here though, when we've done a runner from our husbands. It's such a small world,' Babs remarked.

'It is. I do wish Margot was here too,' Dee said wistfully. She would have loved to have a catch up with Margot. 'Kenny has invited us to the local pub, The Pirate's Head, this evening, if you fancy it. Apparently a few of the villagers will be there as they're having a meeting about raising funds for the local Artists' Studios. What do you think?'

'Sure, it might be fun,' Babs agreed. 'It's nice that you've met Kenny again, isn't it? I was looking forward to you and me time but it's great to connect with some of the villagers while we're down here.' She looped her arm through Dee's. 'Now, how about a walk along the beach and a paddle in the sea?'

'That sounds perfect!' Dee told her. She doubted if she would be paddling but she she knew Babs would.

'This is the life,' Babs said contentedly as they walked along the sand, the breeze blowing their hair. She stopped by a wall and sat down. 'I'm going to take my sandals off and walk barefoot. It's been years since I felt the sand between my toes.'

Dee smiled as she watched her friend slip off her sandals.

Babs always had the gift of enjoying the moment, no matter what else was happening.

'Go on, be a devil and let your hair down. You know you want to,' Babs said, looking up at her.

Dee hesitated then sat down and took her sandals off too. She wriggled her toes in the warm sand. Maybe she would go for a paddle after all.

As if reading her mind, Babs stood up, her sandals dangling on her fingers. 'Race you to the sea!' She darted off across the beach.

Dee paused then followed, catching up with Babs as she reached the water, both leaving their sandals by a nearby rock. They stepped in, letting the cool water flow over their feet. The waves gently rolled in, breaking over their feet.

'Let's jump them!' Babs suggested. She paddled out into the sea towards a white, foamy wave and jumped over it as it broke, splashing water all over her. 'Come on, Dee, this is fun!' She laughed.

Dee hesitated and looked around. The beach was pretty empty, no one was watching them. No one cares if two older ladies lark around in the sea, she told herself. She paddled over to join Babs just as a bigger wave came crashing onto the shore covering her from head to toe.

She spluttered and coughed, pushing her wet hair off her face.

'I'm soaking!' she shouted to Babs.

'You'll soon dry.' Babs laughed as she jumped over another wave.

What the heck, she couldn't get any wetter, could she? Dee thought. Besides it was quite exhilarating. She waded further into the sea.

Babs grinned at her. 'Good job I packed a cossie in my case, I might have a swim tomorrow. Did you bring one? I meant to remind you.'

Dee hastily stepped back as a huge wave tumbled in. 'No, it didn't even occur to me.'

'Shame, you bought some lovely new ones too. Never mind, you can get one in the town in the morning,' Babs suggested.

'It's a bit public to wear a swimming costume.' Dee wasn't as confident about her body now she was getting older. When she'd bought the new tankinis she'd thought she'd be wearing them in the pool of a private villa in Portugal.

Babs tossed her hair from her face. 'Who cares? The older I get, the less I care what other people think.'

'I don't think you've *ever* cared what other people think,' Dee replied with a smile. Actually, it would be good to be as carefree as Babs, and to stop worrying about what people thought. Maybe she would buy a swimming costume and go for a swim in the sea.

When they'd had a paddle, they dried their feet on a couple of tissues Babs had in her handbag, slipped their sandals back on and put the tissues in their pockets then continued their walk across the sand. It was warm and Dee was soon feeling thirsty. She looked around to see if there was a refreshment stall anywhere and spotted an ice cream van a few feet in front of them.

'Fancy an ice cream?' she asked.

'God, yes, I'm parched. Shall we have a 99 again?' Babs asked. 'Double flake this time?'

Dee grinned. This is one of the reasons she loved having Babs as a friend. Her joy for life was infectious.

'Are you on holiday, ladies?' the ice cream man asked as he filled two cones with ice cream and put two chocolate flakes in each.

'Yes, we're down here for the week,' Babs told him. 'Celebrating this one's birthday,' she jerked her finger at Dee.

'Really? Then happy birthday.' The man smiled and squirted chocolate sauce on both cones, then stuck an extra flake in Dee's.

'Thank you.' Babs handed over the money, insisting it was her treat, then they both set off across the beach again.

'I'll have gained a stone by the time we go home,' Dee said as she licked the ice cream before it dripped off her cone.

'There's worse things than having a bit of extra weight,' Babs told her. 'You worry too much about your figure. Stop trying to please Nigel.'

Dee knew her friend was right, but it was hard to change the habits of a lifetime. Nigel had an image to keep up, and as his wife, he pointed out that Dee did too. He kept a firm eye on his weight, and how he dressed, and expected Dee to do the same. Babs and Geoff were both far more relaxed about it and never let the thought of putting on a couple of extra pounds stop them from eating their favourite foods.

'That was delicious, but my hands are all sticky now. I think I've got some wipes in my bag.' Babs opened her bag, she always carried wipes and tissues with her because she was forever spilling things. She took out a packet of wipes, handed the packet to Dee to take one, then took one herself and slipped the packet back into her bag.

'Thanks.' Dee wiped her fingers carefully and looked around for a bin. Suddenly a gust of wind blew the wipe out of Babs' hand and onto the sand in front of her. Before she could get to pick it up a voice shouted. 'Oi, pick that up! Do you realise what harm litter does to wildlife! You holidaymakers are always the same!'

A tall, well-built man with a thick mop of dark auburn hair

and a beard was walking towards them, evidently furious. 'Apart from littering the beach and making it look disgusting, if those wet wipes get swept into the sea, they'll play havoc with marine life.'

Babs glared at him. 'Wind your neck in! I was about to put it in the bin when the wind blew it out of my hand.'

'That's everyone's excuse!' the man retorted.

'Actually, it's the truth!' The man really was so rude, Dee felt compelled to speak up. Babs had retrieved her wipe by now and was marching over to the bin with it. Dee followed suit. They took the crumpled tissues they'd use to wipe their feet out of their pockets and put them in the bin too.

'Make sure you don't drop any litter again, or I'll report you and you'll be fined,' the man said, pointing to a 'don't drop litter' sign beside the bin. Then he strode off.

'What an unpleasant man! Though he is quite striking, rather like a Titan,' Babs said. 'I hope we don't bump into him again or I might not be able to stop myself from giving him a piece of my mind.'

'He was unpleasant but there is a lot of litter on the beach, I can see his point, even if he did judge us too hastily,' Dee said.

Babs pulled a face. 'You're always too forgiving with people.' She took out a tissue and mopped her forehead, making sure she held it tightly in her hand, then returned it to her bag. 'It's getting hot.'

They took a walk around the town, popping into several of the little souvenir shops, coming a full circle to Sunset View. Dee paused as they approached the row of cottages, looking out for Primrose Cottage, Snowy's home. There it was, the second one along, and she could hear a cat miaowing. She glanced over the low wall with an iron gate surrounding the front of the house, and saw Snowy yowling plaintively, scratching at the front door as if asking to be let in. Edna must be out. Dee's eyes flitted towards the bay window, the curtains were closed, and so were the upstairs' bedroom curtains.

'What's up?' Babs glanced over. 'Oh, it's Snowy. It looks like Edna's out, no wonder he came to you for food.'

'Strange for her to go out without opening the curtains,' Dee mused. Checking her watch she saw that it was gone two o'clock. She had an uneasy feeling in her gut. She often visited local elderly people and helped with their shopping, and knew how particular they were about opening their curtains. And how vulnerable they were. And Snowy sounded very distressed. What if Edna was ill? What harm would it do to check? Dee opened the gate and stepped inside the front garden.

'What are you doing?' Babs asked curiously.

'Just making sure that everything's all right.' Dee headed for the front door, stooped down and shouted through the letter box. 'Edna! Are you there?'

Snowy had stopped miaowing now, his dark eyes watching her. Then she heard it. It was faint but audible.

'Help! Help me!'

14

'Edna's hurt. I have to phone an ambulance.' Dee reached for her phone and jabbed at the number nine key three times. The lady who answered calmly assured her that an ambulance would be there as soon as possible, and the police would be alerted too. Whilst Dee was phoning, Babs quickly checked around the back to see if she could get in.

'The gate's locked and it's too high to climb over,' she said.

When Dee finished her call, she shouted through the letter box to ask Edna if she had a spare key, but there had been no answer. What if the poor woman was unconscious and the ambulance didn't arrive in time?

'Let's check under the stones and plant pots, she might have hidden a key there,' she suggested. But they couldn't find one.

Dee checked her watch. Fifteen minutes and still no sign of an ambulance.

'We'll have to see if we can get over the back gate,' she said. 'Come on.'

They both raced around to the back. As Babs had said, it was locked and there was no sign of a keyhole so it must have a bolt, which would probably be near the middle otherwise it would be too high to reach. Dee looked up at the wall. Could she shimmy over that without breaking her neck?

'Can you give me a leg up? I might be able to climb over,' she said.

'Be careful,' Babs warned as she looped her hands together and Dee stepped onto them, heaving herself up the wall. She'd just gripped it firmly when Babs screamed and her hands disappeared, pulling Dee's shorts with her, leaving Dee dangling from the wall, her shorts around her ankles. Whatever had possessed her to wear the elastic-waisted shorts instead of button waist ones?

'Babs! Get me down! You can't leave me like this!' she shouted, clinging on for her life, not daring to look around.

'I fell, sorry,' Babs stammered. 'Hang on, I'm coming.'

'You ladies don't look the type to go house-breaking,' said an amused voice behind her. It was Kenny.

Oh God, of all the people to come along when she was clinging onto a wall, shorts around her ankles, knickers on display – and brief black lacy ones at that. She felt her cheeks burn.

'Edna needs help. I've called an ambulance but they're taking ages. I was trying to get in through the back,' Dee said, between gasps. 'Can you give me a lift over?' And pull my shorts up, please? Dee wanted to ask but couldn't bring herself to voice the words.

'Look, let me help you down and I'll climb over,' Kenny said.

'You will not! Perishing men taking over! She's almost there,' Dee heard Babs say.

Dee could feel her hands slipping. 'Please can one of you—'

Then she felt two strong hands grip her waist and lower her to the ground.

'Thank you!' She brushed Kenny's hands away, reached for her shorts and pulled them up, not daring to look at his face. She had the strong impression that he was holding back laughter. She could kill Babs for putting her in this position.

They all spun around as they heard the sound of sirens and then an ambulance followed by a police car came speeding around the corner, screeching to a halt on the kerb.

'Thank goodness. It was me who called you. The poor lady who lives here is injured. We were trying to get over the back gate to see if we could get in and help her,' she explained as a burly policewoman and a slender policeman got out of the car.

'Leave it to us now, madam, we'll deal with it,' the policeman said. 'Thank you for calling us. We'll see if we can get in the front door.'

Dee, Babs and Kenny all hurried around to the front of the cottage. The policewoman hurled her shoulder at the door and after a couple of attempts it sprang open. The police went inside, calling Edna's name. The paramedics followed, with Dee and Babs behind them. Dee's hand flew to her mouth when she saw an elderly lady lying on the floor, the paramedics kneeling beside her.

'Is she okay?' she asked, watching them worriedly.

'She's alive, but it's a good job you found her when you did. She's been lying here for some time and is very dehydrated.'

As they carried Edna on a stretcher to the ambulance the woman flickered her eyes open. 'Snowy,' she said weakly.

'Snowy is her cat.' Dee dashed forward. 'I'll look after Snowy. I'm Dee and this is Babs,' she pointed to Babs. 'We're staying at Sunset View.'

'Thank you.' Edna closed her eyes wearily.

Dee looked around for Snowy. The cat had disappeared. 'Has he gone inside?' she asked.

'We'll go and have a look, then we'll get the front door secured,' the policewoman told her.

They found Snowy cuddled up in his basket in the lounge. Dee felt so sorry for the little cat, he must be wondering what was happening. And he barely knew Dee, although he'd been happy enough to let her stroke him. Would he let her pick him up and carry him out of the house?

She walked over to Snowy slowly, stooping down and keeping her tone soft. 'Hello, Snowy. I'm coming to look after you until your mummy is better.' She bent down to pick him up but he jumped out of the basket and shot out of the house.

'Take the basket with you, he'll probably come back to you later,' the policewoman told her. 'I'll see if I can find any cat food.'

Dee picked up the basket and took it out of the cottage. The policewoman came out carrying two tins of food and a cat dish, handed them to Dee then pulled the door to. 'The contractor will be here any minute to secure the door,' she said. 'Do you know if Edna has any family we should contact?'

Dee shook her head. 'We're on holiday here, we only arrived yesterday, but you could ask at Moira's Café, a lady called Andi works there and she knows Edna well. It's on the harbour front.'

'Thank you. I'll do that.' The policewoman nodded. 'And if you could give me your phone number, please, in case I have further questions.'

'Of course,' Dee agreed. Then she looked around anxiously. 'Where could Snowy have gone?'

'Don't worry, he'll be back,' Babs assured her.

Dee hope so. She'd impulsively offered to look after him; what else could she do? But what if he had run off and never came back?

15

When they got back to Sunset View, Dee put Snowy's basket in the far corner of the living room, by the French doors. Then she opened the doors and stepped outside.

'Snowy!' she called, hoping that the cat had decided to visit again.

'Is he here?' Babs stood in the doorway, looking out.

Dee shook her head. 'What if he's so scared he's run off?'

'He's lived with Edna a long time, he'll be back,' Babs told her. 'I'll put the shopping in the fridge.' They'd picked up some ham, cheese, lettuce, tomatoes and cucumber, and crusty rolls during their walk around the village.

'I think I'll put some cat food in a dish and leave it on Edna's front doorstep in case Snowy comes back home,' Dee said. 'I won't be long.'

Babs nodded. 'That's a good idea.'

Dee was back in a few minutes and they both sat outside having a cold drink. Then the police phoned to say that they'd traced Edna's son, Martin, and informed him about what had happened, and that Dee was looking after Snowy.

If only she was, Dee thought sadly. She was worried that the little cat was so frightened, it might not come back.

After dinner they popped around to Edna's to see if Snowy had returned. Dee was disappointed to see that the cat food was still in the bowl and there was no sign of Snowy. He could be in the back garden, she guessed, but she wasn't attempting to climb over that wall again. She would go round again in the morning.

'Right, now, let's get our glad rags on and go off to The Pirate's Head. I'm looking forward to having a drink and meeting everyone,' Babs said.

Dee had been hoping Babs had forgotten about that. She was dreading meeting Kenny again after he'd seen her hanging from Edna's gate with her shorts around her ankles.

'How about we get a bottle of wine and stay in?' she suggested. 'We can put a film on.'

Babs folded her arms and looked at her sternly. 'I'm guessing this is because sexy Kenny saw your knickers?'

Dee felt herself flush.

'Look, I'm sorry, that was my fault and I guess it's embarrassing, but you saved Edna's life. That's more important than Kenny seeing your knickers.' She winked. 'And very nice knickers they were, too, by the way. If my shorts had fallen down, all he'd have got was an eyeful of my big white patterned pants! Can you imagine what a sight that would have been?'

'Rubbish!' Dee said, smiling in spite of herself. 'Okay, yes, I do feel a bit awkward.'

'Well, don't. If Kenny's the gentleman he seems to be he won't mention it at all.' She nudged Dee with her elbow. 'Although he might think about it!'

Dee gave her a playful slap. 'Oh, you!'

The Pirate's Head was teeming when they walked in that

evening. Kenny was sitting at a long table with a few others, and waved them over. Dee felt a little bit uncomfortable but as soon as they'd got themselves a spritzer each they wound their way through the crowd to join him. Amongst them was the couple from the restaurant.

'Everyone, this is Dee and Babs.' He turned to the two friends. 'I've been telling them how you both rescued poor Edna. Have you heard how she is?'

Dee wondered exactly what Kenny had told everyone but their faces seemed concerned not amused, so maybe he hadn't said anything. She repeated what the police had told her. 'Edna's cat, Snowy, still hasn't come home,' she said. 'I've left some food out for him and will check again in the morning.'

'It was a good job you realised something was wrong with Edna, and very kind of you to offer to take care of Snowy.' The woman from the restaurant smiled. 'I'm Cath, by the way. And this is my partner, Stu.' She turned to the group. 'We met these two ladies at the restaurant last night, celebrating Dee's birthday.'

'Belated happy birthday, Dee,' Kenny said. The others raised their glasses. 'Cheers!'

'Thank you.' Dee felt a little embarrassed but Kenny continued the introductions. 'This is Teri, Flic and Dot.' Kenny pointed to each person in turn. Dee guessed that Flic was short for Felicity. 'Dee is an old friend of mine and Margot's. She and Babs are on holiday for a week, staying in Sunset View,' he explained.

'We also met earlier,' boomed a voice behind them. 'I caught them throwing litter on the beach.' It was the Titan.

Dee felt her cheeks flush and was about to deny this, but Babs got there before her. 'You most certainly did not!' Babs retorted emphatically. 'As we told you at the time, what you saw was the wind blowing the wipe out of our hands!' She glared at the man in a 'how dare you' kind of way.

'She's right, it was an accident. We tried to explain but you wouldn't listen,' Dee said calmly, feeling the need to support her friend and defend themselves in front of Kenny and the others, albeit in a quieter way than Babs.

'Which has happened to me a few times. I know you care about keeping the beach safe, Glenn, but don't be too hasty to jump to conclusions. Dee is definitely not a litter lout and I'm quite sure her friend isn't either.' Kenny sprang to their defence.

Glenn nodded curtly. 'Glad to hear it.'

Dee could see that Babs was seething and the look she gave Glenn was scathing. She didn't blame her though, the man was a jerk and had no right to embarrass them in such a public way over a hand wipe, for goodness' sake. She took a seat opposite Kenny. Babs pulled out the one beside her and sat down, realising too late that she was opposite Glenn. They would glare at each other all evening now, as she got the impression Glenn was just as stubborn as Babs. Dee fixed a smile on her face and attempted to change the conversation. 'Have you finished your fundraising meeting?' she asked Kenny.

'Just wrapped it up,' he replied. 'We're hoping to raise enough money at the Manor on Saturday to put six months' rent down on the old warehouse, then we can start letting it out into separate spaces for the artists.'

'I think that's such a good idea,' Dee said enthusiastically.

'It is, but we're running out of original ideas to raise funds,' Cath told her.

'Dee does a lot of fundraising, don't you?' Babs turned to Dee. 'I bet you've got lots of ideas.'

'That's useful to know, Dee. What sort of things did you do to raise funds?' Cath asked.

Dee thought about it, some of the things they did, such as Charity challenges, wouldn't work for this. 'How about virtual fundraising events? You could all give an online demonstration of your skills, a painting workshop, jewellery making, glass blowing, etc., for a donation to be used towards the Artists' Studios? Maybe you could have some practical workshops that the public could join in with at the garden party?'

'Or a fun event such as an Open Mic night? A pirate and mermaid fancy dress?' Babs added.

Everyone looked impressed. 'Great ideas, ladies,' Kenny said approvingly.

'It's a shame you have to go back on Saturday, and can't join in the fun,' Teri said.

'That's *if* we go back,' Babs muttered darkly.

'Do I detect man trouble?' Cath asked. 'If you want to offload, we're all ears, but equally if you prefer not to talk about it, that's fine too.'

Babs swigged back the last of her spritzer. 'My husband has decided that, now we're retired, he's going to sell up and live in Spain, whether I want to or not.' She swept her gaze over the group. 'And I don't want to. So I've run away until he takes the house off the market and considers my feelings too.'

Cath clapped. 'Good for you.' The others joined in.

'I think that's appalling.' Kenny's eyes rested on Dee. 'It sounds like you've both "run away". I hope your situation isn't similar.'

Dee could feel everyone watching her and wondered whether to say anything. Her reason sounded a bit immature compared to Babs.

She shrugged. 'It doesn't sound like much but Nigel, my husband, is always going off with his mates golfing and this year he decided to go off with them to Portugal on my sixtieth birthday. So when Babs said she was going away, I thought I'd join her. We looked online for a holiday cottage in Cornwall, found Sunset View and here we are.'

There was another clap at this. All apart from Glenn.

'Well, power to you, ladies,' he said, 'for putting the men in your life in place, but that holiday cottage could provide a home for local working people if people like you weren't prepared to pay extortionate rents for it. People like you are driving the locals out of their own area, making them move away from family and friends.' He pushed his chair back and stood up.

Babs glared at him. 'Oi! It's the landlords that buy the properties and turn them into holiday lets, charging extortionate rents, not the holidaymakers! And you can't blame people for wanting to get away from the rat race for a week or two.'

'Can't I? You holidaymakers take up homes our kids need to live in, litter our beaches with your rubbish, then go home until the next time you feel like a week or two in the sun. You don't care about the damage you do to those of us who live and work down here.' He turned and walked off to the bar to get another drink.

Babs and Dee looked at each other, speechless.

'Well, he's a right ray of sunshine, isn't he?' Babs said.

There was a silence around the table then Kenny said, 'He's a single dad, his wife died a couple of years ago. Last week his young daughter, Sammi, cut her leg on broken glass left on the beach, just missed an artery and could have bled to death. She's all he's got.'

Dee gasped and put her hand to her mouth. 'How awful.'

'So that's why he was mad when he thought we were littering the beach,' Babs said. 'Although he didn't have to be so rude.'

'I know, but Glenn's going through it a bit at the moment,'

Cath added. 'He's struggling to find accommodation he can afford. He might have to move away from the village and he's lived down here all his life That will be a big blow for him, especially as the lady next door is like a grandmother to Sammi. She's looking after her tonight.'

There was a silence around the table as they all digested Cath's remarks. No wonder Glenn was so bitter, Dee thought.

16

'That's tough,' Babs acknowledged. 'But it doesn't excuse rudeness.'

'We know,' Kenny agreed. 'Glenn can be a bit too quick to jump in.'

He'd picked the wrong person to do that to, Dee thought ruefully. Babs didn't take any prisoners and now Glenn had rubbed her up the wrong way, it looked like sparks might fly between them.

'Is there anything else we can help with, we're here for the week?' Dee asked. She liked to be useful and thought it would also be a good idea for Babs to have something to get involved in, take her mind off things. Although, she might have to keep Babs and Glenn apart!

'We have a beach clean-up tomorrow morning, you can join that if you want. Though I'd better warn you that Glenn is the one running it,' Cath said.

Dee turned questioningly to Babs. They had planned to go to St Michael's Mount, but they would have plenty of time to do that later in the week.

'I'm up for that,' Babs agreed. 'And I'm sure we can handle Grumpy Glenn.'

'I'll ignore that.' Glenn had returned now and took his seat at the table. Babs met his gaze defiantly. He shrugged and put his hands up. 'Okay, I admit I was a bit sharp. I apologise.'

'Accepted,' Dee said and Babs added, 'I should think so. After all, holidaymakers bring in a lot of work and income to the area too.'

Glenn gave her a sharp look. 'That's as maybe,' he said grudgingly. 'But if you mean that about joining the Beach Clean-Up, be at Telwyn Beach tomorrow morning at eight.' Glenn took a sip of his beer. 'We need all the help we can get.'

'We'll be there,' Babs replied.

'Do we need to bring anything with us?' Dee asked.

'It will all be provided.' Glenn glanced at their clothes. 'Mind you, it's not a dress up job.'

Babs rolled her eyes. 'Don't worry we're not going to turn up in our glad rags. We do have some common sense.' Her tone was lighter now though and there was also a small smile on Glenn's lips as he replied.

'Glad to hear it.'

Hopefully those two would call a truce now, Dee thought. It would be good to not only be involved with something, but to have a group to socialise with while they were down here. It would make the holiday an even more pleasant one.

The atmosphere lightened considerably after that and the conversation turned to the garden party being held to raise funds for the Artists' Studios the following Saturday afternoon. Someone was making cakes and providing refreshments, and there were stalls for the artists to display their wares and lots of activities going on.

'Is there time to run any "join the artist" sessions?' Dee

asked. 'It might attract a lot of attention if the artists not only showed how they do their crafts, but gave the public a chance to join in too.'

Kenny looked thoughtful. 'That's a great idea, we've only got a few days to go but I could do a painting session and I'm sure some of the artists could put something together. We'll suggest the idea to them and see what they can come up with.'

'For future funds, have you thought of approaching local businesses to see if they'll sponsor any of the artists? Perhaps they could agree on creating something bespoke to promote the business too? For example a glassmaker could make a special glass with the name of the business on it? Or a jewellery maker could make a pendant and earrings that the business can sell in their store. I went to a book festival last year and lots of the authors had pendants and earrings with their book covers on them. They were very popular.'

'Dee, that's brilliant!' Kenny said. 'We're going to have to get together for a promotion ideas meeting before you go back home. It's a shame you don't live down here, we could do with you on the committee.'

'Perhaps you could still be on the committee when you go back home, Dee. We can have online meetings and maybe you could even come down to an event now and again,' Cath suggested.

'I'd love that,' Dee agreed. This is what she'd been looking for, something fresh to get involved with. And the Arts were close to her heart. When she was a teacher she used to do a lot of craftwork with the children in school, and enjoyed making paper flowers to brighten up her flat, and colourful paper bead jewellery, before she met Nigel. Then she got too busy helping him with his paperwork, running the home, and looking after the children. Nigel also pointed out that the set they mixed with were into diamonds, gold and pearls, not home-made paper beads.

'Right, I'm off.' Glenn put his empty tankard down on the table. 'See you both on the beach at eight tomorrow. And remember, old clothes.'

He seemed to have mellowed a bit, thank goodness, Dee thought. She had been worried that he and Babs were going to have an all-out row but Babs had a big heart and after learning what Glenn was going through, Dee knew that Babs would forgive his outburst, although she wouldn't put up with any more of them.

Dee sometimes wished she could be like Babs, but she hated confrontation and arguments. Many a time she'd stayed in her bedroom, hiding under the duvet, as her parents argued and threw things. Their rows were heated and noisy, although thankfully, never got violent, and as an only child she'd found them deeply traumatising. It made her fear any kind of argument and she bent over backwards to keep the peace, trying to look at the bigger picture. It was a habit she'd carried into her married life, squashing her anger and upset with Nigel in order to keep the house peaceful, and life secure for Annabel and Hugh. She had never wanted to make them feel as scared as she had been, worried that things would escalate or that Dee and Nigel would get divorced. Dee had once mentioned this to her mother – as the reason she always tried to keep the peace, when her mother had told Dee that she should stand up for herself more. Her mother had looked at her in astonishment, insisting that she and Dee's father had no idea their arguments had made her feel that way. 'We were simply clearing the air, we adored each other, surely you knew that?' And they must have done because they remained together right until her father died, and her mother had never remarried, dying a few years later. 'Love doesn't mean you have to be a doormat, Dee,' her mother had said, but Dee preferred to be a 'doormat' than have a confrontation. She couldn't deal with arguments and she didn't want her children to have to either.

Now though, the children were grown up and Dee was tired of Nigel taking her for granted, of being overlooked, of always being the one to keep the peace. She could feel the stirring of rebellion growing in her.

When they arrived back at the cottage Dee went straight out into the backyard and was relieved to see Snowy lying on one of the garden chairs. He lifted his head and miaowed at her.

'Snowy's back!' she shouted, hurrying over to the little cat, then sitting on the chair beside him and stroking him.

'Thank goodness for that!' Babs came out with a small dish of milk which Snowy lapped up eagerly. Then he followed them into the house and curled up on Dee's lap on the sofa.

'I'm going to miss you when I go home,' Dee said softly as she stroked him.

'You could always get a cat.' Babs handed her a mug of hot chocolate. 'I think I might get another dog when Geoff stops being a stupid bugger. It will do him good to have a dog to walk, stop him getting any more crazy ideas.'

'Maybe I will,' Dee said. She was going to miss this cottage too. And Port Telwyn. This was only her second day here but she felt more alive and accepted than she'd done for a long time.

When she returned home she was going to talk to Nigel, she decided. Things had to change.

17

BABS

Monday

'Do you think this is suitable "clean up the beach" wear?' Babs asked, walking into the kitchen and doing a twirl. She was wearing bright yellow shorts, a daisy print scooped neck T-shirt and daisy patterned trainers.

'Perfect,' Dee replied. She was wearing shorts again, tailored khaki ones that buttoned at the waist this time, with a plain white V-neck T-shirt, and suddenly felt a bit drab compared to Babs. Maybe she should experiment a bit with brighter colours, she thought. She did like turquoise, which wasn't exactly dull, but she never wore red, yellow or orange, thinking they were too loud. Or was it Nigel who had said that? She'd get a couple of brighter outfits when she and Babs went shopping. 'We've got time for breakfast then we'll be off.' She flicked the kettle on and plugged in the toaster. 'I've been around to Edna's and brought Snowy's dish back – the cat food had gone so I've washed the dish and given him some fresh food.'

'You've been busy. Have you heard how Edna is?' Babs took

the butter and marmalade out of the fridge as Dee put four slices of bread in the toaster.

'Yes, I phoned the hospital, explained that we were the ones who'd raised the alarm and asked how she's doing. Thankfully, she's recovering well but has twisted her ankle and hurt her hip in the fall. The policewoman phoned me a few minutes ago, too, she's been in touch with Edna's son, Martin, who is her next of kin. He's driving down today. He lives in Yorkshire so it's a bit of a trek for him. She asked if she could give him my phone number, and, of course, I said "yes".'

'That's good news – not the injuries, of course. I wonder how Edna will manage when she comes home? Perhaps she'll have to sleep downstairs for a while.'

The toast popped and Dee put it on two plates. 'I wondered about that too. She's not going to manage those stairs until her hip and ankle recover. I guess she might want a stairlift but I don't know how expensive they are and how quickly they can be fitted. I thought that maybe we could go and visit her in Truro hospital later, then we can see if there's anything we can help with.'

'Good idea.' Babs spread a thick layer of butter then marmalade on her toast. 'And how about we go shopping before we visit Edna? There's quite a big shopping centre in Truro, we can get you a cossie so we can go for a swim in the sea.' She bit into her toast and waited for Dee's reaction.

Dee nodded. 'Okay. Why not?'

Babs grinned in delight. It seemed like her friend was getting a little more daring, which was fantastic. She adored Dee but she definitely needed to loosen up a bit.

They finished their breakfast, left Snowy sleeping in their backyard and headed down to the beach, it was already a hive of activity. Babs was surprised at seeing such a good turnout. Glenn called everyone together for a safety briefing.

'Always make sure you wear gloves and be aware of sharp objects.' He passed around a box containing heavy duty plastic gloves. Then he handed out reusable buckets, thick plastic bags, rakes and shovels, a sifter, and hand sanitisers and biodegradable wipes with explanations on how to use them. 'Remember to use sun cream, handle sharp objects carefully and stay hydrated,' he said.

'You'd think we were going on a dangerous expedition in a jungle instead of picking up a bit of litter,' Babs murmured.

Glenn spun around, he'd obviously heard her comment, and fixed her with a steely glare. 'Litter can cause accidents. I don't want to ruin my day by having to rush one of you to hospital because you've cut your hand on a broken bottle or tin can.'

'That's me told,' Babs said, resisting the temptation to salute. Honestly, Glenn could be a bit of a jobsworth, but then he was in charge of the group so had a responsibility to them all, she reminded herself. And his daughter had cut her leg on something dumped on the beach, she remembered, feeling a bit guilty. Sometimes she spoke before she thought. Well, most of the time actually. Perhaps she should try and be a bit more diplomatic, like Dee.

Cath took over then, telling them how to sort out and dispose of wastage, differentiating between trash and recyclables and keeping a tally of the type and amount of trash collected. 'It's important information, and helps with future planning,' she said.

They were divided into groups and assigned a different area of the beach to work on, then off they went. Babs and Dee were in the same team, with a woman called Teresa. Thank goodness they weren't with Glenn, Babs thought as she pulled on her gloves and set about cleaning up the beach. She knew he was only doing his job but she didn't think she'd be able to cope with him watching her every move and calling her out if she did something wrong.

Fifteen minutes in she was amazed at the amount of rubbish she'd collected, and understood why Glenn had been so upset. There were literally hundreds of cigarette butts, numerous plastic bags, broken bottles – which gave her the shivers remembering how she'd walked barefoot on the beach yesterday, not to mention cans, food wrappers, straws, used condoms – yuck! – balloons and rubber bands. All of this could be harmful to wildlife and people. 'I can't believe people can dump all this stuff,' she complained to Dee. 'There's plenty of bins on the beach. It's selfishness.'

Dee glanced at her, amused. 'You sound like Glenn – but yes, it is.'

When they all stopped for a break half an hour later, they all had full trash bags, and recycling buckets.

'What do you actually do with all this?' Babs asked Glenn.

'We weigh and record it, as much as we can. The data is useful to raise public awareness of the amount of litter dumped and the impact of it on the environment. Then I take it in my van to local trash and recyclables pick-up points,' Glenn told her. 'We do three beach clean-ups a month, at different locations, but we can never seem to get on top of the trash.'

Babs looked around at the now clear section of beach and the bags of rubbish they'd collected. Multiply this by the number of beaches in this part of Cornwall alone and she could understand why Glenn was angry. He had a job and his daughter to look after, so it really was good of him to give up his morning to organise the beach clean-up. All the other people here, too, a mixture of ages, giving up their spare time to make a difference. Some of them were retired, like her, so was it to fill their days? Or because life was passing them by and they wanted to grab the days and do something useful with them?

Like Geoff wanting to do something with his life before he got too old? That's why he wanted to go to Spain, he'd said. She could understand him longing for new horizons and adventures, but why couldn't they simply go on more holidays? A couple of cruises, perhaps. Why did he insist that they turn their whole life upside down?

18

DEE

She'd enjoyed the beach tidy up, being part of the community, and liked the idea of being involved with the Port Telwyn Artists' Studios committee even when she went back home, Dee thought when they were back at Sunset View. She had lots of fundraising ideas already. They could do a Facebook page for the group, introducing all the artists and their work, with maybe links to each artist's individual pages. If there was enough interest maybe they could do a GoFundMe page to raise more. Perhaps they could do an online shop too, where the artists could sell their wares, and they could offer workshops on Zoom or YouTube. She jotted down all her ideas, ready to discuss with Kenny later.

Her mind flitted to Nigel in Portugal. She hadn't heard from him since she'd refused to go back home to collect his parcel, she wondered if he'd arranged for it to be redirected, or redelivered on Saturday as he'd be home early that morning. She didn't want to miss the fundraising garden party in the afternoon though, so she and Babs were planning on going home afterwards. It wouldn't hurt Nigel to come home to an empty house for once.

She could hear Babs on the phone in the garden and wondered if she was speaking to Geoff. He'd phoned her several times, trying to talk her into going home, but Babs wasn't showing any sign of wanting to go back. And Dee couldn't blame her.

'Honestly, he makes my blood boil!' Babs exclaimed as she stormed into the lounge.

'Who? Geoff?'

'Yes, bloody Geoff! He's still going ahead with the house-viewing trip to Spain. I've told him that I'm not going and he can cancel any viewings whilst he's away too, because I'm not having people traipsing around my home. I'll double-lock the front door and take the bloody "For Sale" board down!' She sank down onto the sofa. 'He's still going ahead with exactly what he wants and ignoring everything I say.'

'Maybe you should go back and talk. You're not going to sort this out when you're not even in the same location,' Dee pointed out.

Babs shook her head. 'Stop trying to send me back home or I'll be thinking you don't want me here! I'm staying put. I've never been away without Geoff before and it was a bit strange at first, but now, well, I'm enjoying it. It was good to be involved in the beach clean-up today, and the fundraising do next Saturday, instead of the same old life.' She took a deep breath. 'The thing is, Geoff said he's been bored since we sold the shop, well I have been too. I miss the interaction with the customers, the busy days. All this has made me think that maybe we've grown apart. It might be the end of the road for us.'

'Oh, Babs.' Dee turned to face her friend. 'Are you sure that it's not because of this moving to Spain business? You've always seemed to get on so well.'

'We worked well together, we're a good team, but now there's no structure to our day. It's all so "samey" and okay, I've just got on with it but I've felt alive since I came down here. Like I can be myself.' She shook her head. 'I don't want to go back to how my life was before.'

'I feel the same,' Dee admitted. 'I think it's because we're on holiday, we're doing things we don't normally do. The novelty would soon wear off after a couple of weeks. And surely you don't want to throw all those years of marriage away.'

'It's Geoff who's thrown them away,' Babs reminded her.

They both turned as they heard a miaow at the French doors. It was Snowy. 'I think he wants lunch,' Dee said, opening the door so Snowy could come in. Then she took out the opened cat food tin from the fridge and put the remains into Snowy's bowl. He immediately tucked in.

'At least I can tell Edna that Snowy is well, and eating,' she said. Her gaze went to the clock. 'Actually we need to go soon if we want to go shopping before afternoon visiting.' They'd both showered and changed already.

'Should we leave Snowy inside, do you think?' Babs asked.

Dee considered this then shook her head. 'This isn't his home and he might go a bit crazy being locked in here without us. We'll let him back out. We know he's happy enough to sleep on the chair in the garden. Plus it means he can go back and check on his home if he wants to.'

She put a dish of milk outside to coax Snowy out then closed the French doors.

'Right, we'd better be off.'

* * *

'This would suit you.' Babs held up a pair of rose-coloured cropped trousers. 'Why don't you try them on?' They were in one of the many smaller clothes shops in Truro.

Dee looked around, a pair of beige linen trousers in her hand. 'They're a bit bright...'

'Go on, be daring. And look, you could wear this top with them.' Babs held up a black and rose flowered top. Dee bit her lip, the top was definitely too loud for her but maybe she would buy the trousers. She had a lovely white top that would go with them.

'Just try them,' Babs persuaded her. She picked up a red maxi dress too. 'And this. It would look great on you.'

'Okay, I will,' Dee agreed. Babs had an armful of clothes in pinks, yellows, orange and bright green. On impulse, Dee grabbed a black top with tiny rose coloured dots on it, too, then she and Babs went over to the changing rooms.

She was pleasantly surprised when she studied her reflection in the mirror. The trousers fit her beautifully, and the top was a perfect match.

'Let me see,' Babs shouted from the next cubicle.

Dee pulled back the curtains to find Babs waiting, dressed in a Barbie-pink jumpsuit that clung to her in just the right places.

'Gorgeous! I knew they would suit you. What do you think of this?' Babs did a little twirl.

'It's beautiful,' Dee told her.

'Try the red dress on now,' Babs encouraged her.

The red dress looked good, too, and the colour seemed to make her brown eyes even darker. *I think I definitely will wear brighter colours more often*, she decided.

'Are you ready?'

She stepped out to find Babs wearing a lime-green dress that she was almost spilling out of and that clung in all the wrong places. Dee gulped. How could she tell her friend that this wasn't the dress for her. Then she noticed that Babs was giggling. 'Imagine if I walked into The Pirate's Head wearing this. I reckon Glenn's eyes would pop out!'

Dee chuckled. 'Well, you'd certainly make an entrance!'

'This is a no, but that dress is definitely a yes.' Bee nodded in satisfaction. 'Red really suits you, Dee.'

After paying for their clothes they went to get a swimming costume for Dee.

'It's a shame I didn't think to bring the new ones with me, there was a really nice black and white striped tankini amongst them.'

'Forget black and white! Make those eyes pop out!' Babs held up a yellow bikini with a barely there top and G-string pants.

Dee spluttered. 'You must be joking!'

'You should see your face.' Babs eyes were twinkling. 'We'd have worn this if we were a bit younger, wouldn't we?'

'Loads younger, you mean. And I'm not sure I would.' Babs would have though!

'How about this then? One-pieces can be really flattering, especially with a figure like yours.' She held up a beautiful bright blue tropical print swimsuit.

'Actually, that is nice.'

'Go on, try it on. Then you can wear it when we go for a swim tomorrow.'

Babs was right, the swimsuit really suited her, Dee thought. She was surprised how toned her figure looked.

Babs spotted a straw sun hat with a gaily coloured scarf around it and couldn't resist. And, on impulse, Dee bought a white brimmed floppy hat that made her look quite jaunty.

They stopped at the newsagents to get a box of chocolates, a couple of magazines and a bottle of lemonade for Edna, and set off to the hospital.

19

Edna was sitting up and, although pale, looked a lot stronger and was delighted to see them with their gifts.

'Thank you, both, you saved my life. I could have been lying there for days.' She sounded very emotional. 'And you're holidaymakers too, I can't believe that you noticed something was wrong.'

'It was Dee, really,' Babs said as they each pulled out a chair and sat down beside the bed. 'She was the one who thought we should check on you.'

'Actually it was your cat, Snowy, who alerted us. We're staying at Sunset View, as you probably realised, and he visited us. He seemed hungry but we could tell that he was well cared for, and his name and your address was on the disc on his collar. So when I saw him miaowing and scratching at your front door, and your curtains all closed, I had a feeling that something was wrong and decided to check.'

Edna clasped Dee's hand between hers. 'Thank you. Thank you.'

She turned to Babs. 'You too. You helped. And the lovely

policewoman said that you're both looking after Snowy while I'm here. How is he? I'm so worried about him.'

'He's fine, he's made himself at home. See.' Dee showed her a couple of photos of Snowy that she'd taken earlier. One of him eating his food and the other of him curled up in his basket.

'That's so kind of you. So kind.' Edna dabbed her eyes with a tissue. 'All of this has been such a shock to me. I've been getting a bit unsteady on my feet, and when I was lying there on the floor I thought "this is it, Edna, no one's going to find you for ages".' She dabbed her eyes again. 'It's not been easy living on my own since Bert died.'

Dee felt for her. She had seen it many times with the old folks she'd visited, they struggled on alone, not wanting to leave their homes, scared to ask for help in case they ended up in care. 'Your son is driving down to visit you,' she said, then wondered if Martin had wanted to keep it as a surprise.

'After his inheritance I expect,' Edna said bitterly. 'I haven't seen him for ages and now he thinks I'm about to keel over, he's going to play the loving, dutiful son.'

Dee wasn't sure what to say. She knew that there could be some truth in what Edna was saying, she'd seen it happen before, but she didn't want to judge the man until she met him.

Babs leaned over and squeezed the old lady's hand. 'Well, he'll be waiting a long time because there's a lot of life left in you yet.'

Edna nodded. 'There certainly is. Although that won't stop him trying to sell my cottage and putting me in a home. But I'm one step ahead of him.' She straightened her shoulders, looking a bit brighter. 'Has anyone told my sister, Mabel? We talk to each other every week. She'll want to know.'

'I can let her know for you,' Dee offered. 'Can you remember her phone number?'

'It's saved in my mobile. Did you bring it?' Edna asked. 'It's in my handbag.'

Dee shook her head. 'I'm so sorry, I didn't realise and your house is all locked up now. I'm afraid that the police had to break in to get to you and they've temporarily made the door safe.'

'I've got a set of keys hidden. Can you get them, go in the back way and get some things for me, do you think?' Edna asked.

'Of course. Where are the keys?' Dee asked her.

'In the green watering can in the front garden. Thieves never think to look in a watering can. The larger key is for the back gate and the one next to it for the back door,' Edna added.

'Are you sure about this? You don't know us and you're giving us the keys to your house,' Dee said.

'I'm a good judge of character and I know who I can trust.' Edna touched her nose with her forefinger. 'Could you please get my handbag from the lounge, it's by my armchair, and the phone charger is on the coffee table. Then go up to my bedroom, please, it's the first one, and get a wooden box from the shelf at the top of the wardrobe. You'll have to move some jumpers. Please do that as soon as you can. Martin will be here any minute and he's probably intending to stay at the cottage. I don't want him to find the box.'

She really doesn't trust her son, Dee thought. 'Of course. We'll go as soon as we get home,' she promised.

'Thank you so much. And please bring the keys with you, I don't want Martin letting himself in without my permission.'

'We will.' Dee handed over the carrier bag in her hand. 'Meanwhile, we've brought you a couple of things from the corner shop.'

'Bless you both. You're so kind.' Edna's eyes filled up. 'I'm so grateful. Do you think you could pop back later with my hand-bag, the box and my keys? I need to phone Mabel and get things moving as soon as I can.'

Dee promised they would.

* * *

'We'll go around to Edna's first,' Dee said as they left the hospital. 'I don't like the thought of her keys being available for anyone who might find them.'

'Perhaps Martin knows where his mum keeps her spare keys and that's why she wants us to go now, before he arrives.' Babs frowned. 'And I wonder what's in the mysterious box she doesn't want him to find?'

'Maybe it's her will...'

'Could be.' Babs eyes lit up. 'Perhaps she's left the house to the local cat's home instead of Martin and she thinks he'll be furious and try to talk her out of it.'

Dee thought her friend could be right, she'd seen situations like this before when adult children had tried to control their ageing parents' lives. 'I hope that he's not as mercenary as Edna thinks, but unfortunately it does happen and she obviously doesn't trust him. So, I think for now, until we know different, we have to take her word for it.'

As soon as they got back to Port Telwyn they parked up at the back of the cottages, checking to see if there were any cars that could possibly be Martin's there. Not that they had any idea what car he drove but they had the impression it would be an expensive one. The parking space was empty apart from a dirty, dark blue van and a silver car that they'd noticed there before. So they went around to the front garden of Primrose Cottage.

Glancing around they saw the green watering can tucked up

in the corner. Dee picked it up and turned it upside down, and out fell the keys. She grabbed them triumphantly, looking over at Babs who was keeping watch. 'Let's go!'

They hurried around the back and were soon inside the house, going straight to the lounge to get Edna's handbag.

Babs quickly started checking down by the sofa and held up a large grey and black handbag. 'Here it is,' she said, picking it up. She checked inside. 'Edna's phone is in here too.' She picked up the phone charger from the coffee table and popped it into the handbag. 'Now, let's find the wooden box and get out of here before Martin arrives. I know we have Edna's permission to be here but I still don't fancy her son walking in on us.'

'You're right.' Dee headed up the stairs first, Babs behind her. Feeling a bit like an intruder, she opened the first door and stepped inside. It was a cosy, cluttered bedroom, a crotcheted multi-coloured bedspread on the bed, pretty flowered curtains, a large patterned rug on the floor, pictures all over the walls, many of them of Edna with a smiling, dark-haired man – Bert, Dee presumed – and some featuring a little boy of various ages – Martin.

A huge, dark-walnut wardrobe ran across the back wall.

'That must be where she's hidden the box,' Dee said.

Babs was already at the wardrobe, trying to pull open the doors. 'They're very stiff.' She gave an extra hard pull and the door popped open. Babs fell back onto the floor on her backside. 'Owww!' she yelled.

'Are you okay?' Dee hurried over to help her up.

'I think I've got a bruise on my bum!' Babs rubbed it ruefully. 'I don't know how Edna manages to open those doors!'

'I don't think she goes in here often.' Dee regarded the array of dated winter coats, evening dresses, fur stoles and other items of clothing that she couldn't imagine Edna wearing now. They were clearly from the fifties and sixties but still looked in excellent condition.

'These would fetch some money,' Babs said.

Dee looked up at the long shelf running along the top of the wardrobe that was full of hat boxes, shoe boxes and neatly folded jumpers. 'Edna said that the wooden box is at the back. I'm going to need a footstool to reach.'

'There's one!' Babs pointed over to a wooden footstool with a pretty but faded embroidered top which was placed under the window. She went over and picked it up, carrying it back. 'Phew! It's heavy!'

'Good, I don't want it giving way underneath me!'

Babs placed the footstool on the floor by Dee, who manoeuvred it into place with her foot then stepped on it, feeling underneath the jumpers for a wooden box.

'Nothing here,' she said.

'It might be behind it. She obviously doesn't want Martin to find it, so might have hidden it really well,' Babs suggested.

'Good point.' Dee took some of the jumpers off the shelf and passed them down to Babs who laid them carefully on the bottom of the bed. Then she saw a box, smaller than she'd imagined, pushed right at the back. 'I've got it!'

She pulled out the box, surprised at how light it was, and handed it to Babs, who placed it on the bed then handed back the jumpers for Dee to replace on the shelf. Finally, Dee stepped down from the footstool and regarded the box. It was decorated to look like a book, and was the same size as a hardback novel, securely locked with a small bronze padlock.

'Maybe she's got her best jewellery locked in it,' Babs suggested, giving the box a little shake.

Dee thought that was possible. She knew that many older

folks didn't trust banks or solicitors, preferring to keep their precious items hidden in their houses.

She slipped the box under her arm. 'Let's get going. I'll feel happier when we're out of here.'

They headed down the stairs and out of the back door, locking it behind them. Babs opened the gate and peered up and down the street, making sure the coast was clear before calling Dee out.

'I feel like a criminal!' Babs said as they hurried back to their cottage.

'So do I,' Dee agreed. The sooner Edna had her things the better. If only they could take them to her now instead of having to wait for visiting time tonight.

20

'Hello, ladies, how's Edna?' Andi asked as Dee and Babs popped into Moira's Café to tell her about the afternoon's events.

'News travels fast,' Babs said.

'Kenny's been in. He told us about your house-breaking escapades.' Andi grinned. 'Fair play to you both. Edna could have lain there for ages.' Her face sobered. 'She could have died.'

'We're just glad that we got to her in time.' Dee sat down. 'She's doing fine, sitting up and talking. We're on our way to visit her again later but thought we'd pop in and let you know what happened. Also—' she lowered her voice and looked around. The café was almost empty, as it would be closing soon and no one was paying attention, but even so. 'Edna wanted us to get her handbag, with her phone inside, from her cottage and to lock it up. She seems worried that her son might try to persuade her to sell the house and put her in a home.'

Andi pulled out a chair and sat down beside them. 'I think she might be right. She told me that Martin has been trying to persuade her to sell up ever since Bert died a few years ago.' She chewed her bottom lip. 'I think he means well, he can be a bit overbearing though. He could seize on this opportunity to say that Edna isn't fit enough to live on her own.' She leaned back in the chair. 'If I'm honest I think he might be right.'

'You must be close for her to confide in you,' Dee said.

Andi nodded. 'As I said she comes in a couple of times a week since her husband died, looking for company, I think. I always make a bit of time to chat with her and she's told me that Martin's a bit bossy.'

Dee hesitated, wondering if she was breaking Edna's confidence to mention the box, then decided against it. 'Edna said that she wants to phone her sister, Mabel. I think she's hoping to move in with her.'

Andi's face brightened. 'That would be a better move than living alone. Mabel is lovely and Edna gets on really well with her. She's been down to visit a couple of times and Edna's brought her to the café,' she added.

They finished their drinks and had a sandwich and decided to set off back to Sunset View so that they could pick up Edna's things and take them to the hospital. 'Tell Edna I'll visit her tomorrow after work,' Andi called after them.

'We will,' Dee promised.

As they walked back up the hill and turned into the car park, a black Lotus shot out. The driver, a dark-haired man, was scowling.

'Something's upset him,' Babs said. 'Do you think he's Edna's son? He might have been hoping to find the keys and let himself in.'

Dee felt a little uneasy about it all, but they had to abide by Edna's wishes.

* * *

When they got to the hospital the nurse said they couldn't see Edna yet as she already had a visitor, so they grabbed a hot drink from the machine and sat down in the corridor to wait.

A quarter of an hour later a man came out. The same man who had sped past them. He walked by Dee and Babs without giving them a second glance.

'I was right, he must be Edna's son,' Babs whispered.

When they entered her room, Edna was sitting up in bed, a determined look on her face. 'Did you get everything?' she asked as they walked over to the bed.

'Yes, it's all in here.' Dee frowned. 'That man who just left, was that—?'

'My son, Martin? Yes, he's been to the cottage he said, to collect some things for me, but he couldn't find the spare keys. Wanted to know why I didn't keep them in the watering can any more.' She nodded. 'Thank you, ladies. I think you got there just in time.'

Dee handed her the handbag, house keys and the box. Edna opened her handbag and took out her mobile phone. 'Thank you, you've been really helpful and I'm very grateful to you.' She patted the box. 'I've got personal papers in here, my will, the house deeds, savings. I don't want Martin getting his hands on them. I think that's what he went to my house for.'

'He didn't look in a very good mood,' Babs said.

'That's because I won't do what he wants. I've got a twisted ankle and a bruised hip, so Martin said I'm not safe to live on my own and he wants me to move in with him and his wife until my hip is better. But I know if I do that they will never let me come back home. They'll say they'll look after me, but I'll have no life up there.' She pursed her lips. 'They'll make me sign the house over to them, sell it, then put me in a care home saying that they're doing it for my own good. Well, I've got other plans.'

'Well, we've packed in a lot in the two days we've been here!' Babs said as they set off home. 'So much has happened you'd think we've been here for a week!'

'I know.' Dee glanced in her mirror then indicated to turn left. 'Shall we get a couple of bottles of wine for tonight?'

'Let's get some gin or vodka and have cocktails instead,' Babs suggested. 'We could make up our own, that will be fun. Remember how we used to do that back in the day?'

'I'll never forget your Tequila Sting, I had a hangover for days!' Dee told her.

Babs chuckled. 'Maybe we'll forget the tequila, but what do you say to cocktails?'

It would be good to let her hair down and have a drink and a giggle with Babs, Dee thought. And they were in their own house – well, holiday let – so no chance of showing themselves up. Nigel always hated it if Dee got tipsy and never let her forget it if she did something daft.

They made a quick stop off at the supermarket, where they bumped into Andi. She eyed the trolley stuffed with vodka, rum, mixers, crisps and chocolate gateau. 'Are you having a session, ladies?' Andi asked, her eyes dancing with amusement.

'You bet we are, we're on holiday,' Babs told her. Then she added, 'Why don't you join us?'

Dee suppressed a sigh, they barely knew Andi, she wasn't sure she wanted to spend the evening drinking with her. This was typical Babs. When they'd gone away together before they both got married, their hotel room had always ended up as the party room. They'd had some fun though, she remembered. It had been a while since Dee had had fun.

'I'd love to, if you're sure?' Andi looked from one to the other. 'I can't make it a late one though as I'm working in the café tomorrow.'

'The more the merrier,' Dee told her, feeling happier now she knew they wouldn't be having an all-nighter with practically a stranger. 'We don't want a late one either, we're planning on a day trip tomorrow.'

'Want to come back with us now?' Babs asked.

'Can I drop by in an hour or so? I'll take my shopping home and grab a bottle to bring with me.'

'Sure, see you in a bit,' Babs told her.

They'd made a couple of 'tester' cocktails and laid the food out on the table by the time Andi arrived with a bottle of Cointreau, a cocktail shaker and a bag of crushed ice. 'I wasn't sure if you had one,' she said, waving the shaker.

'We don't. You're a star,' Babs grabbed the shaker whilst Dee put the ice in the freezer. 'Now how about I make us all a "Babs Special"?'

'What's one of those?' Andi asked Dee.

'I dread to think,' Dee told her. 'If it's too strong for you, go to the loo and tip it down the sink, she won't know.' She winked.

Andi's face broke into a big grin. 'I'm guessing you've had to do that a few times?'

'Oh yes, and there are times I should have done but didn't and regretted it the next day.' She indicated the sofa. 'Sit yourself down. And please help yourself to any of the snacks.'

'This is so kind of you both,' Andi said. 'I've been worrying about Edna, I should have checked on her, I knew she was living on her own. I dread to think what would have happened if you two hadn't realised something was wrong. The other cottages in this block are holiday lets.'

'She's going to be fine,' Dee reassured her. 'She looked chirpy. Martin was coming out as we went in, he did seem like he might be a bit overbearing.' She told Andi all about the encounter. 'I don't know if he's being a bit overprotective, but Edna is convinced he wants her out of the house to sell it.'

'Have you ever met him?' Babs asked.

Andi looked thoughtful. 'He grew up in the village so we went to school together, not that I've actually seen him for years. He lives in Yorkshire now so I guess he probably worries about Edna falling and really hurting herself. Although...'

Dee and Babs exchanged glances.

'From what I remember of him he can be a bit ruthless, charges ahead if he thinks something is for the best and doesn't always stop to think how it affects others. Edna's said that she's not seen much of Martin since Bert died, so he's hardly the doting son. I know he lives miles away, but even so there's a phone and Facetime.'

'So, you don't trust him either?' Babs asked.

Andi shook her head slowly. 'I'm not sure he'd take Edna's wishes into consideration. He sort of takes over. Edna and Bert wanted a child for a long time, and when Martin came along, I think they spoiled him a bit.'

'Well at least she's got Mabel to stay with; she'll be fine.' Dee patted Andi's hand. 'And she wouldn't want you worrying over her.'

'Here, get this down you. It'll cheer you up.' Babs handed them both a tall glass full of a bright red liquid, topped with cherries. 'No sad faces allowed here.'

Andi took a sip and almost choked. 'Goodness! What's in this?'

Babs tapped her nose and sat down beside them, holding her own glass. 'Knock it back,' she ordered, taking a big gulp of her drink without as much as a splutter.

Andi raised her eyebrows to Dee who took a small sip out of her own glass. It was strong!

'You two seem such good friends. Have you known each other long?' Andi asked, following Dee's example and taking a small sip.

'Years! We were childhood friends,' Babs told her. 'And Dee here never used to be so quiet, you know. She was loads of fun before she got with Nige. Oh, the stories I could tell you.'

Dee felt herself stiffen at the insinuation that she was boring now. Babs was right though, Nigel had stifled her. Well the old Dee was still in there. She wasn't having Andi think she was a bore, no way. She took a long gulp of her drink. 'Yes, me and Babs go back a long way. Culprits in crime, right back to our schooldays.' She took another gulp. The cocktail didn't taste so strong now. 'Babs sneaked some itching powder into class one day and sprinkled it inside the teacher's coat. We couldn't stop laughing when he kept scratching all lesson.' She grimaced. 'The trouble is I didn't wash my hands properly and when I rubbed my eyes some itching powder got in them. It stung like hell and everyone thought I was crying!'

'What about when we went on the double date?' Babs had almost finished her cocktail already. 'This was before we met our other halves,' she told Andi. 'Platform soles were all the rage then and we both turned up in them but I'd only bought mine that day and couldn't walk properly in them. I tripped up and fell onto the table, knocking the drinks everywhere.'

Andi roared with laughter. 'I can beat that! I signed up to a dating app and went out on a date with this guy called Donni. He was good-looking and he knew it. He spent the whole date talking about himself and I was so bored I kept knocking back the drinks, then I spewed up all over him. The memory mortifies me even now.' She looked at Dee. 'You don't seem the sort to have done something like that.'

'Ha, you're joking! She walked around all day once with her

dress tucked into her knickers.' Babs chuckled. 'And did you hear about yesterday when we were trying to get into Edna's?'

The alcohol spurred Dee on to tell the story about her shorts falling down and exposing her knickers to Kenny.

'OMG, I'm literally going to wet myself here,' Andi howled.

'Oh, there's more. We went on holiday to Turkey once and a couple of waiters had the hots for us but they were a bit slimy. So we went around arm in arm all holiday, pretending we were a couple.' Babs grinned. 'Anyone for another one?'

'My turn now. I'll do a "Dee Special".' Dee struggled to her feet. She was already feeling a little light-headed but who cared, they were having fun. And fun was something she hadn't had for a long time.

21

BABS

Tuesday morning

Babs woke up with a thumping head and a missed call and a message from Geoff asking her to phone him urgently, which had been sent almost an hour ago! Immediately she panicked. What had happened? Was he ill? Had Molly or Lennon had an accident?

Geoff answered on the second ring. 'You took your time!' he said belligerently.

'I've just woken up. It was a late night.' After Dee had made her cocktail – which really had a bite to it – Andi had made one too and they'd all been more than a bit sloshed by the time Andi got a taxi home, not trusting herself to make the ten-minute journey without falling over. Babs grinned, they'd had such a laugh. Andi was great company and it had been good to see Dee letting her hair down a bit. She longed to see more of the 'old Dee'.

'Out gallivanting and leaving me to cope with everything here.' Geoff sounded very aggrieved. 'I can't believe that you've swanned off on holiday and left me to deal with all this, Babs. I didn't think you could be so selfish.'

'Me? Selfish?!' she practically screamed the words out. The whole street would hear her at this rate! She lowered her voice. 'What exactly are you coping with? What's happened? Are the kids okay?'

'What am I coping with? I've got another two viewers today. I'm trying to keep the house tidy, sort out all the paperwork and get ready for Spain on Friday and there you are sunbathing and living it up down in Cornwall.' He paused. 'What do you mean? Why wouldn't the kids be okay?'

It's a good job she wasn't in the same room as him or she swore she'd have thrown a cushion at him. 'Geoff, you messaged me to tell me to phone you urgently. I thought something had happened to you or the kids?'

'It *is* urgent. I told you, I've got two more viewers today. It's too much for me on my own. You need to come back and help sort things out. We go away in three days. The flights are early on Saturday morning so we're staying overnight at the airport.'

'You mean that *you're* going away, Geoff. I've told you I'm not coming to Spain with you. And as for not being able to cope, you started all this, so you're the only one who can stop it.'

'I did it for us. I thought it was what you wanted too.'

She sucked in her breath. How could he tell such an outrageous lie! 'You did *not*. I've made it plain – multiple times – that I don't want to go to Spain and you still went ahead.'

'It was a misunderstanding. Look, please come home, Babs, and we can talk about it. We always talked things through. It's not like you to run off like this.'

He was right, they had always talked things over, made joint decisions, but he was the one who had changed that, not her. It wasn't even the fact that he'd gone behind her back to arrange a sightseeing trip to Spain and put the house on the market, although that was bad enough. It was that he'd told her it was *his* house and he could do what he liked with it. She couldn't forgive him for that. She had to admit that she would like to sort things out though, she missed him, and her home.

'We've booked the cottage until the weekend, so I'm staying until then. That gives you time to take the house off the market and think of something else to keep yourself occupied now you've retired, because I'm telling you now Geoff Marston, I am not moving to Spain. Not now. Not ever. And if you try and sell *my* home from underneath me, I'll get a solicitor and divorce you. Then you'll see whether it's your house or not!'

'Divorce? No one said anything about divorce.' She could hear a distinct wobble in Geoff's voice.

'Well, what else can we do when we both want to live in different countries?' Babs demanded. 'And your name might be on the deeds, but a lawyer would tell you that I'm still entitled to half of that house. So, when it's sold you can take your half of the money and buy yourself a home at the top of a Spanish mountain, and I hope you'll be very happy there.'

There was a shocked pause. Then Geoff asked, 'What about you? What will you do?'

'Don't you worry about me. I'll buy a little flat somewhere. Maybe down here!' She ended the call before she burst into tears.

Her life seemed to be spiralling out of control. She'd always thought she and Geoff would be together forever and couldn't believe what had happened over the past few days. Determined not to spoil Dee's holiday, she pulled herself together and went downstairs. Dee was in the garden stroking Snowy.

'I heard you shouting, so I guess that you haven't made up?' Dee asked gently.

'Worse.' Babs sniffed. 'I told him that I want a divorce.' She repeated the phone conversation to Dee.

Her shoulders shuddered and she started to cry.

'Oh, Babs.' Dee put Snowy down and wrapped Babs in a hug.

'I'll be okay.' Babs pulled away, wiped her eyes and fixed a smile on her face. 'I'm sure Geoff will come round when he realises I'm serious.'

Would he though? And did she even want to go back to him after this?

Was this really the end of her thirty-seven-year long marriage?

22

DEE

Babs cheered up after breakfast so they decided to take the trip to St Michael's Mount that they'd planned yesterday, stopping off at Moira's Café first. When they arrived there, a very flustered Andi was trying to cope with a café full of customers alone. There was no sign of Moira and the empty tables were cluttered with dirty cups, saucers and plates.

'Where's Moira?' Dee asked Andi, walking over to the counter with Babs.

Andi finished serving the customer then replied, 'She had to go up to Swindon early this morning. Urgent family business. So I'm holding the fort alone until she returns.' She put her hand to her head. 'And I've got a stinking headache. A hangover from last night.' She smiled. 'It was a fantastic evening though. I haven't laughed so much for ages. Thanks for inviting me.'

'Our pleasure. And as it's our fault you're hungover, let us help,' Dee offered.

'Oh no, it's fine—'Andi started to protest but Dee and Babs were already clearing the tables and loading up the dishwasher, leaving Andi to take the orders. Then they helped her make up the orders and take them to the customers. Finally, when all the customers had been served, the three of them sat down for a break.

'Thanks so much. Moira had to leave so suddenly, she wasn't able to organise any extra help. I've called an agency to arrange for a temporary assistant.' Suddenly a guilty look passed over Andi's face. 'I was hoping to see Edna this afternoon but I'll have to go tonight.'

The door chimed and Kenny stepped in. 'Hello, you two. What a lucky coincidence,' he said as he came over. 'Mind if I join you?'

'Hi, Kenny, sorry but I'd better get back to work. Hopefully the temp will be here soon.' Andi stood up. 'I'll leave you all to chat.'

'Where's Moira?' Kenny asked as he pulled out a seat and sat down. 'And how's Edna?'

'Edna is recovering well.' Dee quickly explained about Moira. She would have liked to confide in Kenny about Edna and Martin but decided it was best not to. She was leaving on Saturday after the fundraising event and she didn't want to cause any trouble or unpleasantness for Edna.

'How're the plans for Saturday coming along?' she asked.

'Quite well actually, we've got a few artists willing to give a demonstration of their craft. That was a fantastic idea of yours, Dee.'

A glow filled Dee at his praise.

After chatting with Kenny for a while, Dee suggested that they visit Edna before going to St Michael's Mount. 'I'm anxious to see if she's managed to contact her sister,' she said.

When they got to the hospital, they found Edna in good spirits. 'I've spoken to Mabel, it's all arranged. I'm going to stay with her for a couple of weeks when they discharge me tomorrow. Andi called too, she's offered to look after Snowy for me, and keep an eye on the house.'

She looked so much happier than yesterday.

'How are you going to get to Brean?' Babs asked.

'Mabel's driving down to get me, then we're going to get some of my things from the cottage, lock it up safely and give Andi the keys. I'd love to take Snowy but he might run away. He's best left here and Andi has promised to pop in on him twice a day. It will only be for two weeks or so until my ankle and hip heals.' She leaned forward and clasped first Dee's then Babs' hands. 'I guess I won't see you two again, but thank you so much for what you did for me. You saved my life. I'm so very grateful.'

'We're glad to have been able to help,' Dee told her.

Babs nodded. 'You take care of yourself and give that son of yours a run for his money!' she said, patting Edna's hand.

'Don't you worry, I will. Martin's gone back to Yorkshire now he knows I'm going to stay with Mabel. He'll be back though once I'm home, trying to persuade me to sell up. Well, he's got no chance!'

* * *

When they arrived in Marazion they discovered that the tide was out so they could walk along the cobbled causeway to the island. Dee had already booked the tickets online. It was a warm, calm day with a clear blue sky and she felt very relaxed as they walked over to the island. 'I came here years ago when Annabel and Hugh were young, so it will be interesting to see how it's changed.'

'It's one of those places we always intended to go to but

never did,' Babs told her. 'It's very quaint, isn't it? Did you go into the castle at the top of the hill?'

'We did, but it's a bit of a climb, so if you don't fancy it, we can just look around the village,' Dee told her.

'Oh no! We must go up. Let's do it now before we're too tired then we can maybe look around the village and stay for afternoon tea in the Harbour Café too? It's mentioned on this leaflet.'

'Wasn't there a story about a giant living here once?' Babs asked as they trudged up the hill. 'Phew! This is a steep climb!'

Dee nodded. 'Legend says that a giant built the island and terrorised the people of Marazion, stealing their cattle, until one day a lad named Jack killed him. Apparently Jack dug a big hole, covered it with straw, then blew on his horn to summon the giant who ran down the hill and fell into the hole. I remember walking up to the castle with Annabel and Hugh and a guide pointing out a heart-shaped stone saying it was the giant's heart and if they knelt down and put their ear to the stone, they'd hear the giant's heartbeat. They were fascinated.'

'That's a bit gruesome, but kids love stuff like that, don't they?' Babs said. 'Where is this stone?'

'I'll show you when we come to it.' Dee panted, stopping for a rest. 'It's been a few years since I've climbed his hill!'

'Maybe we don't need to go all the way to top,' Babs gasped.

When they finally came to the heart-shaped stone, Babs wasn't impressed. 'I'd expect a giant's heart to be bigger than that!' She turned to Dee. 'Did your kids ever say they heard the heart beat?'

'They thought they did, but you know kids. They've got big imaginations. I never heard anything. Fancy seeing if you can hear it?'

'No chance! If I kneel down there I'll never get back up again,' Babs declared.

Dee laughed. 'I don't think I would either! I was a lot fitter back then.' She had lovely memories of their holidays in Cornwall. She wouldn't call them family holidays exactly, as Nigel was rarely with them, and when he did join them he only stayed a day or two. She wondered if Annabel and Hugh remembered those times. And now here she was back again, on her own this time – apart from Babs, that is. And to think that Kenny had come back to live here too. It was almost as if something had pulled her down here.

The village was fascinating, once home to over 300 islanders. There were still about thirty families that lived there, commuting over to the mainland to go to school, work or shop. As an ancient island, it was steeped in history and both Babs and Dee were fascinated to see bronze cast footprints of King Charles, Queen Elizabeth II and Queen Victoria set in the cobbled harbour pathway.

'This was definitely worth a visit,' Babs said as they walked back over the causeway. 'I'm knackered now though.'

'Too knackered to pop into The Pirate's Head tonight?' Dee asked mischievously.

'Absolutely not. But I'll need a short nap first,' Babs replied.

* * *

'Wow! You look fantastic, Dee. That colour really suits you!' Cath said when Dee, wearing her red maxi dress, joined Cath, Stu, Kenny and Flic at the table later that evening. Babs was at the bar getting the drinks. She'd insisted that she buy the first round.

Dee felt a flush of pleasure, especially when she saw the approval in Kenny's eyes too. 'Thanks. Babs persuaded me to go for a brighter colour,' she said.

'She was right to, you should wear bright colours more often,' Kenny said. 'Maybe not as vivid as Babs though,' he added. 'That sure is a dazzling pink.' Then his eyes widened as he stared at something behind her. 'What are you two drinking?'

'Spritzers,' Dee said, puzzled. She turned to see Babs carrying a tray holding two black cocktails with a frothy surface. No wonder she'd insisted on getting the drinks first.

'That's not a spritzer,' Stu observed as Babs put the tray down on the table.

'No, it's an Espresso Martini,' Babs replied. She handed one of the glasses to Dee. 'Try it, you'll love it.'

Dee took a sip and shuddered. 'Wow! There's a strong coffee shot in here!'

'I don't think it's the caffeine you have to worry about,' Kenny said, amused.

'Why don't you all try one? My treat?' Babs said. She was up and at the bar before anyone could object, returning a little later with six more of the dark cocktails. 'I got us another one,' she told Dee.

'That's so generous of you, thank you.' Cath picked up a glass and took a sip. 'It's strong but I like it.'

As they all tucked into the cocktails, the conversation got louder and merrier. Babs turned up the juke box while Kenny got the next round and by the time it was Cath's round they were all dancing to the music and several of the other customers had joined in.

Dee threw her head back, laughing as she danced the twist with Kenny. It had been so good to get away and enjoy herself.

The trouble was she was enjoying herself so much, she couldn't escape the feeling that she really didn't want to go home.

23

BABS

Wednesday

When Babs woke up her bones were aching from all the sightseeing yesterday and the dancing last night, and her head was thumping. She reached for the glass of water and the packet of paracetamol she'd left on the bedside cabinet, guessing she might need them in the morning after the session at The Pirate's Head. It had been a fun evening, but it had made her miss Geoff even more. It had been good to see Dee let her hair down and enjoy herself though, Babs always felt that Nigel stifled her and didn't allow her to be her true self. Whereas Geoff... Babs threw the light duvet back and padded over to the window staring across the rooftops to the sea. She and Geoff had been good together, happy. How had it all gone so wrong so quickly?

Her phone rang and she hurried over to it, glancing at the screen and biting back the disappointment when she saw that it wasn't Geoff, as she'd hoped, but Molly.

'Hello, darling.'

'Mum, Dad said that you're going to divorce him. You're not, are you?'

Babs chewed her lip. 'He's not leaving me much choice, is he? He's determined to go and live in perishing Spain, no matter how I feel about it. So that will be our home sold. I'll be homeless.'

'Oh, Mum, Dad won't do that to you. You know he won't.'

'Molly, the house is on the market and your dad has booked a trip to Spain this weekend to view some houses over there. He's already doing it to me.'

'Look, Mum, I had a long chat with Dad last night when I came back from my flight and he's really down and missing you. Please try to work this out.'

'Me? How can I work it out when I'm not the one doing it? I'm quite happy to stay in our house and live the life we're living. It's your dad who's hell-bent on changing it. Are you saying that I should move to Spain when I don't want to, simply to please your dad?'

'No, of course not.'

'Then how do we resolve this because your dad has made it clear that he's not giving up "his dream" for me?'

There was a silence then Molly whispered, 'Oh, Mum, this is horrible.'

It was horrible. Babs couldn't believe it was happening. 'It is, but your dad is the one you have to talk to, not me,' she said firmly.

Long after the phone call had ended Babs sat by the window, thinking. They'd been together forever, her and Geoff, thirty-seven years married. They had been inseparable, never even had holidays apart until now. Was that part of the problem? Was Geoff worrying that life was passing him by, wanting new experiences? And maybe a new woman in his life. Perhaps that's what this was really all about? Geoff knew she didn't want to live in Spain, but he wouldn't let it go. Was he deliberately trying to push her into divorcing him, not wanting to be the 'bad guy' and actually leave her?

She didn't know how to deal with this. It had all escalated so fast and the situation was running away from her. Suddenly they were heading for divorce and it seemed that the only way she could stop it was to give in to Geoff. Then what sort of life would she have? They'd end up divorcing anyway. She'd come away with Dee on impulse, wanting to make Geoff realise that she was serious and he couldn't decide something as important as this by himself, but what did she do when they had to be out of the holiday cottage on Saturday? Would Geoff have gone off to Spain by himself? Was this really the end of their marriage?

She looked up as Dee tapped on the door. 'Kettle's on. Want a cuppa?'

'Coming!' Babs pulled on her dressing gown and went downstairs.

'Are you still up for going back home later on Saturday so we can go to the fundraising garden party?' Dee asked.

Babs knew that she was diplomatically asking her if she was intending to reconcile with Geoff and go to Spain. No, she wasn't. Which meant that she was potentially going back to an empty house. So yes, she'd be happy to stay over for the garden party too. Then she would have a whole week back at home without Geoff to figure out what to do. And to get some legal advice. She'd be blowed if she'd be showing anyone else around in that time though so the estate agents could cancel any viewings.

'That's fine by me,' she agreed. 'It sounds like it'll be fun.'

After breakfast they went for a walk along the harbour front then popped into Moira's Café for a snack. The agency had sent a young scatty-looking lad to help out.

'He's been mixing up the orders all morning.' Andi sighed. 'I know he's new, but he's supposed to be experienced. I hope he shapes up soon.'

'How was Edna when you visited last night?' Dee asked as Andi made a pot of tea and put it on a tray with two cups, milk and sugar.

'She was very sprightly. They're keeping her in one more day for observation but then Mabel is picking her up tomorrow. They'll be at the house about three in the afternoon, whilst Edna collects some things. She said to tell you in case you wanted to pop in again to say goodbye.'

Dee and Babs both nodded. 'That would be great.'

Suddenly there was a loud crash from the kitchen. 'Oh heck, what's Tyler broken now!' Andi exclaimed, jumping up to find out.

'Poor Andi, looks like she's got her hands full,' Babs said.

Dee nodded. 'Hopefully she'll get more staff soon, or Moira will be back.'

* * *

After a walk around the Maritime museum, which was very interesting, they had another stroll along the estuary, on the outskirts of the village where the new development was taking place. Babs studied the board detailing how the finished development would look.

'It looks amazing, lots of apartments, shops, plenty of job opportunities,' she said. 'It will bring a lot of much needed income to the town, surely?'

Dee glanced over at the muddy estuary. 'It sounds like it will be a big improvement, but the trouble is the locals won't be able to afford most of the housing, so will still be driven out. I can understand Glenn's point, although I do think the basic idea is a good one.'

They carried on around to the warehouse conversion that was going to become the Artists' Studios. Kenny had invited them to drop in, saying he would be there today and could show them around. 'Hello, there, I was wondering if you'd come along,' he said cheerily when he saw them.

'It takes more than a couple of cocktails to knock us out,' Babs told him.

Kenny grinned. 'I bet it does. Great night though, wasn't it? You two have certainly livened up the place.'

Babs saw the colour flood to Dee's cheeks as her friend turned away. Was there a flicker of interest between these two?

'Right, let me give you a tour,' Kenny said briskly, showing them around.

'I like the individual spaces where the artists can work on their crafts but still have support and company,' Dee said a little wistfully.

'Do you think you'd ever go back to crafting, Dee? I used to love your paper beads. I still have one of your necklaces,' Babs said, thinking that it might be good for her friend to have a hobby.

Kenny looked at Dee keenly. 'You're a crafter?'

'Oh no, not really. I did a bit of paper crafting years ago, flowers, jewellery, cards, calendars, that kind of thing. But it was a long time ago.'

'Interesting, we haven't got any paper crafters on board. Maybe I'll put some feelers out to see if we can attract one. We want a diverse selection of artists and craftsmen here. We intend to open it to the public so the more variety the better.'

'I'm looking forward to the garden party,' Dee said. 'It will be good to see all the artists at work.' Noticing Kenny's surprised look, she added. 'We've decided to put our cases in the car once we've handed in our keys on Saturday then go home after the garden party. It's only a couple of hours' drive.'

'Brilliant.' His face broke out into a wide smile. 'And why don't you come to the karaoke at The Pirate's Head on Friday night? It's always good fun. The usual crowd will be there.'

Dee shot an enquiring glance at Babs. Babs nodded. 'Count us in!'

24

DEE

Thursday

'Let's go for a swim today. You haven't worn your new cossie yet and there's only a couple of days left of the holiday,' Babs suggested the next morning as they sat eating breakfast in the garden. Snowy was snoozing on one of the chairs beside them. He seemed to have settled well, but then cats were more adaptable to new 'owners' than dogs, she'd always found.

Dee nodded. 'Good idea. Let's go this morning otherwise we'll get caught up in the day and might not get chance.'

She noticed Babs' startled expression and guessed her friend had expected her to protest, but the old Dee was coming back, the Dee that liked fun and wasn't anxious about doing something wrong, or what she looked like. These few days down in Port Telwyn with Babs, and being accepted by Kenny and his friends, had given Dee her confidence back. She was sure that Cathy and Flic often took a dip in the sea without worrying that their figure wasn't as taut as it used to be.

'The sea will be warmer this afternoon,' Babs pointed out.

Dee shrugged. 'It won't be that cold. Anyway, bathing in cold water is good for you.'

'Who are you and what have you done with my best friend Dee?' Babs teased and Dee laughed.

* * *

Babs was right, it was a bit chilly on the beach. They had both put their swimming costumes on underneath their shorts and T-shirts and as Dee slipped out of her clothes and tucked them into her beach bag, she shuddered. Did she really want to go into that cold water?

Babs was already running towards the sea, her boobs almost bouncing out of her pink and yellow flowered swimsuit. She paused and squealed as her feet touched the water. 'It's blooming freezing!'

Dee was determined not to be put off. She could do this. She ran over to the sea, shivering as a cold wave splashed over her, then braced herself and dived in. She did it! She was swimming in the sea!

'Come in!' she shouted to Babs.

'Okay, I'm coming!' Babs dived in, heading over to her and splashing her.

Dee splashed back, and they both giggled, fooling around like a pair of kids.

'You two are brave going in this time of a morning! Either brave or mad!'

Dee looked over at the beach to see Kenny watching them.

'I'm not sure which we are either,' Dee called back.

'Fancy meeting up at Moira's about two to discuss the arrangements for Saturday?' Kenny asked.

'Sure. See you then,' Dee waved.

Kenny waved in return and walked off.

'Is that okay with you?' Dee asked Babs. 'I'm happy to go without you if you prefer to do something else.'

'You know me, any excuse for a cuppa and a natter,' Babs assured her. 'Now I'm going to have a quick swim then get myself warm again. I'm frozen to the bone!'

Dee was too, but she felt alive, exhilarated.

* * *

They had a warm shower when they got back to Sunset View and sat out in the garden for a while chatting. 'I'm so glad we came away, I feel more relaxed than I have done for ages.' Dee looked thoughtfully at Babs. 'How are you feeling? Have you heard from Geoff lately?'

'Not today. I guess he's too busy packing to go away tomorrow,' Babs told her sadly. 'I really can't believe it's come to this, Dee. I don't know why Geoff's acting this way.'

Dee chose her words carefully, not wanting to upset her fiery friend. 'Have you asked him? Have you both actually talked about it?' She took a deep breath. 'Don't take this the wrong way, but you can both be a bit stubborn, can't you?'

Babs eyes flashed. 'Me, stubborn? He started this.' Then she sighed. 'I guess you're right, we both dig our heels in. But Geoff's been like a dog with a bone over this.'

'I know, but you're not going to sort it if you don't talk to him, Babs. Why don't you phone him and see if you can discuss it? Both talk about how you feel?'

Babs shook her head. 'It's up to him to make the first move. And I'm not discussing anything until he takes the house off the market.'

She looked defiant but Dee could see the tears brimming in

her eyes. She felt like phoning Geoff herself but would that make things worse? She hated interfering, besides Babs said that Molly and Lennon had already tried talking to him.

'Maybe he won't see anything he likes over in Spain and will forget about the idea,' she suggested. She stood up. 'I'll go and do us a bit of lunch now, then it will be time to meet Kenny at Moira's.'

She went into the kitchen and stared out of the window in astonishment as a familiar figure opened the gate of the front garden. Geoff! Should she tell Babs or just let him in? Damn it, they needed to talk and Geoff had made the effort to come all this way. She went to the door and opened it as Geoff walked down the path. He looked tired, she noticed, there were bags under his eyes. He looked pale too. Babs going away had obviously upset him. It's a shame he hadn't come down earlier, but then maybe he'd expected Babs would be back home by now.

'Hello, Dee,' he said solemnly.

'Come in Geoff. I'll let Babs know you're here.'

She walked through into the garden. 'Geoff's here!'

'What?' Babs got to her feet and stood rooted to the spot as Geoff followed Dee outside. They both looked at each other but neither of them spoke. Dee grabbed her handbag. 'I'll leave you two to talk, I need to meet Kenny in the café.' She was out before Babs could protest, if she wanted to that was.

They were actually both supposed to be meeting Kenny to discuss the arrangements for Saturday but maybe Babs would go back home with Geoff. Dee hoped so. It would be great if they could put their differences behind them and get back together. She was sure it was what they both wanted.

'No Babs?' Kenny asked as Dee joined him at a table in the window. Andi was rushed off her feet and Tyler was carrying a tray over to the other side of the café.

Before Dee could answer, a loud crash made them both jump. They looked around and discovered that Tyler had dropped the tray on the floor, though luckily it was almost empty.

'Geoff has turned up. They're supposed to be going on a house-hunting trip to Spain this weekend.' She paused. She didn't want to gossip about her friend, but she was wondering if Geoff would manage to talk Babs into going home, that must be why he'd driven down. Or rather, talk her into going on the trip to Spain with him. One of them had to give in and she wasn't sure which one it was going to be. They could both be very stubborn.

'Problems?' Kenny raised an eyebrow.

Dee took a breath. 'Remember how Babs told you that her husband wants to move to Spain now they're retired, and she doesn't want to? And that he's put their house up for sale, without telling her? Well, he's arranged for them to view some houses in rather remote spots in Spain over the next week. Babs is digging her heels in and I don't blame her. But they've been together a long time, and he's a good man, this is totally out of character for him. I really hope they work it out.'

Ken whistled. 'That's a tough one.' His eyes rested on her, full of kindness and warmth. 'And what about you?' he asked softly. 'When's your husband back?'

'Saturday.'

'And does he often book golfing holidays without you? And forget your birthday?'

She shrugged. 'Nigel's busy with work.'

'You're his wife. And you're important.'

It was a long time since she'd felt important to Nigel, but she wasn't going to admit that to Kenny.

'Not as important as a golfing holiday apparently.' She

shrugged. 'You know how it is when you've been married a long time.' Then she put her hand over her mouth as she realised what she'd said. Poor Margot had died. 'I'm so sorry, that was thoughtless.'

'Please don't worry about it. I know exactly what you mean. Margot and I had got into the habit of taking each other for granted too, but when she was diagnosed with cancer, we realised how precious life was. I'm so pleased we had chance to reconnect before she passed away.'

She could hear the emotion in his voice and didn't know what to say. For a moment they sat in silence, then Kenny leaned forward and looked at the list on the table in front of them. 'Now, where was I?'

'You were about to tell me if there was anything I could lend a hand with,' Dee said lightly.

They discussed table positions, refreshments, seating and other things over two cups of coffee and a slice of chocolate cake. Dee agreed to be at the Manor at eleven on Saturday morning so she could help with everything. She was glad that Kenny and the others wanted her to stay on the committee when she left, at least she'd still have contact with them all. Maybe she could even come down for the weekend now and again.

'I'd better go now, hopefully see you both later at The Pirate's Head. That is, if Babs is still here.' Kenny stood up.

'I'll definitely be there,' Dee replied, wondering how Babs was getting on with Geoff. Should she go home or give her a bit more time to talk?

Watching Kenny leave the café, she messaged Babs.

How's it going? Want me to stay clear for a bit longer?

While she waited for Babs' reply, she stopped and had a quick chat with Andi, who looked frazzled.

'When will Moira be back?' Dee asked.

'Hopefully soon. Tyler is a nice lad but he's driving me nuts!' Andi said. 'If Moira isn't back by the weekend, I think I'll have to ask the agency to send someone else. We can't carry on like this.' She wiped the back of her hand across her forehead.

Dee wanted to offer to help but they only had a couple more days left in Port Telwyn and it wouldn't be fair to leave Babs alone. If she went back home with Geoff today though, maybe Dee could help Andi out for a couple of hours tomorrow. She wouldn't mind. She liked being busy.

Dee checked her phone. Still no reply from Babs.

25

BABS

'What are you doing here? How did you know where I was?' Babs demanded.

'Molly told me. I need to talk to you, Babs.'

'If you're hoping to persuade me to go back with you and help you get *our home* – which *I* don't want to sell – ready for viewers, you've got another *think* coming!'

'I've come to tell you that someone wants to buy the house.' He paused, then added to make sure that Babs understood, 'It's as good as sold, they're organising their funds.'

'So, you've come to gloat. I bet you'll be off as soon as you get your money in the bank!' She scowled, hand on hips. 'Well, it won't be all your money, even though the house is in your name. I'm entitled to half and I'm going to make sure I get it. You're not leaving me homeless! I'm going to see a solicitor about this!'

Geoff sighed and ran his hands over his beard. 'I would never leave you homeless, love. I don't want us to divorce, Babs. I'm sorry about what I said about the house being mine. I didn't mean it. Of course it's your home too.' He shook his head. 'Solicitor. Divorce. I can't believe it's got to this.'

'What do you expect me to do, when you put *our* home on the market and make plans without consulting me?' Babs was struggling to hold back the tears but she was damned if she was going to let him see her cry. Then she saw the tears in his eyes, too, and the bags underneath them, the paleness of his skin and she felt a surge of compassion. He'd come all the way down here to talk to her, she should hear him out. Maybe he was sorry. And he had called her 'love'. He didn't look like he'd come for an argument. And Dee was right, they needed to talk.

'I suppose I'd better put the kettle on,' she mumbled, going inside.

She flicked on the kettle and took two mugs out of the cupboard. When she turned around Geoff had followed her and was now sitting on the sofa, knees apart, hands clasped together. He looked uneasy, unsure. Maybe she'd given him more of a shock going away than she realised. They'd always done everything together, made every decision together. She wished they'd never sold the perishing shop now, then none of this would have happened. She made the tea strong with a dash of milk, just as he liked it, and spooned a sugar in, then handed it to him and sat down in the chair opposite, her own mug on the table in front of her.

'I can't tell you how sorry I am. I shouldn't have put the house on the market and booked the viewing trips to Spain. Not without you agreeing,' he said. He swallowed, fiddled with the neck of his shirt then raised his eyes to hers. 'I love you, Babs. I don't want us to split up.'

Neither did she, but she wasn't going to let him sweet talk her into giving in. 'Then you know what to do. Refuse the buyer's offer and take the house off the market.'

'I really want to do this, Babs. I feel like I'm stagnating. That my life's going nowhere. I don't want to do the same things every day, I want to do something with my life while I still can. I want to have an adventure.'

'It not just your life though, is it? We're a couple and I don't want to go to Spain.'

Geoff licked his lips and fidgeted in his seat. 'The thing is, I haven't been totally honest with you.'

Her breath caught in her throat. He looked serious. What was he going to confess? Surely he hadn't had an affair?

'A couple of months ago I found a lump.'

Her hand flew to her mouth. Oh God, no, was he ill? 'A lump?' she gasped. 'Where?'

'In my— er, you know.'

'Your testicle?' Her heart was beating a drum against her chest now. 'Why didn't you tell me? You need to go to the doctors right away.'

'I did go to the doctors, it was a bacterial infection and they gave me medication for it. And I didn't tell you because I didn't want to worry you.'

'Oh, Geoff.' Babs was by his side, hugging him. 'Are you sure you're okay?'

'I'm fine. Honest I am.' He wrapped his arm around her and they embraced tightly. 'The thing is, it gave me a fright. It made me realise how vulnerable I was, how I was getting older and hadn't done what I wanted with my life. That's when I started thinking about moving to Spain. To have the experience of living in another country. Do something I've never done, before I get too old.'

'Oh, Geoff, why didn't you talk to me? You could have explained so that I could at least understand why you've acted this way.'

'I know. I've been a pig-headed idiot. Molly and Lennon have both read me the riot act. I've gone about it all wrong.'

Babs swallowed. 'So have I,' she admitted. 'I should have realised there was a reason behind all this. You're not a selfish man.'

Geoff kissed her on the cheek. 'Look, I understand that it's a big step but would you at least come with me to Spain to view the properties? You never know, you might see something you like.'

'And what if I don't? What if I still don't want to go? What then?'

He sighed. 'Then we won't go. I don't want to lose you, Babs. I know I was a bit heavy-handed. Please come with me, take a look and if you say no then I promise I will drop the idea.'

She hesitated. 'But then will you resent me for not letting you live your dream?'

He ran his hand over his bald head. 'No, of course not. I promise you I'll turn down the buyer's offer, take the house off the market and forget the idea if you really don't want to move. Please at least come and take a look.'

Babs hesitated. What if she went on this trip to Spain with him and he kept chipping away at her, trying to persuade her to go along with his plan? She didn't want her marriage to end, but she didn't want to be guilt-tripped into living abroad either.

Geoff rested his hand on hers. 'Look, I'll cancel the trip if you want, if that's what it takes to get you back, I'll do it. You mean the world to me, Babs. You always have.' His eyes glistened. 'I'd really like you to give it a chance though. We could look on it as a holiday, spend a bit of time together. It's been horrible without you this week, I can't bear to think of spending the rest of my life without you.'

She could see that he meant it. He would call it all off if she wanted. He was prepared to forget his dream. Well, it wouldn't hurt her to agree to look at the properties in Spain, would it? And she had to admit, a week in the sun would be lovely.

26

DEE

A text pinged in. Dee grabbed her phone expecting it to be an update from Babs but to her surprise it was Yvonne, the wife of Nigel's friend, Andrew, who she presumed was on the golf trip with Nigel.

> I need to talk to you urgently. Call me when you're free.

Dee read the text, puzzled. She and Yvonne were polite to each other, but not chummy. Yvonne had never messaged her wanting to talk before. Had something happened on the trip? Was Nigel hurt? Had Andrew asked Yvonne to contact Dee to let her know?

She quickly hit the call button. 'Yvonne, what's happened? Is Nigel okay?'

'Don't panic. It's nothing like that. Although you might want to do him some damage when you learn what he's done.'

Dee swallowed. 'What do you mean?'

'Look, I'm really sorry to break this to you but I simply can't not tell you. It wouldn't be fair.' She paused. 'Nigel and Andrew, they've been playing away. They've been cheating on us, Deirdre.' On the few occasions that Dee had met Yvonne she'd always insisted on calling her by her full name of Deirdre.

Dee closed her eyes. Not again. She'd thought that was all over with. Nigel had sworn after the last time that he'd never cheat again. It had been five years, and there had been no signs. He was older now. She thought, hoped, he was past all that. Maybe he'd simply got better at hiding it.

'Are you sure? How do you know?' she asked.

'My friend, Katya, you've met her a couple of times, is in Portugal on holiday, in the same resort, and she saw Nigel and Andrew arm in arm with some women. She sent me photos. Do you want to see them?'

There could be nothing in it. They could just be friends, Dee thought. Like she was friends with Kenny. If someone took a photo of her talking to Kenny, that might look a bit suspicious, mightn't it?

'Yes, send them over. There could be an innocent explanation.' She desperately hoped that there was.

'I'll call you back when I've sent them,' Yvonne told her.

A few seconds later her phone pinged. She opened up the message. There were two photos and a short video. She opened the photos first. The first photo showed Nigel walking along the street holding hands with an attractive woman. Dee couldn't remember the last time Nigel had held hands with her. She pressed her fingers on the screen to enlarge the photo, the woman looked to be in her mid-fifties and their hands were clasped close together, fingers entwined. The next photo showed them sitting opposite each other, drinking a beer. Nigel was holding the woman's hand across the table and they were gazing into each other's eyes. She braced herself and played the video. Nigel and the woman embracing, kissing. Like he hadn't kissed Dee for a long time. And definitely not the way you kissed a friend.

The phone rang. It was Yvonne. 'The ones with Andrew are similar. I think there's no doubt that they're cheating on us. I'm booking a flight out to Portugal tonight and I'm confronting Andrew before he leaves. Let him wiggle his way out of this one. Want to come with me?'

Dee couldn't think of anything worse than flying over to Portugal in order to see Nigel with another woman. 'No, I don't. I'll talk to Nigel when he comes back.'

'He'll worm his way out of it, men always do. If we confront them, then they won't have chance to come up with a story.'

'Yvonne, the way I feel right now if Nigel wants to go off with another woman, she's welcome to him.'

'Do you want me to give him a message from you?' Yvonne asked.

'No. I'll deal with it when he comes back home. Thanks for telling me though, and good luck.'

* * *

Andi put a steaming mug in front of her. 'Want to talk or be left alone?'

Dee closed her eyes briefly. 'Just give me a few moments.'

She couldn't believe that she'd said that to Yvonne. And she'd meant it too. She was tired of worrying about what Nigel was up to. She'd had years of it. She'd put up with it so that she didn't disrupt the children's lives, she didn't want them to suffer, and because somehow Nigel had made it seem like it was her fault. That she never had enough time for him so he'd been forced to seek attention elsewhere.

Well now the children were grown up, she only had to

bother about herself. And she didn't want to put up with it any more. Nigel could do what he wanted. All she wanted was to stay down here in Port Telwyn.

She definitely wasn't ready to go back and confront Nigel yet. Maybe she never would be. Yvonne would tell him that she'd made Dee aware of what he'd been up to. Let him make the first move. She'd rather stay down here for a while, get her head straight, decide what to do. She'd go to the estate agents tomorrow and see if they had another cottage she could rent for a while, give her time to think. Right now she didn't *ever* want to go home.

27

BABS

Dee arrived back at Sunset View ten minutes after Babs sent her the text. She was obviously waiting for a reply and it had been really good of her to give Babs and Geoff space to talk. As soon as she heard the front door open Babs took out the bottle of wine that she'd put in the fridge earlier. 'Want one?'

'Heck, yes! Better still, put the straw in the bottle!' Dee sank down onto the sofa and kicked off her shoes. She took the glass Babs handed her and took a long gulp. 'Where's Geoff?' she asked. 'Have you two made up?'

Babs nodded. 'He's apologised. I've agreed to keep an open mind and go on the house viewing trip to Spain with him. And he's promised to forget the idea if I decide that I really don't want to move.' She looked over the rim of her glass at Dee. 'You were right that there was a reason for his behaviour.' She told Dee about Geoff's health scare. 'He didn't tell me because he didn't want to worry me. Idiot! Instead he caused all this mayhem.'

'Poor Geoff, he must have been worried sick. And yes he should have told you. Are you both all right now?'

'I'm a bit shook up about it all. I thought me and Geoff were rock solid but now I know we're not,' she confessed. 'Anyway, Geoff's gone home and I've agreed to catch the train back tomorrow morning. I wanted space to pack and talk to you, not just walk out on you without any notice.' She frowned, suddenly noticing that Dee looked upset and had already downed half of her glass of wine. 'Listen to me banging on, when there's obviously something wrong. What's happened?'

Dee bit her lip and ran her finger alongside the rim of her glass. 'Yvonne, Andrew's wife, told me that Nigel and Andrew are both playing AWAY in Portugal. She sent me photos as evidence.'

Babs almost spilled her wine. 'What, of them actually doing it?'

'No!' Dee retorted, eyes flashing. 'But they're kissing and holding hands and, well, it's obvious that they are more than friends.' She opened the gallery on her phone and showed Babs the pictures and video.

Babs whistled. 'The arsehole!'

Dee finished off her wine with a long gulp. 'Yvonne is flying to Portugal tonight to catch them in the act. She doesn't want to give Andrew the chance to wheedle out of it. She wanted me to go too.'

'And are you?'

Dee shook her head. 'No. I'm not going home yet either. Maybe not at all. It's not the first time Nigel has been unfaithful to me,' she admitted.

'What?' Babs was outraged, but not totally surprised. Nigel was so full of himself and his own importance she wouldn't put anything past him. 'He really is a toerag, isn't he! I'm glad you're leaving him. But why not go home and change the locks? Why should *you* give up your home?'

'I can't do that, it's Nigel's home too and he'll only get someone in to change the locks back.' Dee's hand shook a little. 'I don't want the upset, Babs. I want to keep away and sort myself out. I'm going to see if the estate agents have another place to let and stay down here for a while.'

Babs was astonished. The old Dee would never have made that decision. This week had done her good. It had done Babs good, too, she acknowledged, made her realise how much she rushed in, how stubborn she could be. She should have talked to Geoff, but he should have talked to her as well.

'I hope you don't let Nigel talk you round. You deserve much better than him,' Babs retorted. 'You always have. He puts you down all the time, so you don't realise how gorgeous and amazing you are. Look how well you've fitted in here. You blossom without him around.'

Dee looked startled. 'Well, thank you for those lovely words.'

'I mean them. You're way too good for that slimebag!' She was so mad she could throttle Nigel if she ever saw him. She'd always hated the way he treated Dee but Dee had never seen it. She acted as if she actually thought that she wasn't good enough for HIM. 'Look, do you want me to stay? Geoff can go on this house viewing trip by himself and I'll go home when he returns. I feel like I'm deserting you when you need me.'

'Of course you're not. You and Geoff must go together, it's important. And it's best for me to be on my own so I can sort my head out. I am glad you're staying until tomorrow though, and no need to catch the train I'll drop you back. I want to collect some of my things while Nigel is away. Now, how about we pop over and see Edna? It might cheer us both up.'

Babs looked at her thoughtfully. Dee was strong, and yes she knew people down here so wouldn't be alone. And she did want to go with Geoff, this week apart had been devastating for them both. 'Make sure you keep in touch and let me know what's going on,' she said. 'I want some photos of the garden party, for starters. I'm going to miss it.'

'Of course I will. And you send me some photos of the villas you see in Spain. I wouldn't be surprised if you fall in love with one!'

'I think that's very unlikely. Anyway, we'd better leave the rest of this wine until we've seen Edna. We don't want to turn up sozzled!'

'Good point.' Dee put the bottle in the fridge. 'Shall we get going?'

* * *

A woman slightly younger than Edna, with short grey hair in a chin-length bob answered the door to them. 'You must be Dee and Babs. Edna's told me all about you both.' She smiled. 'Now let me guess,' she pointed to Dee. 'You're Dee.'

'I am. And you must be Mabel,' Dee said.

'That's me. Now we're all introduced come on in. Edna was hoping you'd drop by.'

Edna was sitting in a comfy but 'lived in' brown floral armchair, her bandaged ankle resting on a stool. 'Hello, girls, how lovely to see you again.' She pointed to the matching and equally worn sofa. 'Take the weight off your feet.'

Dee smiled at being called 'girls' at their age. 'How are you feeling?' she asked as she and Babs sat down.

'I'm fine. I have to use a walking frame and hobble about for a few weeks but Mabel will look after me.'

'That I will. And we need to set off soon, I don't want to get caught up in traffic,' Mabel said. 'So I hope you don't mind if I don't offer you refreshments.'

'No worries, we've just had a drink, thank you,' Babs said, not adding that it was wine.

'Well, thank you for popping in. I didn't think I'd see you both again. I know you're going home on Saturday.'

'I'm going home tomorrow,' Babs said. She glanced at Dee.

'I'm staying a little longer. My husband has been playing away – again – and I've had enough,' she said.

Edna and Mabel both looked outraged. 'How appalling! You must leave him,' Mabel declared. 'You deserve better than that.'

Edna leaned forward. 'Are you staying on at Sunset View?'

'No, it's been let to someone else from Saturday but I'm sure they have somewhere else on their books that I can rent.'

Edna and Mabel both exchanged glances and Mabel nodded.

'Well, why not stay here while I'm at Mabel's, it will give you time to sort out what you want to do?' Edna suggested. 'I'd feel much better about leaving my cottage empty if you were living here, and you could look after Snowy for me too. He's got attached to you. That is, if you want to.'

Dee looked incredulous. 'Are you sure? I'd pay you rent of course.'

'You will not. You two saved my life.' Edna pursed her lips firmly. 'We'd be doing each other a favour.'

'Then, yes. Please! I'd love to stay here,' Dee said.

Babs was delighted for Dee, it was the perfect solution.

* * *

Later that evening they went down to The Pirate's Head so Babs could say goodbye to everyone. Andi had joined the group tonight and she called out as soon as they stepped in and waved them over.

'Have you two got your names down for the karaoke tomorrow?'

Babs shook her head. 'I won't be here. Geoff and I have made up and he's persuaded me to go to Spain to take a look at some properties. And he's promised that if I don't want to move there he'll drop the idea.' She placed her drink down on the table. 'It'll be a holiday, at least.'

'I'm so pleased,' Cath said. 'We could all see how much you missed him. Do come down and visit us now and again, won't you? Bring Geoff with you.'

'I will,' Babs promised.

'And what about you and your husband?' Cath asked Dee.

Babs saw that Kenny was listening intently. 'Nigel and I are finished, I'm filing for divorce,' Dee told her. 'I'm afraid he's had one affair too many, although you might think I should have thought that the first time I discovered he was seeing someone else.'

Cath placed her hand over Dee's. 'Not at all. Relationships are complicated and the decision whether infidelity ends your marriage or not is a personal one. We'll be sorry to see you go, though.'

'Well, actually, I'm not going just yet. Edna is going to her sister's until her hip and ankle are better and has kindly asked me to stay in her cottage and look after Snowy while she's away.'

'I'm glad you're not leaving us yet. We need you on the Artists' Studios fundraising committee,' Kenny added.

'Count me in,' Dee replied. 'And, at some point, I reckon I'm going to have to find a job to bring in some income.' She had some savings but they would soon go and who knows how long it would take to sort out a divorce settlement.

'How do you fancy helping me in the café?' Andi asked. 'Moira's daughter is being discharged but she needs care at home, so Moira has to stay to look after her three grandchildren until she recovers. Tyler can only cover until Saturday, and to be honest I don't think I could cope with him much longer anyway. I was going to contact the agency. But if you fancy it, it might tide you over for a couple of weeks, until you can sort something else out.'

'I'd love to!' Dee said immediately. 'Thank you.'

Babs thought that was a wonderful idea. Andi was lovely and it would get Dee out of the house and bring in some regular money. Dee looked delighted too.

'When do you want me to start?' Dee asked.

'We open at eight on Monday morning so if you could be there half an hour beforehand, I could show you the ropes?' Andi suggested. 'Eth, a local student, covers at weekends so I'd only need you on the weekdays.'

'Perfect!' Dee said. She smiled at Babs. 'That's another thing slotting into place.'

Babs had been feeling guilty about going back home and leaving Dee down here by herself, but now – in a matter of hours – she had a home and a job. Even if only temporarily – it made Babs feel easier about going back home without her.

Dee had a rocky road ahead but at least she had the support of friends and she seemed so happy down here. It would give Nigel a shock when she didn't return home, which served him right. He'd treated Dee abysmally over the years. And her best friend deserved much better.

28

DEE

Friday

'What a bloody cheek!' Dee said, exasperated, staring at the text message Nigel had just sent her.

'Nigel?' Babs guessed.

'You've got it! He wants me to get some things from the shops for him and to make sure his new blue and white pinstriped shirt is clean and ironed as apparently we have a function to go to on Saturday evening. "Wear your long royal-blue dress", he's added, "you always look good in that".' She could feel the anger rising in her. 'He's acting as if nothing has happened. There's no "how are you, how's your week been, did you have a good birthday, safe journey home, would you mind doing this for me?", is there?' She tossed her phone down onto the cushion in annoyance.

Babs raised an eyebrow questioningly. 'I take it that you haven't confronted him about his "holiday companion" yet?'

'No, but I'm sure Yvonne has made it clear that I know.' Dee picked up the phone again and started texting a reply.

She didn't think that Nigel would be happy to hear that she wasn't coming home tomorrow and wouldn't be picking up anything from the shop or going to the evening function with him.

He wasn't. Two minutes after she had texted:

No.

Nigel phoned.

'Don't answer it,' Babs advised, but Dee had already hit the button out of habit. She always answered Nigel's calls. She put him on speakerphone.

'Look, Dee, you have to be back—'

She listened, waiting patiently for a pause in his tirade then replied. 'I don't *have* to do anything I don't want to do. I'm not coming home and that's final. Why don't you ask your new girlfriend to run your errands for you?'

There was a stunned silence. Dee could imagine Nigel's astonished face, his jaw dropping, his eyes widening. His mind would be whirling, trying to think of a way of talking himself out of this. Babs gave her a thumbs up.

'I don't know what Yvonne has been telling you, but she's got it all wrong. We met two women golfers and went sightseeing with them a bit, that's all. We tried explaining it to Yvonne yesterday, when she arrived and caused a scene.'

Dee could imagine Yvonne storming furiously in and berating them both. She took no prisoners. She glanced at Babs who rolled her eyes.

'Save your lies, Nigel, I've seen the photos and the video, you did a lot more than sightseeing.'

'It's not what you think, Dee. I'll explain when I get home.'

'Don't bother, because I really don't care. If you want

someone else, you can have them. I'm staying here until I decide what to do.'

'Staying where? What do you mean? You're leaving me?' He sounded incredulous.

'I'm divorcing you, Nigel. Goodbye.' She ended the call and took a deep breath.

Babs clapped. 'Wow, you really told him. Good for you.'

Dee looked pale but resolved. 'I can't believe I've told him I'm divorcing him! I am though. I'm sick of his selfishness and I'm not standing for him cheating on me any longer. Hopefully I'll be able to find somewhere else to rent when Edna returns home. It will get easier once summer is over, I should be able to get a winter let.'

'Of course you will! You can come and stay with me and Geoff if you're stuck,' Babs offered.

'Thank you, but I'll sort something, I'm sure I can get a room in a B&B if nothing else.' She'd take whatever she could find until the divorce was sorted out. There was no way she was going back to Nigel she thought determinedly. Another message pinged in and she automatically glanced at her phone. Nigel again. What did he want now?

> I can't believe that you're leaving me after all the years we've been together because of a bit of malicious gossip.

She could imagine his lip curling, the tight, cold expression on his face as he wrote it.

> Well, stay there if you want, you'll soon miss your house and the luxury lifestyle I've provided. I'll give you another week to think things over. If you haven't returned by then, I'll be divorcing you!

She read it out to Babs.

'The slimeball. I hope you take him for every penny you can. You put so much into that marriage and he wouldn't be where he was without you,' Babs said furiously. 'I still think you should stay in the house though. It is your home, too, after all. Why should you have to walk away from everything? He might say that you deserted him. Remember that Nigel's a solicitor,' she warned her. 'He knows how to play the game.'

'He's also very persuasive.' And condescending. And knew how to make her feel as if she was being stupid, overreacting. 'I need some space to get my head straight. And I'll get a solicitor too. Nigel won't be able to get out of paying me what I'm entitled to.'

She was outraged and deeply hurt by his behaviour. The fact that he denied he'd done anything wrong made things worse. Why couldn't he man up and admit it? But then he never had before until he was forced to, had he? And then there was always some excuse for his infidelity, and it was usually – according to him anyway – Dee's fault.

As soon as Babs had packed, Dee drove them both home. She saw Babs' face darken when she saw the 'For Sale' notice outside their house. Geoff must have been watching for them because he came straight out to greet Babs, hugging her tight. 'I'm so glad you're back.' He pointed to the sign. 'We'll take it down when we return from Spain, if you decide you definitely don't want to go.'

'You bet you will,' Babs said emphatically.

They both asked Dee in for a drink but she politely refused, thinking that they needed some time alone to sort out their marriage. And she wanted to get back to her house, grab her things and return to Port Telwyn. She didn't want to stay long enough to have second thoughts. She had to be strong.

* * *

Parking her car in the drive, she stepped out and looked at the detached house with the wide picture windows and separate double garage that had been her home for many years. Nigel had chosen it, but she had loved it too. It was large, spacious, with a generous front and back garden. Ideal for a family to grow up in. They had some happy years here. Some sad ones too, she acknowledged, remembering the times she'd struggled to hold it together when Nigel had another one of his affairs, the nights she'd nursed a sick child alone while Nigel had been in a hotel on the other side of the world. Or out at a business meeting. She'd believed him then, well at least tried to. Her focus had been on holding her family together, protecting their children. Now there was no one but herself to consider and she'd had enough.

Shoulders back, she walked determinedly to the front door and put her key in the lock. Pushing it open she saw a small pile of letters on the carpet. Stooping down to pick them up she closed the door behind her and sifted through them. Half a dozen birthday cards, a note informing her that Royal Mail had tried to deliver a package, maybe the one Nigel had wanted her to go home and collect – and a couple of letters for Nigel. Then she remembered that Hugh had told her he'd posted her a present so she put the note in her handbag, along with the birthday cards, intending to collect the parcel before returning to Cornwall. She left Nigel's letters on the small hall table and headed straight into the kitchen to make herself a drink. Everything was exactly as she had left it, of course, as no one had been home. She glanced out of the window at the large garden with its neatly mowed lawn, colourful flowerbeds, the ornamental fountain in the middle, and the decked area to the right.

Perfect for entertaining. She'd lost count of the times she'd spent all day cooking then the evening hosting Nigel's friends or clients. In the summer they'd sat out in the garden, on cooler days they'd used the dining room. She'd always made sure everything had been perfect, the house and garden immaculate. If she'd succeeded, Nigel would put his arm around her when the guests had gone, tell her that she'd done well, kiss her on the cheek, even help her tidy up and stack the dishwasher. If she'd done something to displease him, he would retreat into his study, leaving her to tidy up, then go to bed alone.

She made a filter coffee, wanting to savour these last few moments in the house that had been her home for so many years. Sipping it slowly, she made a list of the things she wanted to take with her. The family photo album, her memory box containing paintings the children had done, their school records, cards they'd made for her, the craft box her parents had bought her that she hadn't used for years, her laptop, her jewellery box containing her great grandmother's ruby brooch. She went up to fetch the jewellery box, sitting down at the table with it and her coffee. She took out the brooch and placed it in the palm of her hand. Her mother had always told her that it was valuable and to guard it carefully. She'd get it valued at the garden party tomorrow, hopefully it might be worth enough to enable her to rent a cottage when Edna returned, just until the divorce settlement came through.

Divorce.

She sat for a few minutes mulling over the word, taking in the enormity of what she was doing. She was walking away from her marriage of thirty-five years, their family home, and starting afresh. It was a daunting prospect. There had been happy memories here as well as sad ones, especially in the earlier years of their marriage. Their children had grown up here, the house had been filled with the sounds of the children's laughter once. She and Nigel had loved each other once. Well, at least she had loved him. She had no idea if he had ever really loved her, or had simply seen her as an asset. They had muddled along, but had there ever really been a strong connection? She had never felt that Nigel loved her more than anything in the world, his love had always been conditional on how well she 'behaved', how tidy she kept the house, how she played the part of the dutiful wife.

She shook her head. Maybe she was being unkind, dismissing all their years together so lightly, but certainly over the past decade they had grown further and further apart, she could see that now. She had, God willing, twenty or more years to enjoy her life, and she wasn't going to waste them being a doormat for Nigel. She was going to build a new life for herself, one where she could be who she wanted to be. She was tired of dancing to his tune, she wanted to live her life her way. Scary as it was, and she had no idea what she would do, but she knew that she had made the right decision. Her marriage to Nigel was over.

She finished her drink, put the cup in the dishwasher, picked up her list and went upstairs to pack.

29

Dee stopped off at the post office to get the parcel – it was a gorgeous pale lemon cashmere jumper from Hugh – then headed back down to Port Telwyn. She took her things to Sunset View, leaving them in a corner of the lounge, intending to sort it all out tomorrow when she moved into Edna's cottage. Then she went out into the garden to see if Snowy was around and was delighted to see him curled up on one of the chairs around the table. She put her phone down on the table and sat down beside him, stroking his head. 'I guess you're missing Edna, aren't you, boy?'

Snowy jumped onto her lap and curled up, purring softly. Dee stroked his soft fur, deep in thought. The last few days with Babs had been exactly what she'd needed. It had taught her to widen her horizons, try different things, be more herself. Her and Babs had always bounced off each other, complimented each other, as best friends should. Babs providing the gaiety and spontaneity and Dee providing the calm and reason that Babs sometimes needed. She was glad that Babs had talked to Geoff and they'd both made up, but she would miss her. Babs' company had given it all a holiday feel. Now though, she was well and truly on her own. 'I have you, don't I, boy, at least until Edna comes back?' she murmured, and Snowy swished his tail as if he understood. When she'd found herself a permanent home, she'd get herself a cat. Or a dog. Or maybe both, she decided as the little cat nestled deeper into her lap. Dee closed her eyes, rested her head back a little and felt herself relaxing. She could do this.

The ringtone of her phone interrupted her thoughts. She leaned over and glanced at the screen. It was Andi. A friendly voice was exactly what she needed right now. She picked it up and pressed answer. 'Hi, Andi.'

'Hi, just wondering how things are going and whether you'll be at the karaoke tonight?'

Dee smiled, feeling lighter. She had only been here a few days but people had been so welcoming. 'I'll be there. But I'm not promising to sing.'

Andi chuckled. 'You don't have to if you don't want to. Mind, you won't be able to keep me off the stage. I always fancy myself as Madonna once I've had a couple of drinks.'

Dee could imagine that. It sounded like a fun evening, just what she needed to take her mind off things. She wished that Babs was still here, she'd be up for a sing-song. She felt a little unsure on her own, she and Babs would have giggled as they decided what to wear. She knew Andi and a few of the others, she'd be fine, she told herself.

A little later, Dee went back inside to get changed, pulling out her new rose trousers from the wardrobe, the pretty black and rose top she'd bought to go with them, and put them on, then studied her reflection in the mirror. She looked so different. Bright, bubbly.

Suddenly her phone rang again. She glanced at the screen, it was Babs wanting a video call. She pressed answer and there was Babs' friendly face smiling at her. 'Just checking in to make sure you're okay before we leave for the hotel,' Babs told her.

'I'm good, don't worry. How are you? Is it good to be home? Are you and Geoff all right now?'

'Yes to both. I'm looking forward to going actually. A week in the sun will be nice. Are you off to the karaoke? What are you wearing?'

Dee held out the phone so Babs could see.

'Oh, brilliant! You look totally gorg. What shoes are you wearing?' Babs asked.

'I was wondering about that. Maybe my black ankle boots?'

'You'll knock them dead.' Babs grinned at her. 'Have a good time and send me a video if any of the gang get up and sing a song.'

'I will,' Dee promised. 'Send me lots of photos of Spain.'

They chatted for a little longer then Geoff said it was time to go. He joined Babs, waving to Dee, and she felt so happy for her friend that they'd made up.

The call from Babs had really cheered her up. She pulled on her ankle books and picked up her bag. She could do this.

Suddenly there was knock on the door. Puzzled, Dee went to answer it and found Andi standing on the doorstep. 'I thought you might want a bit of company walking into the karaoke.' She paused, noticing Dee's outfit. 'Hey, you look great!'

'Thank you. So do you,' Dee replied. Andi was dressed in ripped, skinny washed-out jeans, a rust coloured vest and knee length fringed brown suede boots.

'Ready to go?' Andi asked.

Dee nodded and pulled the door shut behind her. She really appreciated Andi calling for her, she felt more at ease going to The Pirate's Head now.

The rest of the gang were already at the pub when they arrived that evening. Cath waved them over to two empty chairs.

'Just in time, the karaoke starts in five minutes,' Kenny said. 'Fancy doing a song?'

Dee was about to refuse when Andi glanced at her, a big grin on her face. 'How about singing "These boots are made for walking" with me?'

Her eyes were twinkling with mischief and suddenly Dee wanted to join in, wanted to act impulsively, to laugh, to dance and sing. 'Perfect!' she agreed.

It was a lively evening. Kenny was the first one up and he sang 'Save the Last Dance For Me' in a surprisingly deep, soulful voice, his eyes resting on Dee's as he sang the chorus. Then Cath and Stu got up and sang 'Does Your Mother Know?' with hilarious antics, and another couple sang the smoochy 'I've Got You, Babe'. They were obviously in love, and it made Dee think of Babs and Geoff as it was their song. She remembered them both dancing to it at their wedding, and Geoff had crooned it to Babs once when they'd both got a little tiddly. Nigel had disapproved, of course. Dee videoed that, and Cath and Stu's song, and sent it to Babs. She knew her friend would enjoy seeing them.

Then it was Dee and Andi's turn. Everyone at the table cheered them on as they both walked over to the karaoke area, Andi playing to the crowd, waving and bowing, Dee feeling very self-conscious. She'd hadn't done karaoke since her student days! She soon got into the stride of it though, it was difficult not to with Andi's enthusiasm, and they both exaggeratedly stamped across the stage as they sang the chorus and Dee imagined herself stamping over Nigel – metaphorically of course. When they finished, they were greeted with claps, cheers and whistles. Andi's eyes were sparkling and Dee felt her cheeks flushing. She hadn't enjoyed herself so much for ages.

'You two were fab,' Kenny said as they took their seats. 'I've videoed it and will send it to you later. I'm sure Babs would love to see it.'

'Thank you.' Dee picked up her glass for a much-needed drink. Babs would be astonished when she saw that, she thought with a giggle.

It was Glenn's turn next. As he took the mic and coughed to clear his throat, the pub went silent, as if they'd heard Glenn sing before and it had been worth listening to.

He started singing Roy Orbison's 'Crying' and you could hear a pin drop. Dee swallowed the lump in her throat as she listened to the poignant words, which she was sure were a tribute to his late wife. How sad to have that kind of love, and lose it. She had never loved Nigel that way, nor him her, she realised.

She felt so comfortable with this group, and life down here in Port Telwyn, as if she belonged. She hoped that somehow she could stay here, become part of this community that she'd already grown to love.

30

SATURDAY

A text came through from Nigel as Dee was eating breakfast the next morning. He'd obviously arrived home now.

> I thought that once you calmed down you might have realised how ridiculous you were being!

She ignored it and finished her bowl of cornflakes.

The phone rang. She answered it automatically. 'You're making more of this than it is. I met Chrissie on the golf course and we went sightseeing together. There's nothing more to it than that. Those photos have been doctored,' Nigel told her, his tone soft and persuasive.

'Why would Yvonne's friend doctor photos of both Andrew and you with other women? And what about the video? Are you suggesting she computer generated it?'

'I wouldn't put it past her. She's never liked Andrew so she's causing trouble.'

'But why cause trouble for you?'

'Look, darling, you know what it's like when you're away. You get friendly with people—'

'You promised me that you wouldn't cheat on me again. And this was my birthday week! You went off with someone else on my sixtieth birthday.'

'That's what all this is about, is it? Because I went away on your birthday! You've been away too. And you're still away!'

'Only because you left me on my own. And I haven't been with another man.'

'So you haven't even talked to another man all the time you've been down there?' There was an edge to his voice and Dee felt her cheeks flush as she thought of Kenny. Nothing improper had gone on with her and Kenny, she reminded herself. They were old friends.

'I've had enough of this! You've cheated on me. AGAIN. We're finished.' She ended the call.

She sat trembling for a while, she couldn't believe that she'd actually stood up to Nigel. She made herself a cup of strong coffee and pulled herself together. She couldn't fall apart. She wasn't going to let him break her down. She had too much to do. She had to hand the keys in for Sunset View this morning and before then she had to pack and move her things to Edna's, then meet Kenny at eleven.

For a moment she felt overwhelmed by it all. Was she doing the right thing? Uprooting herself miles away from everything she knew. Staying at Edna's was only temporary. Her job at the café was only temporary. Would she be able to find somewhere permanent to live and a job?

Another text pinged in. She took a deep breath then opened it.

> If this is the way you want to play it, I'll have no option but to cancel your bank and credit cards. You want to start a new life on your own, go ahead, but you're not doing it with my money.

She closed her eyes, leant her head back and took a few deep breaths. Nigel was trying to force her to come home by making her penniless, but he wasn't going to succeed. He'd built his career on her back, she had been his unpaid PA, housekeeper, driver, childminder and a dozen other things. He couldn't take everything from her. She would call a solicitor on Monday during her lunch hour and find out what her options were. Meanwhile, she had to pack, move her things to Edna's, then go to the garden party. She'd promised to help and she had no intention of letting her new friends down.

She cleaned and tidied Sunset View, then took her few possessions around to Edna's. As Primrose Cottage was only a few doors away, it didn't seem worth packing them into her car then getting them back out again, so she took them around bit by bit, leaving them all in the lounge. She hadn't really taken much notice of Edna's cottage the other couple of times she'd been here, she'd been more worried about how Edna was, but now she noticed how dated it was. Sunset View had been repainted, modernised, and looked so spacious. Whereas Primrose Cottage was clean and cosy but it was old-fashioned and dark. There was no archway between the small galley kitchen and the lounge – Edna had left the dividing door open to let in the light so she hadn't really noticed this before. The wooden staircase was still the original dark wood and the furniture was faded and worn. It was clean and comfortable though, and she was grateful to Edna for allowing her to live here.

Dee took her suitcase upstairs and put it in the guest room. She wouldn't unpack now but it would be good to get the large case out of the way. As in Sunset View, there was a gorgeous view of the sea. The room was basically clean and tidy, like the rest of the house, although it could do with a vac and a polish. She would do that and put clean sheets on the bed when she returned from the Manor.

Right now she had to hand in the keys to Sylvia and go. She'd promised to meet Kenny at eleven and it was almost ten already.

* * *

As she pulled up in the Manor car park a phone call came in from Annabel. 'What's going on, Mum? Dad said that you want a divorce and you're going to live in Cornwall!'

Dee sighed. She could do without this right now but obviously Annabel was upset. She quickly explained about Nigel cheating on her in Portugal. 'I don't want to badmouth your dad, Annabel, but this isn't the first time he's cheated and quite frankly I've had enough. So yes, I want a divorce and at the moment I'm staying down here to give me time and space to sort myself out.'

'Oh, Mum, that's awful! I can't believe it, Dad's acting all hurt and hard done by and it's his fault, he's been a total jerk. Are you okay? You must be heartbroken.'

'I've been better, but don't worry about me, I'll be fine.'

'I'm so sorry. But please don't stay there forever. Because Hallie will miss you, Mum. And so will I. And I still have your birthday present here.'

'I'll miss you both, too, darling, but I have to put myself first now. You and Hugh have your lives, it's time I lived mine.' She softened her tone. 'I'll come and see you soon and you can come and stay for a weekend when I'm settled, you can give me my present then.'

'Where are you going to live? Are you still in that holiday cottage? Surely it'll cost you a fortune to stay there.'

'I've moved out today, I'm looking after a friend's cottage a few doors up while she recuperates at her sister's. She had a nasty fall and hurt her hip and ankle. I'll text you the address later. I'm afraid I have to go now. Give Hallie a big hug from me. I'll be in touch soon, I promise.'

She got out of the car and walked over to the large grounds at the back where the garden party was being held. It was already a hive of activity with the people unloading boxes and laying out their goods. She was surprised at the big selection of crafts on display – exquisite glass items, delicate jewellery, soaps and candles, carved wooden house signs, seashell ornaments, paintings, home-made fudge, cakes, printing services and greetings cards. Dee stopped at the first stall, there was a large display of various cards but there were no paper flowers, decorations, jewellery, or origami figures like Dee used to make. Was there even a market for that? She paused at Glenn's stall to admire the exquisite blue glazed pottery he was putting out. There was a young girl with long auburn hair, who looked about eight, sitting on a stool beside him, tucking into a bag of crisps.

'Did you do this?' she asked Glenn, trying to keep the surprise out of her voice. It really was beautiful.

'Aye, that's my job – that and part-time bartender when Sammi here is at school.' He jerked his thumb at the young girl who smiled at Dee then jumped off the stool and ran over to join two other girls who were waving at her.

'It looks very...' she paused, stopping short of saying 'professional' in case Glenn took that as an insult. She knew from experience how prickly he could be.

He raised an eyebrow. 'What? Professional?'

'Well, er, yes, for want of a better word.'

'It's a good word to use, I am a professional. I've been doing this for years,' Glenn told her.

Dee traced her finger lightly over an azure-blue jug. It was expertly glazed and smooth to the touch.

Glenn picked it up and held it to the light. Dee gasped, the way the light caught it made it look almost translucent. 'That's stunning!'

'Thank you.' He put the jug back down. 'Do you do any crafting?'

'I used to do paper crafts a long time ago, when I was a primary school teacher. I doubt if I could remember how to do it now.'

'You won't know until you try. It might be good for you to have a hobby, with what you're going through. Creating things is a good way of channelling your emotions. When my wife died, I was full of anger and grief but I knew that I had to get myself together and function for Sammi's sake. Pottery helped me do that. Mixing and moulding the clay is so relaxing.' His eyes met hers. 'And you look to me as if you need a way to channel your emotions and clear your mind, if you don't mind my saying so.'

And there she was, thinking she'd been doing a good job of acting upbeat, in charge. Obviously not.

'Maybe I'll take it up again,' she said.

Dee made her way over to the back section where, as she had suggested, there was an extensive area set up for the artists to run workshops. Kenny was there, putting up a large wooden table. She went over to him. 'Hi, how's it going?'

He smiled at her. 'Hello, Dee. I wondered if you would make it. You're moving into Edna's today, aren't you?'

'Yes, I've taken my stuff around and left it to sort out later.' She replied. 'What time is Simon Hemingford arriving?'

'He's doing the official opening at one thirty and then he will be valuing people's heirlooms from two thirty.' Kenny took out a couple of wooden easels and stood them up on the table. 'We're hoping he'll be a big attraction.'

'I'm sure he will be. I've got something I want him to value for me.' Her grandmother's brooch was safely tucked away in her handbag. She hoped it was worth a few hundred at least, she needed every penny she could get, especially now Nigel was threatening to cancel her bank cards.

31

Dee watched in admiration as Kenny stood some paintings on the easels; a beautiful landscape, a flowering bush, a ship on a stormy sea with flashes of lightning crashing across the sky, the same sea on a sunny day with the water shimmering.

'I'd love to be able to paint like that,' she said. 'You're so talented.'

'Thank you, but it's been years of practice. Perhaps, you could give it a try?' Kenny suggested. 'It might be good to have a hobby, distract you a bit from everything else that's going on.'

Dee nodded. 'Glenn said the same. Are you running a workshop?'

'I am. Feel free to take part, if you want.'

'I might just do that.'

Dee left him to finish preparing his stall and hurried over to join Andi and Cath at the refreshments tent. 'Right, what do you need me to do?' she asked, rubbing her hands together.

'A hand in putting out all the cups, saucers and plates would be very appreciated,' Cath told her.

'I'm on it. Show me where they all are.'

* * *

Crowds flocked into the manor grounds. Dee was sure that it helped that it was a warm, sunny afternoon and that a popular celebrity like Simon was officially opening the event. He was charismatic and charming, and was greeted with cheers and applause when he finished his speech. Then people went off to see – and buy – the wares on display at the stalls, and either watch the crafts people at work or have a go at doing the crafts themselves. Dee was pleased that she'd suggested leaving a list on each stall for people to sign up if they were interested in attending workshops at the art studio when it was open, that would be added income for the artists as well as generating interest in the project. She helped Andi and Cathy serve the never-ending stream of customers wanting refreshments for an hour or so then took a break so that she could ask Simon to value her grandmother's brooch.

There was quite a queue around Simon Hemingford already. Most people had smaller items such as watches and jewellery but there were a couple with paintings and one with a very old teddy bear. It was fascinating watching Simon value the items. Some people were overjoyed with the amount, but others were disappointed that it wasn't worth what they'd expected. Which would it be with her grandmother's brooch, Dee wondered?

Simon's eyes sparked with interest when Dee passed him the brooch, briefly explaining its history. 'If I'm not very much mistaken, this is Edwardian.' He held the brooch in his open palm and looked through the magnifying glass at it, turning it over and examining it from all sides. 'It definitely is. I would say that this is worth at least £4,000, maybe more.'

Dee clasped her hand over her mouth. 'Really?' she could hardly believe it.

'Definitely. Would you like me to put it in an auction for you?'

Dee nodded. 'Yes, please.'

'Wait until the end of the valuation session and we'll discuss it,' Simon told her.

Dee moved away from the group so Simon could continue with the valuations, her head in a whirl. A sum like that would really help her, it would pay a couple of months' rent on a flat for a start. And she would need some money for solicitors' fees.

At the end of the valuation session, Dee went to talk to Simon, handing the brooch over, getting a receipt, and giving her details. He arranged to contact her when he had offers to buy the brooch. 'I can transfer the money straight into your bank,' he told her. 'Minus my small fee, of course.' He mentioned what Dee thought was a very reasonable fee.

Dee felt like a load had been lifted from her shoulders. Thank you, Grandma, she thought silently. The times Nigel had suggested she sold that brooch, but she'd hung on to it saying that it was sentimental. Even now she was sad to let it go but she was sure her grandma would understand.

* * *

'I forgot how wonderful it was to be involved in a community project like this,' she said later as she sat down to have a much-needed break. The crowds had dispersed a lot now and the crafts people were starting to pack away their stalls. 'And it's revived my interests in paper crafting. I'm going to start it up again, as a hobby. It will keep me busy and give me a purpose now Nigel and I are over.'

'Are you certain it's over?' Andi cocked her head to one side questioningly. 'Your husband is a solicitor, isn't he? I'm guessing that you have a big house and luxurious lifestyle?'

'Happy to give it up, and my two-timing controlling husband, for a lovely peaceful life doing exactly what I want. I've decided that I'm going to try to stay in Port Telwyn.'

'Good for you,' Andi told her. She finished her drink. 'Now, I'd better dash back to the café to help clear up. Are you still on for helping out from Monday?'

'Definitely. Nigel has threatened to cancel my bank cards so it will be great to earn some money of my own.'

Andi raised her eyebrow. 'He's a real piece of work, isn't he?' She leaned forward. 'Well, if it was me, I'd withdraw a load of cash ASAP, in case he carries out his threat.' She winked and walked off leaving Dee staring after her thoughtfully.

* * *

Dee had been so busy helping that she hadn't had time to join in Kenny's painting workshop, but she'd enjoyed the day, which was followed by a pleasant evening with Kenny and the others at The Pirate's Head. When she finally got back to Primrose Cottage Dee fed Snowy then rolled into bed, exhausted.

She awoke to find sun streaming through a gap in the curtains and someone ringing the door bell. *Goodness, morning already!*

The rings were more persistent now, as whoever it was had their finger pressed permanently on the bell. She glanced at her phone. No messages and – gosh, it was gone eleven – she must have literally zonked out! Who wanted her so urgently on a Sunday morning? Pulling on her dressing gown she went down to find out. Opening the front door she was astonished to see Nigel standing on the doorstep.

'Annabel told me where you were staying, so I thought I'd come and see you, talk this misunderstanding through face to face,' he said firmly.

He must have driven down more or less as soon as he woke up this morning she realised.

Much as she didn't want to let him in, she didn't want to be arguing with him on the doorstep, so she led the way into the lounge, determined not to offer him refreshments, or make him welcome in any way.

Nigel glanced around dismissively then sat down in one of the armchairs. Dee took a seat opposite him, her nerves on edge.

Nigel was at his most persuasive. 'Look, Dee, can't we put this all behind us and get on with our lives? Arguing is so pointless. I promise I'll make up for going away on your birthday. I'll book us a holiday together. You name where you want to go.'

'I don't want to go away with you. I don't want to live with you. I've had enough of our one-sided marriage,' Dee told him.

His face contorted in anger. 'You've had a bloody good life with me, Dee. A nice house, no money problems, you've wanted for nothing.'

'Except a husband who loves me, who puts me first now and again.'

'For God's sake, woman, we've been together thirty-odd years. Surely you've gone past harking after all that sloppiness now.'

'Well, you haven't. You just prefer to do it with someone else.' Dee met his eyes. 'Are you still in touch with her?'

'With who?'

'The woman you went to Portugal with.'

He couldn't meet her eyes. He was lying.

'Don't bother to answer. I know that you are. Well, that's fine. You're welcome to her. I'm done. I've told you, I want a divorce.'

'Don't be ridiculous! How will you live? You can't afford to rent a place, without my money you won't have an income.' He sneered. 'I've warned you I'll stop your bank cards, and I mean it. I'm not funding your lifestyle when you've deserted me.'

Anger soared through her. How bloody dare he! Making out she was deserting him when he had cheated on her, time and time again, never mind the appalling way he'd treated her. 'Do your worst, I'll manage until the divorce settlement,' she told him firmly. 'I'm entitled to half the house, and some money from the business. I was your unpaid PA for most of our marriage.'

'I'll be damned if I sell the house and give you half,' he stuttered.

'You'll be damned if you don't. We can separate quietly, if you agree to me having half the house and a financial settlement. Or we can fight this through the courts, and believe me, Nigel, I know enough about your shady dealings to bring down your company and leave you penniless. So, what's it going to be?' She couldn't believe the words that were coming out of her mouth, that she was actually standing up to Nigel.

Nigel looked incredulous too. He was so red-faced, she thought that he might explode. 'How dare you blackmail me!'

'And how dare you cheat on me, again, and expect me to keep turning a blind eye!' She folded her arms. 'I'm serious, Nigel. I want a divorce and a fair settlement.' She paused. 'And seeing as you insisted that I didn't work once the children came along, so I couldn't have an income of my own throughout our marriage, you can pay the rent on my home until the divorce goes through, and my solicitor's fees. Obviously if you don't fight the divorce and go for a fair settlement, those fees will be less.'

His face drained of colour. 'I don't know what's happened to you, Deirdre, but you've changed. You're cold, and hard, and money-grabbing.'

'I've woken up to how you treat me and am no longer prepared to be walked all over,' Dee told him. 'I'll get my solicitor to contact you regarding the financial settlement. And I'll be back in a week or so to pack the rest of my things.' She nodded. 'Goodbye, Nigel. Enjoy your life, because I certainly will enjoy mine.' She opened the front door.

She was shaking after he left. She didn't know how she'd found the courage to stand up to him face to face. Nigel always had a way of talking her round, making her think she was being unreasonable, making her feel like she'd imagined things.

Well, not this time.

Then she remembered his repeated threat to cancel her bank cards and Andi's comment when she'd told her about it. She picked up her laptop, signed into their joint bank account and transferred a considerable sum of cash into her private account.

Then she texted Babs and told her the latest developments.

I'm proud of you!

Bab's reply pinged back.
I'm proud of me, too, Dee thought. *I'm finally fighting back.*

32

BABS

Sunday afternoon

'Exactly how far out is this house?' Babs asked from the back seat of the dusty four-by-four which was bouncing along the dirt track up and down mountains. She looked out of the side window and felt dizzy, she hadn't realised they were that high up. She hoped there was no oncoming traffic because there was nowhere for Santiago, the estate agent, to do a turn and the thought of him having to reverse down this narrow mountain path was terrifying.

Santiago's eyes met hers in the mirror. 'A few more minutes, *señora*.'

'It's beautiful, isn't it, Babs? So peaceful. Look at all these olive trees. No traffic or noisy neighbours here,' Geoff said excitedly.

No life either, Babs thought but she didn't want to say anything. Geoff had looked so happy and relaxed since they'd arrived in Spain that she didn't want to burst his bubble. It was because he was on holiday, people always relaxed on holiday, she told herself. He was enjoying the adventure of it all. He'd promised he wouldn't move if she didn't want to, so she was trying to be fair, to give it a chance. They were going further and further up the perishing mountain, she noticed in panic. Why did people build houses so high up?

Finally, they came to a stop. 'Here we are!' Santiago announced.

Babs stared at the huge pale yellow house in front of them, what she could see of it anyway, as most of it was surrounded by a crumbling wall and big iron gates. This looked like a mansion. Surely it couldn't be in their price range. Geoff was out first, racing around to open the door for Babs, much to her surprise. She couldn't remember the last time he'd done that. 'Isn't this amazing!' he exclaimed.

Amazing isn't the word she'd have chosen to describe it but before she could express her opinion the gates opened and an elderly Spanish man stepped out, smiling broadly. *'Buenos dias.'* He kissed Santiago on both cheeks.

'Buenos dias,' Santiago replied, turning to Babs and Geoff. *'Señor* and *Señora Marston.'*

He indicated the man. 'This is Miguel. He is the owner.'

'Bienvenido,' Miguel kissed Geoff on both cheeks. *'Bienvenida.'* Welcome. He did the same to Babs. Then he indicated for them to come in.

'Come, *señora*, come and look around. You will be... how do you say—?' he thought for a moment.

'Dazzled.' Santiago finished for him, leaving the car outside and following Miguel through the gates.

Dazed is more what Babs felt as she looked at the orange and lemon trees scattered about the huge garden which seemed to stretch on forever.

'Come! Come!' Miguel beckoned. He'd locked the gates

behind them and was leading them over to the huge, sprawling house. Pushing open big wooden doors he beckoned them inside, leading them through the lower level of large, high-ceilinged rooms at top speed. Babs barely had time to notice that they all had tiled floors and were filled with dark wooden furniture. Talk about a whirlwind tour!

'This is a typical Spanish home,' Santiago told them as they followed Miguel up narrow spiral stairs to the upper floor, to more huge, dark rooms. He flung open heavy wooden blinds and the sun poured into the room.

'The Spanish leave the blinds closed in the daytime to keep the houses cool,' Santiago explained.

Miguel stepped out onto the balcony. 'Come!' he beckoned.

They all followed him out. Babs gazed at the expanse of land around them, the mountains rising up at the back. They must be about halfway up the mountain, she realised.

'It takes your breath away, doesn't it?' Geoff exclaimed.

It certainly did, but not in the way Geoff meant, Babs thought. 'Where's the nearest village?' she asked.

Santiago spoke to Miguel in rapid Spanish then turned to her, a big smile on his face. 'Only a twenty-minute drive.' He held out his hands. 'Look at the wonderful view. You will wake up to this every morning.'

'It's marvellous,' Geoff agreed. He turned to Santiago. *'Muy bonita casa.'* He enunciated the words in what he thought was a Spanish accent. 'That means "very pretty house",' he informed Babs.

Babs rolled her eyes. 'Do you have anything a bit nearer civilisation?' she asked.

Santiago sighed and exchanged a knowing look with Geoff. 'Always, the ladies, they want the shopping, the cafés...' He shook his head as if Babs was being frivolous. 'Do you not think this is beautiful?' he asked. 'The mountains, they are majestic.'

'It is, but I was thinking somewhere not so far from the village. And not so high up,' Babs said. 'We're getting older now, you know. This house will be difficult for us to manage.'

Santiago sighed again. 'I will see what I can do, *señora*.'

After saying goodbye to a beaming Miguel, who thrust a carrier bag of lemons in their hands – 'You take, fresh from my trees' – Santiago set off again along the bumpy mountain track. By the time they reached the next house Babs felt like she'd been on a fairground ride.

'This house is only ten minutes' drive to the village,' Santiago said as he opened the door for her again.

More iron gates, this time they opened automatically as they approached and Santiago drove through, the gates closing behind them. The sprawling house – white with a terracotta roof – looked modern, as if it was recently built, and was surrounded by olive trees.

Now this is a bit more promising, Babs thought.

'This is a new house, but it isn't quite finished,' Santiago told them as he took a set of keys out of his pocket and opened the front door. 'Unfortunately the owners split up and went back to Sweden. They've left me to sell the house.'

He led them into a huge room which was completely bare apart from a few wires hanging out of the wall. 'This is the kitchen.'

'It's massive!' Geoff exclaimed.

'What are those wires?' Babs asked, eyeing them suspiciously.

'For the cooker and other... appliances, *señora*.'

The lounge was huge, too, with wide picture windows which Geoff was already gazing out of. There was no rail on the stairs and the bedrooms had no doors. Santiago led them to a huge bathroom, empty apart from a claw-footed bath along one side, which again hadn't been fitted.

It was like a shell, Babs thought. No kitchen, no bathroom, nothing.

Geoff was excitedly deciding what he would put here, and there, declaring how wonderful it would be to design the interior of the house however they wanted. Babs was speechless.

'Come and see the pool. Imagine yourself swimming in this, or gliding across the surface on a lilo,' Santiago said.

He led the way out the back, down some steps, around the corner and there in front of them was a huge pool, full of clear blue water. It looked cool, tempting. For a moment Babs imagined swimming in it. She walked along the side to the end, intending to walk further down the garden when Santiago gasped and pulled her back. 'Careful, *señora,* the fencing, it is not finished yet.'

As he pulled Babs back she gazed down in horror at the sheer drop down the mountain. If she'd gone a few steps further... She shuddered.

Geoff had joined them now. 'Wow!' he gasped.

'It's a view...' Santiago paused again to try and think of the English translation to what he wanted to say. 'A view to die for!' he said triumphantly.

'That's what I'm scared of!' Babs said faintly.

33

DEE

Monday

Dee arrived bright and early at Moira's Café on Monday morning, ready for work. Andi's face broke into a bright smile when she saw her. 'I'm so glad that you've agreed to do this, it's so much more comfortable to work with someone you know and get on with, isn't it?'

Dee felt flattered at Andi's remarks, she was pleased to be working with her too. 'I'm pleased that you asked me, it's good to feel useful, plus I could do with the extra income now I'm divorcing Nigel,' she said.

'Well, I'm very glad to have the help,' Andi told her.

It didn't take Andi long to show Dee the ropes and by the time the first customers came through the door Dee was serving them confidently.

Halfway through the morning, Snowy turned up. Almost as if he'd been looking for Dee. 'I don't believe it, the cheeky rascal,' Dee said as Snowy curled up on one of the cosy chairs in the window. 'Sorry, I'll shoo him out.'

'No, let him be, he isn't doing any harm. He must be missing poor Edna and now you're living in her cottage he's latched himself to you. He'll probably go away as we get busier.'

Dee went over and stroked the cat. 'Did you hear that? You can stay until we get busy.' Snowy purred contentedly.

Dee washed her hands and set to helping Andi put out the cakes. 'Did you make these?' she asked.

'No, we have a woman in the village who makes them for us, thank goodness. Baking isn't my forte.' She glanced at Dee as she took some delicious-looking fruit slices out of a plastic container. 'How are you settling at Edna's?'

'It's very comfortable. I sent Sylvia from the local letting agents an email early this morning, to ask if they had anything on their books free within the next couple of weeks. I'll take a flat even, until the divorce is sorted.'

'You're definitely going ahead with it then?'

'I am.' In between buttering some baguettes whilst Andi put cheese and ham on them, ready for the midday rush, she told Andi about Nigel turning up yesterday. 'I'm going to book an appointment with a local solicitor during my lunch break. With the divorce settlement I reckon I should be able to get a small cottage or apartment.'

'Prices are high around here, but I'll keep an eye out too,' Andi told her.

'Thank you. I appreciate that.' Dee glanced over to see if Snowy was still asleep in the chair and was astonished to see him now curled up on an elderly lady's lap, enjoying being caressed. 'Look at that cheeky cat!'

Andi looked over thoughtfully. 'That's Mrs Samson. Her husband passed away a few months ago, she's only just started to venture out of the house. They were childhood sweethearts and she's lost without him.'

Babs and Geoff went to school together, which sort of made them childhood sweethearts, even if they didn't meet up with each other again and start dating until a few years later, Dee thought. Babs had sent her a lengthy text last night detailing all the unsuitable houses they'd seen so far. Dee had chuckled as she read it:

> One of them was so far up a bloody mountain I swear I could touch the clouds if I stood on tiptoe! And another one had cracks so wide in the walls they were like train tracks.

Babs seemed in good spirits though, thank goodness. Dee was so pleased that she and Geoff had worked things out because she was sure they would both be lost without each other, although it had been nice to have Babs' company for a while. *I can manage,* she told herself, *I have friends already, a job, even if it is only temporary, and hopefully a home until I sort myself out too.*

It was a busy morning, lots of the customers were regulars and Andi greeted them cheerfully, introducing Dee. Snowy was a big favourite with the customers, with many of them allowing the little cat to sit on their laps, and stroking him.

'I think we should make Snowy the café cat,' Andi said. 'There's a lot of people who come here alone, and stroking a pet is very therapeutic.'

'What a lovely idea,' Dee agreed. 'Do you think Moira would approve? We probably shouldn't start off something that she won't agree with and will stop when she returns as the customers will be disappointed.'

Andi grabbed two clean cups to serve the next customer. 'Moira's naturally concerned about hygiene, but she does allow customers to come in with their dogs. Plus, I think Snowy is an asset. Mind you, a cat with dogs might cause a riot!' She poured tea into one of the cups. 'Besides, when Moira returns Edna will be back home and you won't be looking after Snowy, so he probably won't come in.' She left the words 'and you won't be working in the café either' unspoken.

Dee realised she already felt a bit sad at the thought of not working at Moira's Café. She'd only been here a few hours and already she was loving it.

Snowy was finding his feet now and went from table to table, allowing himself to be stroked and cuddled by the customers, occasionally standing by the door waiting to be let out – probably for a toilet call – then coming back in again a few minutes later. He seemed to be very settled here, Dee thought. She would miss Snowy when Edna got better and returned home. She'd already decided that when she got her own place she would get a pet – a cat probably although she would love a dog to take for walks. It was a good feeling to know that she could make whatever decisions she wanted over her future. She could have as many pets as she liked, live wherever she wanted, have a job. She hadn't realised just how much Nigel had suppressed and controlled her. That was the trouble when you'd been with someone a long time, you tried to please them, moulded yourself into how they wanted you to be and then that was it, you didn't know who you were any more.

* * *

Kenny popped his head around the door after lunch. 'How's it going?' he asked.

'I haven't broken anything or scalded a customer so far,' Dee said with a smile. 'Are you here for a cuppa or did you pop in to check on me?'

'Both,' Kenny admitted. 'I'll have my drink outside, please, I've got my dog, Toffee, with me.' He glanced over at Snowy, a smile on his lips. 'And it would be chaos if he saw a cat in here.'

'Yes, Snowy seems to have made himself comfortable.' Dee took a teapot off the shelf. 'I didn't know you had a dog.'

'He's been a bit under the weather so I've kept him cosy indoors but he's picked up now so I thought a walk would cheer him up.'

That's why she hadn't seen Kenny walking the dog. 'I'll bring your drink out to you,' she offered.

'Thanks. Do you have time to join me for a quick catch-up?'

Dee hesitated, it was almost three o'clock.

'Take a break and chat for a while,' Andi told her. 'It's not too busy. I'll take my break when you come back.'

So a few minutes later Dee took out a tray laden with the teapot, two mugs, a small milk jug and packets of sugar.

Toffee, a beautiful tan and black leggy mongrel, barked and raised his head but didn't move. Dee patted him fondly. 'I've always wanted a dog but they do tie you down a bit, and I'm going to need to get another job once Moira comes back, so it wouldn't be fair to leave it in the house all day.'

'Why don't you "borrow" one then?' Kenny asked.

Dee pulled out a chair and sat down. 'What do you mean?'

'People who love dogs but don't have the time or space for one get together with local dog owners so they can take their dogs for walks, dog sit, even look after them while their owners go on holiday. So you have the fun without the responsibility. We've got a local app for the people who live in Port Telwyn and the surrounding area. Some of the owners are elderly or working and appreciate a helping hand.'

'That sounds perfect. I love walking and it would be good to have a dog to accompany me. How do I sign up?'

'How about meeting me in The Pirate's Head tonight for a bite to eat and I can show you?'

'Perfect. I finish here about six and need to go home to freshen up, so I can be there for seven?'

'I'll be there.'

They exchanged a smile and Dee felt a little flutter in the pit of her stomach. She liked Kenny, he was easy to talk to and pleasant company. It had been a long time since she'd spent time like this in another man's company. *Don't get ahead of yourself, Kenny is just being pleasant and friendly because you're old friends and he knows you're having a tough time*, she told herself.

Feeling her cheeks go hot she bent down to stroke Toffee, to allow herself time to compose herself. Then she stood up. 'I must get back to work, it's starting to get busy again. See you later then.'

He held up his mug. 'You will.'

'You two seem to get on well,' Andi said with a waggle of her eyebrows as Dee went back inside.

Dee blushed. 'Yes, it's nice to catch up with an old friend, and everyone has been so welcoming.' She washed her hands and put her apron on again. 'Kenny was telling me that you had a "share a dog" app where you can match up with a dog owner and share taking the dog for walks and stuff. He's going to tell me about it later.'

Andi grinned. 'Oh yes, I've heard of that. It's a great idea, and there are several working and elderly people in the village that use the service. And of course, it's a very complicated app. You definitely need Kenny to talk you through that over a drink.' Dee got the idea that Andi was teasing her but she didn't mind. She was rather excited about the 'sharing a dog' idea. She'd miss

Snowy when Edna returned home. It would be good to have a pet around and she couldn't commit herself to one of her own yet, not until she'd sorted out her living and work situation.

34

Snowy followed Dee home, so she fed the little cat who then curled up on one of the chairs. Dee glanced at the litter tray, it was clean as Snowy had been at the café all day. She put fresh water in the bowl and a bit of dried cat food in another bowl, in case Snowy got peckish. Then she went up for a quick shower and changed into jeans and a top. She'd phoned the local solicitor's office at lunchtime and booked an appointment for Thursday to start the divorce rolling. The sooner she sorted it, the sooner she could get on with her life.

She went over to Snowy, who was still curled up on the sofa, and stroked him. 'I have to go out again, are you going to be okay here by yourself?' Edna had told her that she often left Snowy in when she went shopping and he always used the litter tray.

Snowy lifted up his head and miaowed as if he understood, then laid his head back down on his paws again. He seemed perfectly comfortable.

'I won't be long,' Dee told him, grabbing her handbag. It was warm so she didn't need a jacket. She wondered briefly how

Snowy would be with a dog, but then, at the moment, she would only be borrowing one to take for walks, so that shouldn't affect the little cat.

Flic, Stu and Cath were at The Pirate's Head with Kenny when Dee arrived. Stu waved and called her over.

'Kenny's been telling us that you're thinking of signing up to the "Local Dog Walkers" app?' he said when Dee had got herself a wine spritzer and sat down to join them.

She noticed to her surprise that Toffee was lying by his feet. The little dog waved his tail at her and she bent down and stroked his head then replied, 'Yes, I'd love a dog to take for a walk, it's better than walking alone, and if it helps someone else then that's great.'

'Do you have an iPhone or Android?' Kenny asked her.

'Android,' she told him, taking it out of her handbag. Nigel always insisted that Androids were more flexible and had better cameras.

'This is the app. You'll find it in the Playstore,' Kenny told her, showing her the icon – a white dog in a dark blue circle with Local Dog Walkers written around it.

She installed the app and signed up – which was so easy she could have done it by herself but it was good of Kenny to offer to help. She took out her credit card to pay the small fee of £10 a year, but to her dismay it was declined. Nigel had kept his threat of cancelling her cards. Thank goodness she'd moved that money into her own account.

'Problem?' Kenny asked.

'Nigel has cut off my access to the joint account.' She took out her personal account card. 'It's okay I have my own account.'

To her surprise there were quite a few dog owners looking for people to share their dogs – people who worked, young mums who didn't have time, elderly people who no longer had the energy.

'What sort of dog are you looking for?' Cath asked.

Dee considered this. 'I don't really mind. I think it's more important to me who I help by looking after it,' she said after a moment's thought. 'I think I'd like to help out an older person, it must be really difficult for them to walk their pets and often they're the only "family" they have.' She thought of some of the elderly people in the village she lived in – or should that be, used to live in – they often didn't see anyone from one week to the next, especially if they were housebound. It would be good to help someone like that look after their dog, and also probably provide a bit of much needed company. She remembered the elderly lady who had spent a couple of hours in the café that afternoon, making a pot of tea last, and stroking Snowy, wondering if she had a pet. If she didn't, was it because she couldn't look after it by herself.

Finally Dee selected a Cavalier King Charles Spaniel called Betsy, owned by an elderly couple, Stan and Brenda Slater. Their daughter had signed them up for the app, concerned that no one had time to exercise the dog. They lived a few minutes' drive away. Dee sent them a message offering to walk the dog for them, then settled back to join in the conversation which had now turned to the Artists' Studios.

'We raised loads on Saturday, which is great, but we're still a few grand short of what we need before we can open,' Kenny said. 'It would be good if we could get all the funds we need by September, to give the artists time to move in and establish themselves for Christmas. Being in a large, bespoke studio space should increase their customer reach and sales.'

'We get a lot of visitors in the summer, maybe we can hold more fairs, or raffles even, to raise the money,' Cath suggested.

'I could ask Andi if we could have a collection tin in the café,' Dee said. 'People might put in their odd bits of change, it will all add up.' Another idea occurred to her. 'Maybe we could even have some displays of the artists' work? A photo board perhaps? People might be willing to support it if they can see where the money is going.'

'That's a good idea,' Kenny agreed. 'I knew that you would be useful to have on the committee.'

Dee felt her cheeks glow at Kenny's praise. 'We should run it past Moira too, although I'm sure she won't mind. It's all for a good cause after all.' She picked up her glass. 'I'll mention it to Andi tomorrow and ask her to talk to Moira about it when she calls for her daily update.'

They discussed other ideas to raise funds, with Dee writing them all down. She seemed to have become the unofficial PA. She hoped no one thought she was taking over, but the others didn't seem to mind. Then, about halfway through the evening a message came in from the Local Dog Walkers saying that Mr and Mrs Slater wanted to meet her to discuss sharing the care of Betsy. Dee arranged to pop round the next day after work.

'I hope they like me,' she said to Kenny as she patted Toffee, 'and that Betsy is as friendly as your dog.'

'Of course they will, you'll be a godsend to them,' Kenny told her. 'We'll be able to take both dogs for a walk along the beach at the weekend.' He grinned. 'That'll be fun.'

Dee smiled. She and Kenny had fallen into an easy friendship, which she enjoyed, and she liked the idea of them both walking the dogs together.

Kenny insisted on walking her home. 'I'd ask you in for a coffee but Snowy is in and I'm not sure how he'll be with Toffee,' Dee said.

'No problem, we don't want to unsettle Snowy, he's got

enough to deal with as Edna is away. Anyway, it's time I was off too.' He nodded at her. 'Bye, Dee.'

'Bye.'

She watched as he turned around and walked down the hill. Memories of him with Margot all those years ago flashing across her mind. Margot had been so full of life, she bet that Kenny missed her so much. At least Nigel was still alive, and it was her choice to leave him. She was glad that she had met Kenny again, it seemed that right now they both needed a friend.

Snowy came to the door to greet her when she opened it, running out into the front garden to do his business and then coming straight back in.

'You're missing Edna, aren't you?' Dee asked as she stroked the little cat, who miaowed softly as if he understood what she'd said.

Dee made herself a mug of warm milk and honey and sat down to watch TV for a while, stroking Snowy. Then she scooped him up and took him up to bed with her. The cat snuggled down on the duvet beside her and was soon asleep while Dee lay for a while, her mind buzzing. She was about to finally drop off when a text came in. She groaned. Not Nigel again. She was tempted to ignore it but curiosity got the better of her and she grabbed her phone from the bedside cabinet. It was from Babs. She opened it, anxious to hear how her friend had got on. Babs had written:

> Not seen anything I like so far, and still don't want to live here. Can't wait to get back to the UK. How are things with you?

She'd attached a couple more photos of the houses they'd viewed recently and Dee was surprised when she saw that one of them was almost at the top of a mountain, and the other looked like it was in the middle of a forest. There was no way her friend would live anywhere like that, she wouldn't have thought that Geoff would want to either. He was a people person, he'd loved working in the shop, so had Babs. They were the sort of people who were the centre of the community. Surely, they should be looking at smaller properties in villages where there was a bit of life going on? These houses were all old, huge and remote. What was he thinking of, taking Babs to see houses like this? It was almost as if he wanted her to refuse to move.

35

TUESDAY

Dee mentioned her idea about having a collection tin for the Artists' Studios, and a wall display for their work to Andi when she arrived at the café the next morning.

'I think that's a great idea, I'll run it by Moira when she phones me for a catch-up.' Andi promised.

'Thanks so much,' Dee said. 'I see we have our visitor again.' She pointed over at Snowy, who had followed Dee and was now curled up in a chair in the bay window.

'He's made himself comfortable already!' Andi remarked. 'We might need to rename this place The Cat Café.'

Dee chuckled. 'I think Moira might have something to say about that.' She pulled on her apron, fastened it at the back, and set to work.

A few minutes later, Moira phoned and Andi went into the back to talk to her. 'Moria's agreed to the collection tin and the wall display of the artists' work,' she said when she returned.

'That's great. Thanks for asking. I'll let the others know later. How is Moira? Is her daughter out of hospital yet?' Dee asked.

'She's coming out of hospital tomorrow but she's going to

need help for a while. Moira is very worried about her. She said that it could be a few weeks before she can come back to the café.' Andi unwrapped a loaf and started spreading butter on the sandwiches. 'Are you all right to help out for that long or shall I get agency staff?'

Dee felt sorry for Moira and her daughter but working at the café was a much-needed solution for her current money worries. At least now she had a small income as well as a roof over her head for a few weeks. 'More than happy to work here until Moira can return. It gives me chance to sort out my own situation.'

'Brilliant.' Andi took some ham and cheese out of the fridge, handing the ham to Dee. 'We make a good team and I don't fancy getting used to someone new.'

Dee smiled at her. She was surprised at how much she enjoyed working at the café, it had a real community feel. It made her feel useful and wanted, as if she had a part to play. And she was delighted that Moira had agreed to supporting the artists. She wanted to text Kenny and tell him straight away but the café was due to open in a few minutes and there was still a lot to do. She'd just have to wait until she had a break.

It was a busy morning. Snowy had become quite an attraction and many people came in to stroke him, ordering a drink and snack while they were there.

'He's good for business,' Andi said with a smile as Snowy got down from his chair and went to join a young family, sitting very calmly while the little girl petted him. 'I don't know what we'll do when Edna comes home.'

Dee didn't know what she would do either, she'd really got attached to the little cat.

When the rush finally calmed, and they could sit down for a much needed break, Andi asked Dee how her evening had gone.

'Really good. I've downloaded the app and got a meeting this evening with a couple who need someone to walk their dog. I'm so glad Kenny suggested it.'

'It was very helpful of him. And to offer to download the app for you. Such a difficult thing to do,' Andi teased.

Dee flushed. 'He was just being kind,' she said a little defensively. She didn't want anyone thinking that she was hanging around with another man when she'd only recently broken up with Nigel.

Nigel didn't even wait to break up with you before he jumped into bed with someone else.

The words flashed across her mind and she felt her cheeks flush. Heavens, what had prompted that thought, jumping into bed with Kenny wasn't even on her mind.

'Ooh, do I detect a blush?' Andi cocked her head to one side. 'Do you fancy our Kenny?'

Dee shook her head quickly. 'I told you we're old friends.' She could hear the sharpness in her voice and saw the surprise register across Andi's face. There had been no call for her to snap like that. 'Sorry, it's just that, well, Nigel and I were together a long time – and Margot was a very good friend of mine. Besides, I wouldn't know what to do with anyone else. I barely dated before Nigel. I'm a novice as far as the dating game goes.'

'Bless you, it'll come naturally to you when you are ready to spread your wings again.' She leaned forward and whispered conspiratorially, 'Besides, in my experience all men do the deed basically in the same way.' She pushed her chair back and stood up. 'Ah, here come the afternoon surge of customers.'

I hope I haven't upset her, Dee thought as Andi walked off. She liked Andi, and she didn't mean to make things awkward between them. She couldn't help wondering though if everyone else was thinking the same thing about her and Kenny. Maybe she should keep her distance for a bit?

She was still mulling over Andi's remarks when Kenny came in with Toffee. 'How's it going?' he asked. 'I don't mean to nag, but I wondered if you'd managed to have a word with Andi about Moira allowing the artists to display their work?'

Dee clapped her hands to her forehead, she'd been so put out over Andi's words that she'd forgotten to text Kenny about Moira's decision. 'Oh gosh, I'm sorry, we've been so hectic.'

He placed his hand gently on hers and she felt a flicker of... something. 'It's fine, I know you're working. I didn't mean to put any pressure on you. There's no rush to ask her.'

'No, no. Andi did ask her and she's agreed.' Dee filled him in as she served him his coffee and tea cake.

'That's amazing. I'll let the others know. Thanks so much.'

She nodded, her eyes moving to the next customer in the queue. 'Can I help you?'

She was aware of Kenny walking away and wished she had longer to speak to him. By the time she had a free moment, he had gone.

'Excuse me, I wonder if you might like these?' a young mum asked, handing her a pile of magazines. 'I hate to throw them out and I thought maybe people would like to read them as they sat and drank their cuppas?'

'Thank you. I'll ask the manageress,' Dee said, taking the magazines off her; most of them were women's magazines but there were a couple of gardening and travel ones too. If Andi didn't want them, she would take them home and read them herself, it would keep her busy in the evenings. Except this evening as she had to visit the Slaters.

'Sure, let's put them on the table with the condiments and cutlery, then people can help themselves. Anything that keeps the punters here longer.' Andi grinned and Dee's spirits lifted. She'd obviously forgiven her for snapping earlier.

* * *

After work she went to visit the Slaters. They were a lovely, friendly couple, and Betsy, their little dog, was a real sweetie, coming straight to Dee and allowing herself to be stroked. 'She doesn't do that to everyone, she knows a kind person when she sees one,' Brenda said with a smile.

'She's gorgeous. How old is she?' Dee asked as she fussed the little dog.

'Almost eight, but she still has lots of energy.' Brenda grabbed her walking stick to get out of the chair. 'Let's go for a walk now and see how she is with you?'

Dee was a bit taken aback. 'Are you sure?' she asked doubt-fully as Brenda got to her feet, leaning on the stick.

'I can walk, but I'm slower than I used to be. Betsy will need me with her, I can't just send her off with you.'

She should have thought of that. Brenda hobbled into the kitchen and took a lead from a hook by the door. Immediately Betsy got to her feet, barking, tail wagging.

'She always loves a walk. We'll only go round the block.' Brenda handed Dee the lead. Immediately Betsy ran over to her, yapping loudly.

'Okay, girl.' Dee stroked the little dog then slipped the lead onto her collar. 'Let's go for a walk.'

Brenda handed her some doggy bags and a couple of treats. 'Whenever you call her and she comes to you, give her a treat,' she said.

Dee slowed her pace to match Brenda's and they walked around the block then over to the waste ground when she let

Betsy off her lead. The little dog shot off happily, running around and barking. She stopped to do her business and Dee scooped it up into the bag, tied it up and put it in the bin provided.

'See if she'll come to you,' Brenda said, so Dee called the little dog who came scooting over.

'Good girl,' she patted her and gave her a treat.

Brenda nodded her approval. 'I think you'll do nicely.'

They chatted as they headed back, Betsy walking obediently on the lead but stopping every now and again to sniff at something. Brenda told her how they had three children and five grandchildren, but they'd all moved away. 'They can't afford to live here any more,' she said sadly. 'There aren't even any houses to rent, they're all holiday homes.'

It was clear that she missed her children. 'Do they visit you?' Dee asked.

'Now and again, but they're all working and it's a bit of a jaunt.' Brenda sighed. 'We're okay, me and Stan, but we're not getting any younger and things are getting a bit much for us. We could do with moving ourselves, truth be told, but it's such an upheaval, we can't face it. And it would take months to clear our house. We brought all our kids up there, the loft is full of their old toys and clothes.'

It was such a shame. No wonder Glenn and the others were so angry about the new development, Dee thought. It was affordable homes that were needed, not luxury apartments and shops. But the developers were probably looking to make an enormous profit, and that's likely all they cared about.

Back at the Slaters' house, Stan made them all a hot drink and she sat down to talk to them for a few minutes. She could see that they were quite isolated, only having each other for company.

'How often would you like me to walk Betsy?' she asked as she sipped her tea.

'Maybe every other weekday and once at the weekend? Our garden is big enough for her to stretch her legs, but she does need a walk as well.' Stan looked at her questioningly. 'Would that be okay with you? If it's too much, then whatever you can manage.'

'That's fine. I'll come Sundays, Tuesdays and Thursdays, if that suits you both? I'll collect her when I finish work. And if I give you my number, you can let me know if you need anything from the shops, then I can bring it with me. I work in the café in the village so it's no trouble to me.'

Both their faces lit up. 'Oh, bless you, dear, that's so kind of you. We do find it a little difficult to get out and about. Not that we want to complain, we have each other and our health even if we are a bit doddery,' Brenda said.

'It's a pleasure,' Dee told them. 'I'll see you on Thursday around six then.'

'Perfect,' Stan said, and Brenda clasped Dee's hands. 'You're a godsend.'

Dee patted Betsy goodbye and set off home, her mind preoccupied. There must be plenty of other people in the village like the Slaters who need a smaller home, but didn't want to leave the village. It was a shame this developer hadn't chosen to build self-contained apartments for older folk, then the houses would be released for families to live in. Could they afford to buy them though? Could she, when the divorce finally went through and she received her settlement? Would she be able to stay in this village that she had – even in this short space of time – grown to love so much. Strange that she'd only been here ten days but she'd really fallen for the place, it had immediately felt like home. More than her house of thirty years did.

36

BABS

Tuesday

'What do you think?' Geoff asked. 'You have to admit that it's beautiful.'

'And no mountains, *señora*,' Santiago said, opening his arms wide. 'This is better, no?'

The house owner, who Santiago had introduced as Alonso, beamed and held out his arms wide too.

There were mountains in the distance, Babs noticed – there seemed to be mountains everywhere in Spain – but the house was in a valley and the land was flat. It was also the only house around for miles, at least it seemed to be, although she could see a couple on the horizon.

Babs looked around her at the orange and lemon trees, the purple bougainvillea, the brilliant blue sky, the acres of olive trees. The absence of people, shops, life. There was no way she could live here. And every house they'd been to so far had been in a similar location.

'It's beautiful, but it's *too isolated*.' She turned to Geoff. 'Think about it, Geoff, do you really want to live here away from everyone? Just the two of us rattling around in a big house, all this land to tend to?' She thought again of poor Edna, and how she could have lain injured for days before anyone had realised. And she lived in a busy little village. If something happened to Babs or Geoff they would have no one. She couldn't bear to live like that. She loved having people around her. And thought that Geoff did too.

Geoff avoided her eyes, looking down at the ground as he scuffed the hardened soil with his toe. 'It's peaceful. And there's plenty of room to put up Molly and Lennon, and the grandkids when they have some.'

'There is, but they'd be bored stiff after a day. What would they do here?' she pointed out.

'There is the pool, *señora*. And all this fresh air is good for the children. They can run around and play,' Santiago said persuasively. He and Alonso led the way around the land – there was too much of it to call it a garden – pointing out the various trees. Geoff hung on to every word.

'What's this?' Babs asked as they came to a small concrete shed.

Santiago asked Alonso who replied in rapid Spanish.

'That's the pump house, *señora*,' Santiago translated.

'Pump house?' she repeated.

'*Si*, the water, it is pumped up from the well and then sent to the house. All the... workings... are in here.'

'"Well"? You mean we have to pump the water up in a bucket?' Babs asked faintly. She looked over at the house. How many times a day would they have to carry buckets of water over? 'There is no running water?'

'No, no.' Santiago sighed and was silent for a moment as if

wondering how to explain. 'There is no town water. We are too far. The water, it is pumped up from the well.'

'How?' Geoff asked. Even he looked worried now.

'By the electric. Then it is sent to the house. You turn on the taps and the water, it comes out.'

'And if the electric goes off there is no water?' Babs asked, just to make sure she'd fully understood.

'Sadly, no. But it will soon come back on again. Let me show you.' Santiago spoke to Alonso and they both led the way back to the house. Babs and Geoff followed. They walked into the kitchen and turned on the taps. Water came gushing out. 'See. It is no problem.'

Suddenly the kitchen light went off and water stopped running out of the taps.

'Ah, the electric, it goes sometimes.' He shrugged his shoulders. 'It will be back on soon.'

Babs shot Geoff a look of dismay and was relieved to see that he was alarmed by this too.

The next house was nearer to the town and had town water. It also had a chicken run and a cockerel. This time the owners were out. 'The seller, he say that you can have the animals,' Santiago said. 'They give many eggs.'

Geoff's eyes lit up. 'Imagine that, Babs. Our own fresh eggs.'

Babs wasn't impressed, hens were noisy and messy. 'How far away are the nearest shops?' she asked.

'Very near, maybe ten minutes,' Santiago told her. 'Come see the views from the terrace.'

He led them up the terracotta steps to the huge terrace. Babs tried to ignore the cracks in the walls and the balustrades, there had been cracks in most of the houses they'd seen, Santiago had said that it was normal because of the heat. She looked across the land. It did look beautiful from up here, she had to admit. She imagined herself sitting on this terrace with a glass of wine, enjoying the peace and quiet.

Suddenly a cacophony of barking burst through the silence. It sounded like at least a dozen dogs were all vying with each other to be heard. She peered over the balustrade. 'Whose dogs are those?'

'They are from the rescue centre over the road. You will soon get used to the barking. You will ignore it and sleep on,' Santiago assured her.

'You mean that they bark at night too?'

Santiago shrugged. 'They are dogs, *señora*. Who knows when they will bark?'

Chickens, a cockerel and now dogs. This certainly wouldn't be a peaceful life. Babs looked over at Geoff who was still gazing in awe at all the land.

Suddenly there was a screech below and a scrawny black cat went running past, a rat dangling from its mouth. Babs screamed and clutched Geoff's arm. 'That cat, it's got a rat!'

Santiago studied her thoughtfully for a moment. 'Perhaps a town house would suit you better, *señora*?' he suggested.

Babs nodded.

Santiago took out his phone. 'My friend, Maria, she has town houses. I will contact her for you.' He dialled a number and started to speak in rapid Spanish.

'Tomorrow, Maria will meet you in the square in the town and take you to see some townhouses,' he said when the call was finished.

At last! Now we might find something more suitable, Babs thought.

Geoff was silent all the way back in the car. Babs wondered if he was sulking because she'd asked to view some town houses.

She waited until they were back in the villa and broached the subject.

'I think it's a good idea,' he agreed. 'We need to see as many properties as possible, and I think you would be happier living in a town.'

Actually, I'd be happier living in the UK, Babs thought, but she didn't say anything. She had promised to give Spain a fair chance.

They drove out to a nearby Spanish restaurant for supper and had a glass of wine on the terrace before they went to bed. It was an enjoyable evening and Babs felt more relaxed when they went to bed that night. Maybe a house like this, on the outskirts of the town would be okay.

The next morning they were woken by barking. It sounded like it was coming from the villa's garden. Geoff jumped out of bed and hurried over to the window, pulling open the blinds. Sunlight poured in. Babs joined him at the window. Two border collies were running around the garden barking trying to round up what looked like a herd of goats who were chewing the hedge.

'We must have left the gate open when we came back last night,' Geoff said. 'I hope the goats don't destroy the garden.'

Babs sank down onto the bed. She was glad they were going to see town houses today. Surely there were no goats, rats, barking dogs and huge drops off a mountain in the town.

* * *

The town houses were big and spacious, there were people and shops around, but it was obvious Geoff didn't like them. And Babs had to admit that she didn't fancy living in a town either. There were no gardens, only courtyards or terraces and they were all very noisy. They could hear the next-door neighbours talking. And their dog barking.

'You don't like?' Maria asked, looking worried as she showed them around the final house. They had already viewed five.

'Well—'

Geoff butted in. 'Not for me,' he said adamantly. 'Too dark and no views.'

Maria smiled. 'No problem. We have big apartments with beautiful sea views. Tomorrow I will show you them.'

Now that was more like it, Babs thought happily. She fancied living by the sea. She could imagine Molly and Lennon would visit a lot then.

37

DEE

Dee arranged with Andi to finish work early on Thursday so that she could see the solicitor. It wasn't something she was looking forward to doing, but she knew she had to get the ball rolling. Edna would be back home in a couple of weeks and, although Dee was on a few estate agents' books, none of them had come up with a place for her to rent yet. Sylvia had suggested she tried further afield but Dee really wanted to live in Port Telwyn.

The solicitor, a man called Mr Peabody, was very helpful, assuring Dee that she would definitely be entitled to half the house and some of Nigel's private pension. 'We'll start the ball rolling with an application for a decree nisi on the grounds of adultery,' he told her.

Adultery. Divorce. It all seemed so unreal. She knew that was what she wanted though, that it was the right thing to do. She was also pretty sure that Nigel didn't think she would go ahead with it and would be shocked when he got the solicitor's letter.

She went home to change quickly, grab a sandwich, feed

Snowy and then hurry to the Slaters' house to walk Betsy. They were delighted to see her and the little dog danced around happily when she saw the lead. Dee took her over to the sand dunes which the locals called the Towans, letting Betsy off the lead for a while. On the way back she stopped to look at the new estuary development. It was coming on leaps and bounds and she was impressed with how aesthetically pleasing it was looking so far. The designer had taken a lot of care to ensure that it fitted in with the surroundings.

The Slaters insisted she stay for a cup of tea and a chat so it was gone seven by the time she set off for Primrose Cottage. As she was about to put the key in the door her mobile rang. She fished it out of her jeans' pocket and looked at the screen. Edna. She immediately pressed to answer.

'Edna. How are you?'

'I'm fine, dear,' Edna said. 'How are you? Have you settled into Primrose Cottage?'

'I love it. It's very cosy.' She paused, Edna had probably phoned her to inform her of her imminent return. 'I'm guessing that you'll be back home soon.' She pushed open the door and stepped inside. 'Well don't worry, I'm on the books of all the local letting agents and am sure they'll find me something soon. If not, I can go to the local B&B.'

'Are you definitely intending to stay in Port Telwyn then?'

'I'm hoping to, if I can find somewhere suitable to buy. I've started divorce proceedings against Nigel, and it seems that I'm in for a decent settlement. Plus, I have some savings.' And Simon had messaged her to inform her that there had been a lot of interest in her grandmother's brooch, so it was being auctioned this weekend. Hopefully that would be another few thousand to add to the pot.

'I'm pleased to hear that. I'm really enjoying staying in Brean with Mabel. I won't be coming home yet, so there is no rush for you to leave the cottage.'

Dee was relieved, not only because she didn't have to move out yet but also because she knew that it was going to be a long time before Edna could manage on her own and she was worried how the elderly lady would cope. She would keep an eye on her, of course, but she was at work all day and there was the nighttime too.

'That is so kind of you. Are you absolutely sure? I will pay you rent of course,' she added.

'A minimum rent to cover the bills would be appreciated, and I wonder if you could look after Snowy for me until I come back? It sounds like he's taken to you.'

'Of course I will,' Dee promised. 'I'll send you regular updates so you can see how he's getting on.'

They talked for a bit longer, agreeing a very affordable rent in exchange for Dee keeping the house tidy and contributing to any bills. Edna said that it would be at least a month before she was ready to come back. 'And when I do, you're welcome to stay until you can find your own place to live. It would be nice to have the company,' Edna told her.

That was wonderful news. Dee felt a lot more positive when she finished the call, hopefully it wouldn't take too long to sort out the divorce settlement and the sale of the house then she could get a home of her own. Until then she was happy to stay here. It was so kind of Edna.

Things were turning out better than she had ever expected.

38

BABS

Friday

'There! What do you think?' Maria, the estate agent, asked, sweeping her arms to indicate the panoramic view of the coast in front of them.

It was beautiful, breathtaking, Babs acknowledged. All the apartments Maria had shown them today had been modern, clean, gorgeously decorated and furnished. Like something out of a magazine. But they still didn't feel like a home. Not the sort of home that she could relax in. She was sure that Geoff would feel the same after a while. At the moment it seemed he would settle for anything she wanted as long as they could live in Spain.

The trouble is, she knew now for definite that she didn't want to live in Spain.

Geoff was leaning over the balcony, exclaiming in admiration. '*Es maravilloso*. I could sit here all day.'

'It's beautiful, but it's very quiet.' Babs didn't want to keep putting downers on it but there was no way she could live anywhere like this. She'd be bored. She could see that Geoff liked it though. What should she do? She could understand that his health scare had made him rethink his life. It had shocked her too. Now though, she felt that they were at a crossroads. She'd thought her and Geoff would grow old together, sitting there holding hands in their twilight years, reminiscing about the past. She never dreamed that once they both retired, their lives would be turned upside down.

Maria excused herself to take a call from another prospective buyer, warning them that, 'You must decide quick or it will be gone.' She left them to sit on the terrace with a glass of fresh orange juice each, to discuss their decision.

Beside her Geoff coughed, trying to get her to look at him. Babs kept her gaze fixed firmly on the sea, trying to work out what to say to him. 'You hate it, don't you? You don't want to move to Spain?' he asked quietly.

Babs looked out at the sea, felt the warmth of the sun on her arms and closed her eyes. She tried to imagine this being her life. Just her and Geoff living here in this apartment. Then she thought of Molly and Lennon and the children she hoped they would have someday, the shops she loved to browse around, going to the theatre, meeting up with Dee, all the things she loved to do in the UK. She thought about living in Spain, getting used to the heat, the mosquitos – she swatted one away, groaning when she saw the tell-tale red swelling on her arm – struggling to understand the language. That had been a real problem this week although English was spoken a lot in the coastal areas.

'No, I don't.' She forced herself to meet his eyes and swallowed when she saw the sadness there. 'I'm sorry, Geoff, but I definitely don't want to live here.'

He looked shrunken, defeated, the sparkle had gone out of him like the air from a balloon when you prick it.

I've stopped him living his dream, she thought sadly. *But it's my life too and if I come out here, I won't be happy.*

They told Maria their decision and she shook her head as if in disbelief.

They barely spoke on their way back to their villa and Babs felt that they'd lost something. The past few weeks there had been a distance between them but now it was a chasm. For years they had been a team, united, bringing up their family together, running the shop, overcoming all the hurdles that had come their way, but all that was gone and now they were as awkward with each other as if they were strangers. It was horrible.

And there was only one way she could see to fix it.

39

DEE

Saturday

Mid-morning on Saturday a message pinged in from Simon. He was auctioning Dee's grandmother's brooch today.

> What's the lowest offer you want me to accept?

She considered this. She had no idea what the brooch was worth, Simon said about £4,000, but she would be grateful for anything. She sent a text back.

> What do you suggest?

> I think we should set a reserve for £3,750.

> I agree.

She was happy to leave it to Simon, he knew what he was doing and she trusted him.

Meanwhile, she wanted to tidy up a little. Edna had kept

the house fairly clean, but things like curtains and windows were a lot for a woman of her age. She'd give it all a deep clean, as a thank you to Edna. She was sure the older woman would be delighted. She took off the cushion covers and put them in the washing machine, then took down the curtains and started cleaning the windows. She'd just finished doing the lounge windows when Simon phoned her to tell her that the brooch had sold to an online bidder for £5,750. She couldn't believe it. That was a clear £5,000 profit, taking out Simon's commission. That, and her wages, should see her through until the divorce settlement came through, especially as Edna was allowing her to live in the cottage for such a minimal rent. The financial pressure was off. 'Thank you, Grandma,' she whispered, sending a silent prayer to her late grandmother.

Another message pinged in. It was from Kenny asking if he could pop in and see her as there was something he wanted to talk about regarding the Artists' Studios before they met up with the others tonight.

'Of course, I'm in all afternoon,' she replied.

'Half an hour okay?'

'Perfect.'

They'd sit out in the garden, she decided. It looked like June was going to be a warm month and already the temperature was well into the mid-twenties. She went upstairs to quickly freshen up and change out of the jeans and T-shirt she'd worn for cleaning, brush her hair and apply a bit of make-up. She glanced at her watch. She needed to get a move on, Kenny would be here any minute. She'd put a jug of home-made lemonade into the fridge this morning, she took some ice cubes out of the freezer and dropped them into the jug then took two clean glasses out of the cupboard. Right on cue, the doorbell rang.

'No Toffee?' she asked in surprise. Kenny usually took his beloved dog everywhere with him.

'I thought I'd better leave him at home, I don't want him upsetting Snowy.' Kenny followed her inside. 'He's had a long walk this morning so he's happy to stay and sleep.'

'A wise decision, although they will have to get used to each other at some point as Edna kindly said I can stay here until my divorce is settled,' Dee remarked as Snowy wandered in through the back door and curled up in his basket.

'You've put in for the divorce?' Kenny asked.

'Yes, I saw the solicitor on Thursday.' Dee picked up the jug of iced lemonade out of the fridge. 'Shall we sit outside?'

'Sure.' Kenny picked up the two glasses and followed her out, they both settled down at the little table in the back garden. Dee filled the two glasses, handing one to Kenny then took a sip of her drink, letting the cold lemonade slide down her throat before replying more fully to his question. 'The solicitor said the decree nisi will be through in a few weeks providing Nigel cooperates and doesn't delay for time.' She'd been surprised at that. 'Hopefully we can then work out a fair financial settlement. I don't expect that Nigel will be on his own for long.'

'Does that bother you?'

'Not at all. He wasn't faithful when we were together so isn't likely to be now we've split up, is he?'

'You were right to leave him,' Kenny said. 'It will take you a bit of time to adjust, but you'll make a new life for yourself, you'll see.'

'I'm sure I will. To be honest, I still can't take it all in. I can't believe that I'm living on my own after all these years.'

'It takes time. It took me years to get over losing Margot. Although I guess a bereavement is different,' Kenny said.

He was right, losing someone you love was surely much

harder than a divorce, her divorce anyway. She and Nigel had grown apart. Babs and Geoff still loved each other, and it would be awful if they split up. Come to think of it, she hadn't heard from Babs for a couple of days, she'd have to message her tonight and see how the house viewing trip went.

'What was it you wanted to talk about?' she asked, suddenly remembering his message.

'I wanted your opinion. You might be able to look at things more objectively as an outsider – I mean as you don't permanently live in the village,' he added hastily. 'A local businessman wants to invest in the Artists' Studios. He said he wants to give back to the community.'

'That's very noble of him! And I don't see any problem with that,' Dee said. Unless it was the person rather than the money people would object to, she realised. 'Who is he? Are you allowed to say?'

Kenny's eyes met hers over the rim of his glass. He put it down on the table. 'He wants me to keep it a secret.'

Dee frowned. 'Why?'

'If I tell you, will you promise not to breathe a word? It's top secret so I need you to promise not to divulge it to the others yet.'

Dee considered this. She didn't really like secrets but this was fantastic news for the Artists' Studios and she wanted to find out more. She really did want to be involved, it was a cause she believed in, and she wanted to encourage the talented artists she'd seen at the garden party.

'I promise,' she said firmly.

'He's a property developer and at the moment is involved in a lot of backlash over a new development he's planning.'

Dee tapped her fingers on the table as she considered this.

'Do you think he's doing this to improve his public image or because he genuinely wants to help?'

Kenny frowned. 'I've no idea. Does it matter?'

'It could be important. In my experience people who have something to gain will put in more of an effort than people who don't.'

Kenny leaned back in his chair, a slow smile playing on his lips. 'Good point. And I'm guessing that you are very apt at dealing with business people who have something to gain?'

Dee levelled her gaze at him. 'I've been involved in a lot of fundraising. The people who have given the most generously tend to fall in a few groups.' She counted them off on her fingers. 'Those who want to avoid paying tax so will give to charity instead to improve their public image, those who are trying to sweeten people up so that they can avoid protests against something they are planning to do, and those who are genuinely altruistic and want to pay back to society or – in the case of a medical charity – have lost someone to the disease the charity represents.'

'That certainly makes sense. I think our backer wants to get the community on board before he goes ahead with his next development.'

'Have you any idea what he's planning?'

Kenny looked guilty and suddenly she knew.

'He's in charge of the harbour development, isn't he?'

Kenny's face said it all.

'Yes. He's planning on building a deluxe shopping mall, with top class restaurants and shops, as it's on the outskirts of the village it should bring a lot of trade into the village too and jobs for local people,' Kenny explained.

'And will wipe out the natural beauty, plus bring in thousands of extra holidaymakers, which will push up the house prices even more and drive out the locals.'

Kenny nodded. 'True. Glenn is up in arms about it, as you know, and I doubt he will agree to us accepting the money. A couple of the others might not either, as a matter of principle.'

Dee quirked her eyebrow. 'How do you feel about it?' It would be interesting to see what take Kenny had on this.

'To be honest, I don't know what to do. We've been fighting this development for a while, but I think we're onto a lost cause.' He scratched his cheek. 'The money the developer is offering to put into the Artists' Studios is a large amount. It will allow us to finish the refurbishments and let out the studios at a reasonable price. But...' He raised his eyes to hers and she could see the concern in them. 'Are we selling out the village to make our dream come true?'

She could see his dilemma. 'Are you going to tell the others?'

'Eventually. I wanted to discuss it with you first, get your take on it. You're level-headed and don't have a personal interest like the rest of us, so might be able to see it all a bit more clearly.'

'What's this businessman's name?' Dee asked.

'Gordon Frost,' Kenny told her.

'Gordon Frost.' Dee repeated in disbelief.

Kenny's eyebrows knitted together and stared at her. 'Do you know him?'

'I did. A long time ago,' she replied, her mind going back to that last encounter. Fancy Gordon being behind the harbour development plan. He had moved away to Exeter years ago, after discovering that Nigel and Gordon's wife, Lydia, had been having an affair. Gordon had said at the time that he and Lydia had a marriage in name only, and that he'd been more hurt by Nigel's betrayal than Lydia's.

Should she have left Nigel then? She had certainly consid-

ered it, she had been devastated when she'd learnt about Nigel
and Lydia's affair, but the children had still been at school and
she had been loath to disrupt their lives. So eventually she had
forgiven Nigel, choosing to believe that it was a mad moment of
temptation and it would never happen again.

Only it had. Several times.

It was no use bothering about it now, what was done was
done, as her mother used to say.

'What do you think?' Kenny asked.

Dee's mind was still going over her last encounter with
Gordon and how much to tell Kenny. Just be truthful, she
decided. You're not responsible for what Nigel did. And Gordon
isn't responsible for Lydia's actions. They had all been good
friends before then, and she knew that Gordon cared about
people, about the environment.

'Actually, Gordon's one of the good guys, although, yes, he's
in business to make money.' Slowly she told Kenny about how
Gordon was a client of Nigel's and they'd been good friends,
often going out for dinner together, then Gordon had discovered
that Lydia and Nigel had been having an affair. 'He pulled his
business, threatened to destroy Nigel financially but when he
found out that I was staying with Nigel he backed down, said he
wouldn't put me through any more distress. He and Lydia split
up and he moved away.'

She could see that Kenny was mulling this over. 'Do you
think that if Gordon knows you're involved, he wouldn't back
the Artists' Studios?'

'I don't see why. He was always a fair man, and none of it was
my fault. Actually, what I wanted to suggest was that I come
with you when you have your meeting with him.'

Kenny tilted his head to one side, waiting for her to
continue.

'Gordon was someone who cared about people, and gave a great deal of thought to things, including – as I remember Nigel complaining about – where he builds his developments. From what I know of him, I'd guess he's convinced that this development is good for Port Telwyn, and that he is genuinely trying to help the community by donating money to the Artists' Studios.' She took a swig of lemonade. 'I'm wondering if we tell him how hard local people like Glenn are finding it to stay here, because of the cost of housing, we could persuade him to make a section of the development affordable for the locals – either to rent or buy.'

Kenny digested this for a moment. 'You reckon you could talk him into that?'

Dee considered this. It had been years since she'd seen Gordon, and she was sure that his business would have gone from strength to strength since then. 'It's worth a try.'

'Okay, then let's do it. He wants me to meet him on Thursday morning at ten thirty to discuss it. Are you free then?'

'I'll ask Andi if I can do the afternoon shift,' she told him. It would be a squeeze, as she had an appointment with the solicitor at lunchtime, but she should be able to fit it all in and didn't want to miss this meeting.

'Great.' Kenny finished his lemonade then stood up. 'Well, I'd better be going. I'll leave you to your spring cleaning.'

'Thanks, see you later.' Dee saw him to the door.

He turned at the doorway. 'You're full of surprises, Dee.' Then he briefly kissed her on the cheek and was gone.

Dee stood on the doorstep for a moment, watching him walk down the hill, her hand on her cheek where he'd kissed it. Something stirred in her, something she hadn't felt for a long time.

40

MONDAY

Dee placed the toasted tea cakes, butter and jam on a tray along with the two cups of coffee and picked it up ready to take to the people on the table in the corner. She was halfway across the café when the door opened and Babs walked in, pulling a suitcase behind her. Dee almost dropped the tray in shock. She grasped it firmly and quickly scrutinised her friend. Babs didn't look happy, there were bags under her red-rimmed eyes. Obviously the trip to Spain hadn't gone well, and judging by the suitcase, Babs and Geoff had split up again. Could it be for good this time?

Andi came to the rescue. 'I'll deal with this. We're not too busy, take a break and see what's up with Babs.'

Dee thanked her and hurried over to her friend who was now sitting at an empty table, her suitcase leaning against the wall.

'Babs,' she said, horrified at how distressed her friend looked. 'What's happened?'

'I've left Geoff. Can I stay with you until I sort myself out, please?'

'Of course you can.' Dee gave her a big hug then sat down beside her. 'Why though? I thought Geoff said he would drop the idea of living in Spain if you didn't want to.'

Andi appeared at the table with a tray laden with a pot of tea, two mugs, a milk jug and a sugar bowl. 'I thought you might need this.' She squeezed Babs on the shoulder comfortingly then went back to serving the other customers.

Babs bit her lip and her eyes misted over with unshed tears. 'He has dropped the idea but he's so miserable, Dee. I feel like I've ruined his dream. I've stopped him from doing what he wants with his life. I'll be unhappy if we live in Spain, he's going to be unhappy if he doesn't live there. The best thing we can do is part and let each other live our lives as we want.'

'Does it have to be that drastic?' Dee poured out the tea, adding sugar to Babs' mug before passing it over to her.

'There's no other way. I want Geoff to be happy.' Babs painted a bright smile on her face. 'Anyway, never mind us. What about you and Nigel?'

'I've filed for divorce.'

'Good for you. I was worried that you'd go back to him. I never could stand him.'

'What? You never told me that!' Dee said, a little annoyed.

'Of course not, how could I? You obviously saw him differently. He treated you awfully and you seemed scared to have fun around him,' Babs pointed out.

Dee had to acknowledge that Babs was right.

'Geoff isn't like Nigel though, Babs. Surely there must be some solution. It's clear you both love each other and want to be together. Can't you compromise?'

'We tried to compromise. I told you, we looked at mountain houses, countryside houses, town houses, beach apartments... but I couldn't see myself living in any of them. I like the UK. I like to be by my friends and family. By you! I don't mind going to Spain for a holiday, but that's it.'

'Then does it have to be all or nothing? How about a holiday home?'

'I think that would cause more problems. Geoff would want to stay over in Spain as much as he could and I'll be travelling back and forth, basically living on my own. Plus there's the cost.'

'Look, can't you talk to Geoff about how you feel? He's great. He's not like Nigel. He's been a good husband to you, Babs. You can't just give up on him over this.'

Babs eyes flashed. 'Yes and I've been a good wife to him too! I've compromised all my life if you think about it. Geoff might not criticise me like Nigel does you, we both let each other be free. But it's Geoff's parents' house we lived in, his parents' shop we worked in. I worked in that shop whilst bringing up two children because Geoff wanted to keep the family home and the family business. And I loved him and wanted him to be happy. Whereas, you had time to spend with your kids.' Tears were spilling out of Babs' eyes now, and she wiped them away with the back of her hand. 'Everyone thinks good old Geoff, lets Babs be as loud and crazy as she wants, but what about good old Babs who's supported Geoff in what he wanted to do for years?'

Dee was so astonished, she had never heard Babs rant like this before. 'I thought you two were happy...?'

'We were... are... but you're talking as if I don't compromise when I always have but no one has ever seen it. Geoff and I worked all the hours under the sun in that shop. When we had to sell it I thought it might be time for us, that we could do things together, go away more often. Instead he shuts himself in the shed or garden and I'm hours on my own. Then he finds a lump he doesn't tell me about, discovers it's benign thank goodness, and again doesn't tell me. But it frightened him that much he decides we're going to live in Spain, whether I want to or not.'

She looked defiantly at Dee. 'And somehow I'm in the wrong for not wanting to go. Like what I want doesn't matter? Just because Geoff hasn't cheated on me or put me down like Nigel did to you, doesn't mean he's perfect. And now, because for once, I put my foot down and don't want to do what Geoff wants I'm the bad wife! How fair is that?'

Dee stared at her aghast. She had never thought of it like that. Yes, in a way she'd envied Babs because Geoff was so lovely, but Babs was lovely too. And she *had* always backed Geoff, until now. She remembered how Babs had even worked in the shop when the children were very young, taking them with her, sleeping in the pram, playing in a playpen in the backroom, building Lego quietly in the corner. She hadn't meant to insinuate that Babs didn't appreciate Geoff or that she had to do whatever he wanted.

She held out her arms. 'I'm sorry.'

Babs collapsed into them and they hugged.

'I'm sorry. I didn't mean to rant.' Babs sniffed, pulling away and blowing her nose. 'I know you meant well. I don't want to split up, I love Geoff. But I don't want him to give up his dream and be unhappy.' Her voice wobbled. 'It isn't the life I want though, Dee. And if we stay together, one of us will be miserable and we'll probably both end up resenting each other. The best thing we can do is set each other free, and stay friends. Then Geoff can go and live his life in Spain.'

'And what about you?' Dee asked softly. She hated to see her friend so upset and could see that this wasn't an easy decision for her.

'I was hoping that I could stay with you until I've sorted something out, if Edna doesn't mind,' Babs said. 'I know you have to be out of the cottage when Edna comes home, but maybe we can find somewhere else to rent together until we both get our settlement from our divorces?'

Dee hugged her. 'Of course you can. I'll be glad of the company. I'm sure it will be fine for you to move in with me. I'll check with Edna, but I'm positive it will be okay.'

'Thanks. You're a good friend,' Babs said with a wan smile.

Dee gave Babs the keys to the cottage and told her to make herself comfortable. As soon as she got the chance she'd phone Edna and see if it was okay for Babs to sleep in her room. She'd be finished work in a couple of hours and they'd sort it out then.

'I noticed the suitcase,' Andi whispered as Dee returned to help serve. 'I hope Babs is okay.'

So did she, Dee thought.

As soon as she could take a break, Dee phoned Edna and explained the situation. 'Of course Babs can have my room, dear, although I will need it back when I return,' Edna said.

'We'll both rent a place together then,' Dee promised her. 'Once summer is over, we should be able to get a winter let.' Then maybe both their divorces would be through and they could each buy somewhere more permanent.

When Babs made that toast to 'The Runaway Wives' the night she walked out on Geoff, neither of them knew how prophetic it would be.

41

BABS

Wednesday

Babs tossed and turned all night, her mind in turmoil as she went over her last conversation with Geoff. She knew she was right to call it a day. What was the point of them staying together to both be miserable? Geoff wanted to be in Spain and she didn't. It was heartbreaking, after all these years of marriage. She would miss him terribly. A lump formed in her throat and tears filled her eyes, as she thought of a life without Geoff.

He had taken the house off the market as soon as they'd come back, as he'd promised, but he had gone about with such a long face, hardly talking to her. She didn't want that. She'd prefer to end it now while they were still friends, than hang on until they both hated each other. So she'd told him to sell to the people who'd made an offer and they'd split the proceeds. There was enough for Geoff to buy himself a *finca* in the middle of nowhere, and for her to get a little flat. Hopefully.

Now, at sixty years old, she had to make a new life for herself. Thankfully she could stay with Dee until she sorted herself out. But, much as she loved it down here in Port Telwyn, for her it didn't feel like home. It was okay while she was looking on it as a holiday, but now she knew that this was it, her new life, she felt like someone had spun her round and placed her in a strange country. She had no idea what to do with herself. Dee seemed happy here and she'd got involved with the Artists' Studios and had made a nice network of friends. She intended to make her life down here, but Babs didn't want to. She wanted the life she had. The life with Geoff.

Stop hankering after what you can't have, she told herself sharply. Geoff wants different things now. So you either go along with that or make a break. That's the only choice you've got.

She must have dropped back off to sleep because the sound of the front door closing woke her up. She glanced at the clock. Eight thirty. Dee must have gone to work without waking her. She quickly showered, dressed and went downstairs. Snowy was asleep in his basket in the kitchen. He miaowed when he saw her, stretched, got out of the basket and went to the back door. Babs opened it and the cat shot out into the back garden; she followed him. She could smell the sea air and hear the seagulls squawking as they pattered across the cottage roof. There were worse places to live. Perhaps she'd get used to it eventually. She just needed to keep busy until she adjusted. When Geoff had sold the house, she would have some money to buy herself a little flat. Or maybe she and Dee could buy a place together. Would that work? They'd been friends for a long time, but were completely different personalities.

Could she even find a way to settle down here as Dee had done? Dee already had a job in the café – albeit temporary – and had filed for divorce and seemed happier than Babs had ever seen her. But then she and Nigel had lived almost separate lives for years. They always seemed more to exist alongside each other, rather than with each other. Whereas, Babs and Geoff...

She shook the kettle to check there was enough water for a cup of tea then switched it on. She'd just made herself a mug of tea when the doorbell rang. Persistently. As if someone had their finger on it.

'Okay, okay, I'm coming!' she walked into the hall and opened the door, stepping back in surprise when she saw Molly and Lennon standing on the doorstep together. 'What are you both doing here? And so early too! You must have left at the crack of dawn.'

'Hello to you, too, Mum,' Lennon said. 'Are you going to let us in?'

'Yes of course.' She stepped aside 'It's lovely to see you both but, Molly, aren't you supposed to be in Thailand?'

'I've been given forty-eight hours compassionate leave,' Molly said as they followed Babs into the kitchen.

'Compassionate leave?' Babs spun around, her hand going to her mouth. 'Why? What's happened?'

'My parents are splitting up after thirty-seven years of marriage, because they're too pig-headed to come to a compromise, that's what,' Molly said, pulling out a chair and sitting down on it.

'So we thought we'd better get together and try to talk some sense into both of you.' Lennon pulled out another chair and perched on it.

'Well, much as I appreciate you both caring, and coming all this way to check on me, I'm afraid there's nothing you can do. Your father and I have made the decision to split and that's it.'

'You know that Dad's got someone interested in buying the house?' Lennon asked her.

'Of course I do. That's what brought things to a head. He'll give me half of the money and I'll get myself a little flat.'

'Where?' Molly asked.

'Coffee?' Babs asked them, stalling for time.

They both nodded. 'Well, where are you going to live?' Lennon repeated Molly's question.

'I haven't decided yet.' She spooned coffee into the cups and added milk.

'Neither has Dad. You have a buyer for the house but neither you nor Dad have anywhere else to live. You're both intent on splitting up, yet have no idea what you're going to do next.'

'Your dad is going to Spain.' Babs poured hot water into each cup, gave it a stir and handed one to Molly and one to Lennon. 'And Dee's said I can stay with her until I sort myself out.'

'Dad's not going to Spain.'

Babs almost dropped her mug. 'What? Where's he going then?'

'He doesn't know. We went to see him last night. He's in a right state. He said he's got to sell the house so he can give you your half of the money and he doesn't know where he's going to live.'

'What do you mean?' she looked incredulously from one to the other of them. 'All this is because your dad wants to go and live in Spain and I don't want to.'

Lennon sighed. 'That's just it, Mum. He doesn't want to live in Spain without you. He actually said… he can't bear to think of life without you.'

Babs felt anger roaring through her. 'This is emotional blackmail! He's only saying that because he's hoping I'll feel guilty and agree to go. Well, I won't!'

Molly looked at Lennon. 'What if you bought a holiday

home there? And a little place over here? Then you both get what you want.'

'Dee suggested that but it wouldn't work. Your dad wants to live there permanently and I don't.'

'Mum, Dad still loves you. Do you still love him?'

'Of course I do but that's got nothing to do with it. We both want different things out of life now. It's time to go our separate ways.'

'If we were married and this was one of us, you would tell us to sit down and sort things out,' Molly told her.

'We've tried that, but there's no solution to this.'

'You'd ask us if we'd considered every option,' Lennon pointed out.

'What other options are there?' Babs asked confused.

'You don't know unless you talk to him about it,' Lennon told her.

Babs had no idea what to say. Her kids seemed convinced that there was a way around this but she couldn't see one. 'Maybe I'll phone your dad later.'

'Better still, talk to him now... He's in the car. He wanted to come down with us.'

Babs was dumbfounded. This was a turn of events she hadn't expected.

'Mum?' Molly looked at her beseechingly. 'Please at least try. You're both unhappy so what have you got to lose?'

She looked at her son and daughter. Molly had taken leave to come to see her, Lennon was a workaholic, but had clearly taken time off to pick up Molly and Geoff then drive down to talk to her. She nodded slowly. 'Okay, but I'm not promising anything.'

* * *

Geoff came in and Molly and Lennon made an excuse about wanting to explore the village, and headed out.

'Hello, Babs,' Geoff said quietly.

'Geoff.' She was at a loss what to say but Geoff continued.

'We need to talk, Babs, you've got it all wrong. I don't want to live in Spain without you. I don't want to live anywhere without you.' He pulled out a chair and sat down, resting his head on his hands. 'I've been a fool. I told you that lump gave me a scare. It knocked me sideways. I felt like I hadn't done enough with my life. I wanted a new adventure before I got too old, but all I've done is wrecked the happy life we had together.' He lifted his head and the love shone from his eyes. 'I don't want a place in the sun, Babs. I want to live my life to the fullest with you, the woman I adore. Please come back home.'

Babs went to him immediately and wrapped her arms around him. 'Oh, Geoff, I don't want to live without you either.' They hugged each other tight and it felt so good to have Geoff's arms around her.

'I'm sorry, love, causing all this stress,' Geoff mumbled.

Babs took a breath. 'The kids and Dee both suggested we buy a holiday home in Spain...' It wasn't what she wanted, but she didn't want to lose Geoff either.

Geoff shook his head. 'The truth is, Babs,' he paused, 'when we went to Spain to look at the houses, I realised that I didn't want to live there, but I felt so foolish after all the trouble I'd caused that I didn't like to admit it. I pretended to be enthusiastic because I didn't want to back down after causing all that fuss. I guess I just wanted to do more with my life and I seized on that as the answer, but it isn't.'

'Then let's do more. Let's plan some weekends away, there's lots of the UK we haven't seen. Or go on more holidays, a cruise even.'

Geoff nodded. 'It's worth a try. Anything's worth a try for us to be together.' He touched her cheek with his hand. 'I'm sorry, I've been pig-headed. I should have talked about this with you. And I'll never forgive myself for saying it wasn't your house. I don't know what came over me.'

'I think we're both as stubborn as each other. We dig our heels in and that's it,' Babs said.

He wrapped his arms around her waist. 'All this has made me realise just how much you mean to me. Can we put it all behind us and start again, do you think? Will you come back home?'

'It's made me realise how much I love you too. And yes, I'd love to come back home.' They hugged and kissed again.

'Let's promise each other that we won't be so stubborn again. We almost lost each other and I couldn't bear that,' Geoff said, a choke in his voice.

'Neither could I.' Babs squeezed his hand tight. 'Now, let's message and tell the kids the good news, then I'll tell Dee too. She's working in the café today. She'll be so happy for us.'

Molly and Lennon messaged back to say they were having breakfast in a café the other side of town and would be back in a couple of hours.

'Is that where Dee works?' Geoff asked.

'No, she works in the café by the harbour. I think the kids are giving us a bit of space.' Babs picked up her handbag. 'Maybe we can have some breakfast too.'

They walked down the hill towards Moira's Café, arm in arm.

'Dee's definitely divorcing Nigel then, after his shenanigans?'

'There's no way she'll forgive him this time. She's not been happy with him for a long time and this was the last straw. She's going to buy a cottage and live down here.'

'A fresh start then,' Geoff said. 'Very brave of her, but I'm glad she's leaving Nigel, I never did like him. I hope she won't be lonely here though.'

Babs pushed open the door of the café. Dee was sitting at the table in the window, beside Kenny. Papers were spread out on the table in front of them and they were both laughing. 'She's got a lot of friends here already. I've never seen anything like it! She's like the Dee I first met at school. I think she'll be fine,' Babs said.

Geoff's gaze rested on Dee, she looked so alive, then over to Kenny. 'He looks a bit more than a friend.'

'I think so too. Dee knew him and his wife a long time ago, but he's a widower now.'

Geoff gave her hand a squeeze. 'Well good luck to her. She deserves to find happiness after how Nigel's treated her.'

'She does,' Bab agreed. 'Let's go and tell her our news. She'll be thrilled for us.'

42

DEE

Thursday

'I hope you don't mind, but I've brought someone else with me, she's on the committee for the Port Telwyn Artists' Studios too,' Kenny said to Gordon as the receptionist showed them into his office.

The man behind the desk raised his head, then his eyes registered pleasant surprise. 'Well, if it isn't Dee Walton! How lovely to see you again!' He stood up and walked around the desk to give her a hug. 'How are you? Do you live down here now?' He released her and looked into her eyes. 'You look well.'

Gordon looked well, too, although he'd aged, and what little hair he used to have had gone. 'Yes, I'm renting a cottage at the moment and am looking to buy.'

'So you've finally left the cheating bastard then?'

'Only recently, but, yes. I should have done it sooner.' She shrugged.

'I'm not going to argue with that. You deserve better.' Nigel turned to Kenny and shook his hand. 'Pleased to see you again, Kenny.'

'Thanks for agreeing to meet us,' Kenny replied.

'A pleasure. Now sit down, both of you, and tell me what you wanted to talk about.' Gordon returned to the other side of the desk and sat down, indicating for Kenny and Dee to take the two seats opposite. 'Is it to discuss my offer of backing the Artists' Studios?'

Dee nodded. 'Yes, Kenny told me all about it. It's a great idea but I wanted to ask if you've made provision in your development for accommodation for the locals.'

Gordon frowned. 'What do you mean? This housing project will be of enormous benefit to Port Telwyn. It will really put it on the map, and make it a tourist attraction on par with St Ives or Newquay. Actually, I've been quite frustrated by the local response, given it will bring people into the area, providing jobs and accommodation.' He folded his arms and leaned back in his chair. 'And a condition for purchasing the apartments is that they are actually lived in. There will be a clause that they aren't to be sublet as holiday homes.'

'I noticed that, but a lot of locals won't be able to afford that accommodation,' Kenny pointed out. 'And Port Telwyn is a small village, we don't have the infrastructure to support an enormous build like this. We'll need another school, doctors—'

'The council is on board so I'm sure they are aware it will have to provide more facilities. They've agreed that it's a good idea, bringing job opportunities and income to the area, and without that the locals will have to leave to find work,' Gordon told them.

'The locals will have to leave anyway. The apartments are way out of their price range. Unless you provide some affordable housing for locals to buy or rent,' Dee pointed out.

'I'm running a business, Dee,' Gordon reminded her. 'I owe it to my shareholders to make a profit.'

'A business that will benefit from looking out for local people. You can't just come into an area like this, give a bit of cash for the artist project to sweeten the locals, and not think about their needs,' Dee retorted.

She saw the surprise in Gordon's eyes as he sat up a bit straighter.

'Have you any idea how difficult it is for the local people to find somewhere they can afford to rent? They're having to move out of an area they grew up in.' She was on a roll now. 'We have a friend with a young daughter, a local artist. He's a widower and the landlord has recently increased his rent *again*.' She knew that Gordon's own daughter had been widowed at an early age, leaving her with two children, so she hoped he would have some sympathy here. 'Plus, there's all the inconvenience the locals are having to put up with while you build your development. The access road is often blocked with diggers and lorries, then there's the noise and upheaval.'

'Point taken.' Gordon nodded. 'It seems to me that you've thought a lot about this so what exactly have you decided I should do?' Was that admiration she heard in his voice?

'Well...' she glanced at Kenny, wondering if she's said too much but he was looking at her admiringly too. 'We've had a look at some figures.' They'd both spent hours planning this yesterday.

Gordon listened intently as Kenny took a folder out of his backpack and outlined their plan, suggesting that the area at the rear of the proposed development, nearer to the town, could be reserved for people who actually live locally or can prove that they come from this area.

'Means tested of course so that they go to those who need it most,' Dee added.

'These are the sort of prices people can afford,' Kenny handed him a piece of paper. 'The buyers paying top price will have the sea views and the bigger apartments, of course. But you're far more likely to get the locals behind you if you can cater for their needs too.'

Dee could see that Gordon was studying the figures. 'It's an interesting proposition. Give me a while to consider it and think over the numbers.'

'Thank you.' Dee breathed a sigh of relief.

'I'm still happy to donate to the Artists' Studios, that will be a gift. This,' he pointed to the proposal, 'will be a business decision. I'll get my people onto it, see if we can make it work. I can't promise to match these figures but I'm with you on the idea of providing for the locals.' His gaze went from one to the other. 'This friend of yours who has to leave his property soon... You say he's an artist. Does he have another job?'

'He's a part-time bartender, he has a young daughter to look after, so can only work in the daytime,' Kenny said.

Gordon nodded. 'He needs something quickly then.'

Dee saw his point, affordable housing would be too late for Glenn. 'He might be able to get something temporarily, in the meantime. And there are plenty of others like him,' she said quickly.

Gordon stood up. 'I promise you I'll give it some thought.' He stepped out from behind the desk, and shook Kenny's hands. 'I'll be in touch.' Then he gave Dee a hug. 'Nice to see you again, Dee. Take care of yourself.'

As soon as they were outside, Kenny gave a whoop of joy. 'That went really well. With Gordon's input we can finish the

Artists' Studios and open them up.' He hugged Dee. 'And it's all thanks to you!'

She laughed, more to cover the feelings that were sweeping through her at his embrace. 'Of course it wasn't, you played your part too.'

'I can't wait to tell the others. I'll WhatsApp the group and see if they can meet up tonight. If you're up for that?'

'I'd love to.' She felt like she was walking on air. They had the grant for the Artists' Studios, and she really believed that Gordon would do his utmost to provide affordable housing. 'Do you think Glenn will agree? He might think it's a betrayal to accept money from Gordon. He's been one of the biggest protesters about the development.'

'I don't know,' Kenny said thoughtfully. 'Fancy a drink?' he asked as they neared the town.

'Oh, I can't. Sorry. I've an appointment with my solicitor and then back to the café. But I'll see you in The Pirate's Head tonight.' She would have loved to be able to say yes. It had been such a positive morning and they had a lot to talk about, but she needed to get this divorce moving. Edna would be returning home soon.

The solicitor hadn't heard back from Nigel's solicitor yet but from what Dee told him about Nigel's finances the solicitor was confident that she would get enough to afford a decent cottage for herself, and a regular bit of pension each month, too, which would keep the wolf from the door.

It had been a good day all round.

* * *

After work, Dee set off for the Slaters' to take Betsy for a walk, stopping to have a cup of tea and a chat with them. Then went home for a shower before heading to The Pirate's Head.

Kenny had waited for her before telling everyone the news, and it was greeted with claps and cries of 'well done' by everyone except Glenn. He was sat with a face like thunder, arms crossed. 'Well, you come sailing down here, wave your magic wand and think you can put everything right. This bloke is only saying he's thinking about it because he knows you. He'll dangle you on a thread, then say he can't afford to do it, you'll see. Meanwhile, the protests will have lost their momentum, and the building work will carry on.'

'Gordon has always been a man of his word. If he can do it, he will,' Dee said.

'He's a businessman, he's in it for the profit. He thinks he can buy us with a few grand to set up the Port Telwyn Artists' Studios, but how does it help the rest of the villagers? Even if he does make some of the properties "affordable housing", it won't help people like me. I can only work part time, as I've got Sammi to look after, so there's no way I can afford that rent.'

'He's got a point,' Cath said.

Just then Kenny's phone pinged. 'It's from Gordon,' he said, surprised. There was a silence around the table as they all waited for Kenny to read the message.

'He wants to know if Glenn might be interested in a care-taking job with a live-in two bedroomed flat. It's on the ground floor with a garden and will be available in a couple of months, meanwhile there is a mobile unit he can live in. He said that he needs someone to look after the development, starting as soon as possible. And it's a permanent position.'

A silence descended on the table and all eyes turned to Glenn, who was staring at Kenny, speechless.

'Is he serious?' he finally asked.

'He's asked me to tell you to contact him for a meeting ASAP,' Kenny said. 'I can pass you his number if you're interested?'

Glenn seemed to be struggling to make a decision. Cath leaned over and patted his hand. 'Don't let pride get in your way, lovely. This development is going ahead with or without you. You might as well get a job and a roof over yours and Sammi's heads out of it.'

Glenn swallowed, took a swig of his beer, clearly struggling to contain his emotions. His eyes were wet, Dee realised. He was fighting back tears. He must have been so worried about finding somewhere else for him and Sammi to live. Then he nodded. 'Send me the number then, and I'll see what he has to say.'

43

A FEW WEEKS LATER

The sound of her mobile ringing jolted Dee awake on a Sunday morning. Who could be ringing her at this time? She glanced at the clock, eight thirty. She been up early for work all week and had been hoping to get a lie-in. Yawning she reached for her mobile, her breath catching in her throat as she realised it was Annabel calling her.

'Annabel? What's wrong? Is Hallie okay?'

'Yes, but Dad...'

Nigel? Dee sat up straight. 'What about your dad?'

'He's in a bad way, Mum. He's not eating or shaving, and he's drinking far too much. Drinking away his sorrows, no doubt! He's a mess.'

She found that hard to believe. Nigel was always cool, composed, in control.

'You've got to come home, Mum. I dread to think what's going to happen to him. He might have a heart attack. Or a stroke.'

This was nothing short of emotional blackmail. 'You do remember what your dad did, don't you? He had an affair.

Again. He went away with his mates on my sixtieth birthday and he had another affair,' she repeated slowly. 'And you want me to forgive him? Again.'

'I know and it's horrible, but he's really sorry. He really misses you, Mum. Hallie misses you. She wants her nanna and grandpa together again. She's really upset, Mum.'

'That's low, Annabel. You know that I adore Hallie, but you can't blackmail me into staying with your father to make her happy. She has you and Gareth, her parents.' Dee paused. 'Tell me, if Gareth had an affair, would you forgive him and carry on as if nothing has happened?'

'No way!' Annabel retorted, then Dee heard her take a breath. 'But, Mum, you said yourself that you've forgiven Dad before and he really is sorry. He desperately wants you to give him another chance.'

'He's said this before and nothing has changed.'

'He's older now, Mum. He said it was a last fling. Besides, you're both too old to start again. You can't live in that cottage and work in a café for the rest of your life. Surely you miss your lovely home? Your old life?'

'My old life was empty and shallow. I prefer my new life.'

'So you don't care about Dad any more? You don't care if he has a heart attack?' She could hear the tears in Annabel's voice. 'I know Dad has acted terribly but I can't believe you can be this hard.'

Dee sat up in bed thinking when Annabel had ended the call. She had hardly heard from Nigel since she'd told him she wanted a divorce, she'd presumed that he'd accepted her decision and was as glad to get out of their mockery of a marriage as she was. Had it affected him more than he had let on? Was he really upset, drinking away his sorrows, as Annabel had said.

Finally, she decided that she would go back and check on

him. There were still a lot of her things in the house, she could use the excuse that she had come back for those and see if Annabel's concerns were valid.

Texting Kenny to tell him that she would have to miss the meeting tonight, as she had urgent business back in Bristol, she set off after breakfast.

* * *

Nigel's car was in the drive when she got there and the lounge curtains were drawn. She frowned. It was almost midday. Nigel was never home on a Saturday morning, and certainly was never in bed.

She took her key out of her handbag and let herself in, wondering whether to shout to let Nigel know that she was there. Something urged her to keep quiet so she closed the door softly behind her and listened. She couldn't hear anything. She went into the lounge. An empty bottle of Scotch was on the coffee table beside an empty glass. It looked untidy, as if the vacuum hadn't been put around for ages. She frowned and went softly into the kitchen. Dirty crockery and glasses were piled on the draining board, a basket of washed clothes that hadn't been hung out stood by the washing machine. The place looked like a tip. This wasn't like Nigel at all. Maybe her asking for a divorce really had hit him hard.

Suddenly she heard footsteps coming down the stairs. She turned as Nigel stood in the doorway. He clearly hadn't shaved for days and his clothes seemed to hang off him as if he'd lost a lot of weight.

'Dee, you've come home!' he said, holding out his arms for her to step into.

She couldn't. She couldn't take a single step towards him. She was astounded that her leaving had had this effect on him. She'd thought he hadn't cared about her, yet clearly he was distressed. She swallowed and licked her lips. 'I came to pick up some more of my things...'

He looked crestfallen. On the verge of tears. Calm, always in control, Nigel looked as if he was going to break down. 'You're not going again, are you?' He gasped, clutched his chest and staggered over to the chair, almost collapsing into it.

'Nigel? Are you okay? Do you need me to call you a doctor?'

He swallowed. 'I don't need a doctor. I need you. You will come back, won't you?' His eyes searched for hers, held them. 'Please say you will. It was a mistake with that woman. A stupid mistake. She meant nothing to me. You're the only one who means anything to me. You're the only one I need. I love you so much and I swear that I will never cheat on you again. If you give me another chance I'll do everything in my power to make you happy.'

Astounded, she sat down beside him. It had been a long time since Nigel had told her he needed her. That he loved her. She felt blindsided. He'd cheated on her time and time again. Treated her as if she was nothing. Yet...

Nigel reached out and grabbed her hand. 'Please say you'll come back. Please. I can't live without you.'

Dee thought of Port Telwyn, and Snowy, of Kenny, Andi and the others, working in Moira's Café, of the new life she'd started building for herself. How happy she was living down there. She couldn't give all that up.

Yet she couldn't bear to see Nigel like this. After all the years they'd been together. Their children, little Hallie. She at least owed him the chance to talk.

'Why don't you go and have a shower then we can talk about things. See if we can sort something out,' she suggested. 'I'll make us a drink and some scrambled eggs and toast.'

He got slowly to his feet. 'Thank you. You won't regret it.'

She watched dumbfounded as he walked slowly out of the kitchen. It was like looking at a different man, as if he had aged ten years. Had she done that to him?

She put the kettle on, and loaded up the dishwasher as she waited for the kettle to boil. She decided to take Nigel's coffee up to him. As she pushed open the bedroom door she heard Nigel's voice, clear as day, on the phone.

'She's fallen for it, hook, line and sinker. All I have to do is keep her here until the contract is signed and then we can be together. Only one more week, darling.'

She froze, almost dropping the mug. What was going on?

She walked closer to the bedroom. 'It was so clever of you to suggest not shaving and wearing larger clothes so that it looked like I've lost weight. Annabel was really shocked when she came! I knew she would tell Dee and Dee would come running back. She's so gullible.' She heard him give a little laugh.

'Yes, Steve Connor is signing the contract on Friday, he's a real family man. You know what these Bible Belt Americans are like. He'll pull the deal if he gets wind that Dee is divorcing me for adultery.'

Another pause. 'No, don't worry. It's all in hand. She's downstairs right now, making me breakfast.' He gave a triumphant laugh.

Dee pushed the bedroom door open, and Nigel's jaw dropped. 'Actually, she's upstairs, packing the rest of her things. And she's going to send a message to Steve Connor telling him that we're getting divorced and exactly why.'

'What!' Nigel spluttered. 'You've misheard—'

'I know exactly what I heard, Nigel. And I've recorded it so don't try and wheedle your way out of it. Goodbye. I hope you and whoever you're speaking to on the phone will be very unhappy together.'

44

She didn't feel any sadness, only relief, as she drove back down to Cornwall. She was now rid of Nigel forever and free to live her own life. True, they would always have the connection of the children, Hallie and any other future grandchildren, but his decisions no longer influenced hers. He could play golf whenever he liked, go and have an affair with whoever he liked.

And so could she.

The thought sneaked into her mind, along with an image of Kenny. She was about to push it away but instead she let it stay there, linger for a moment. The car behind her sounded its horn, reminding her that the traffic lights had now changed to green, and she set off again. She couldn't wait to get back down to Primrose Cottage and her Nigel-free life.

She'd messaged Kenny earlier and told him that she couldn't make the meeting this evening but now she could, so when she arrived at the cottage she messaged again to tell him her plans had changed again.

He phoned her immediately. 'Is everything okay? I got the impression that you had to go home urgently.'

'I thought I did, but it turns out that it was a false alarm.'

'I'm about to walk Toffee, fancy joining me and telling me all about it? Or not, whichever you prefer.'

A walk along the beach was just what she needed. 'Sure. I can be there in fifteen minutes, if that's okay?'

'Perfect. I'll wait by the harbour for you.'

Dee quickly changed into jeans, T-shirt and trainers then messaged Andi to tell her that she was back and would pick Snowy up in an hour or so.

When she reached the harbour, she saw Kenny standing in front of a newly erected board. It said:

Lyndon Developments, we build homes not houses

Kenny rubbed his chin. 'Gordon isn't too bad, after all. I get the impression he really does care.'

Dee looked around. It was wild, rugged and beautiful. She could see why Glenn and many others were against the development. But it was a lot of unused land, and people needed homes. It would be great if Gordon could provide some homes for the local people.

'It will bring in a lot of money and jobs,' she reminded him gently. 'And it does look like a beautiful development. It will be a big attraction.'

Kenny shrugged. 'I guess you can't stop progress. Come on, let's walk the Towans.'

Kenny took Toffee off the lead as soon as they were on the sand dunes and the lanky mongrel hurtled off barking and wagging his tail wildly. Betsy would enjoy it up here, too, Dee thought, she would have to bring her one day.

As they walked, they talked. Dee told Kenny all about Nigel's latest trick and he was outraged on her behalf, saying it was a terrible stunt to pull. 'I hope you get a fair divorce settlement from him, it doesn't seem like you can trust him. He'll probably pull every stunt in the book.'

'He won't, because I know a bit too much about his dodgy business practices, he won't want his business partner knowing about them or his latest stunt. All I want is half the house and my possessions. The rest he can keep.'

'You're entitled to more than that, surely? What about a share of his pension, and he must have a bit of money in the bank.'

Dee gazed across the Towans down to the sea below. 'My solicitor said the same, and if he can do that without too much hassle, then good. But I don't want to fight for anything. Half the money from the sale of the house so that I can buy myself a new home will do me. I've got some savings myself and working at the café will tide me over for a bit.' She turned to him. 'I just want to be free to start my own life and leave Nigel to live his.'

Kenny nodded. 'I understand.'

For a moment his gaze held hers, then he turned away to call Toffee to heel. The dog came immediately and Kenny stooped to attach his lead on his collar.

Dee watched him. 'I'll have to bring Betsy along next time and introduce her to Toffee.'

'That's a great idea.' Kenny stood up and turned back to her, holding the lead carefully in his hand. 'Time to get back, I think.'

They walked back in companionable silence, both deep in their thoughts. It was on the tip of Dee's tongue to ask Kenny if anything was bothering him, but she held back. It seemed intrusive, he'd tell her if he wanted to share. Besides, she'd agreed to drop in and pick up Snowy from Andi.

Andi was about to close up as Dee walked in. Snowy was curled up on a chair.

'Hello, Snowy.' Dee sat down by the cat and he purred contentedly. 'How's he been?' she asked.

'Perfectly happy. I think he's adopted this as his second home,' Andi said. 'The customers are all taken with him.'

'The little traitor,' Dee said with a smile. 'Honestly, Snowy will miss all this attention when Edna comes home.' She resolved to check on Edna's progress as soon as she could.

Andi came over with two cups of coffee and a plate of biscuits, putting them down on the table where Dee was now sitting. 'I thought you might need this,' she said, sitting in the chair next to her.

'Thank you, I do,' Dee replied.

'How did things go with Nigel?' Andi asked.

'It was a set up,' Dee told her. Andi had become a good friend in the short time she'd known her and Dee felt very comfortable telling her what had happened with Nigel.

'The toerag!' Andi retorted. 'How low can you get? I'm glad you saw through him.'

Dee rubbed her forehead with her fingers. She couldn't believe how easily she'd been taken in, but also how devious Nigel had been. 'Me too. I didn't want to go back but I was so worried by what Annabel said I thought I should. And Nigel looked really awful when I turned up at the house so I could see why Annabel was taken in. I almost was.'

'It's an old trick, not shaving and wearing bigger clothes, I saw a programme about coercive control and apparently a lot of men do it, try to make their partners feel guilty so that they go back to them.' Andi bit into a biscuit and chewed it before adding. 'It's a good job you took him that cup of coffee upstairs and overheard him.' She leaned forward. 'If I was you, I'd take him for every penny you can get. He doesn't deserve to get away with how he's treated you.'

'Enough money to get myself a little cottage will do me,' Dee said. 'I can provide for myself.' At least, she hoped she could. She had a good few years yet before she got her pension. Thank goodness Nigel had run her through the books as his secretary until he joined this new company a few years ago, so she had a pension coming. It had been a tax saving device for him and she'd never drawn a wage but to be fair she'd always had a card to their joint bank account and had been free to draw out what she wanted, until he recently stopped her card, that was.

'I've meant to ask, have you heard how Edna's getting on?' Dee asked.

'I have, and actually she wants you to phone her.' There was glint of something in Andi's eyes. 'Phone her now if you like, I don't mind.'

Something in her manner made Dee dial Edna's number. Edna answered after a couple of rings, she sounded very sprightly. 'Hello, dear, how's Snowy being?' she asked.

Dee filled her in. 'And how are you? You sound much better.'

'Oh, I am. It's done me the world of good to stay with Mabel. We're both rattling around alone in our houses and it's been good for us both to have company. In fact—' she paused. 'I wanted to talk to you, dear, because we've decided that we're going to live together permanently. I'm selling my cottage and going to move in with Mabel.'

'You're moving away from Port Telwyn?' Dee asked in surprise. She knew that Edna had lived there most of her life.

'I am. It's a pretty village, dear, but that hill is a killer, and it's a lonely life now. Martin rarely comes to see me, he's so busy working. Mabel has a modern apartment overlooking the sea here in Brean, it's so much easier to keep clean and there's so much to do. I'm going to give her half the proceeds from the cottage so that it's both our apartment, and some of the money to Martin, which will help him get on the housing ladder. That will keep him happy. Mabel is giving some of the money I pay for my share of the apartment to her children to make life easier for them now. It makes perfect sense to help our children when we're alive, and they need it, rather than to make them wait for us to peg it. Although, we're keeping a contingency fund for our old age, of course.'

Dee was really taken aback but she could see why Edna had made this decision. She must have been lonely, and was probably scared that she might fall or be taken ill again and not be discovered so quickly. 'What about Snowy?' she asked.

There was a pause. 'I was wondering if you might be able to find a home for him? He's a lovely cat, but I don't think he will settle in Brean. I'm worried that he might run off.'

'I can keep him if you want. I'm hoping to buy somewhere in Port Telwyn when my divorce is settled. I'd be happy to take Snowy with me,' Dee told her.

'That's another reason I phoned you, dear. Why don't you buy my home?' Edna suggested. 'That would be the perfect solution.'

If only. Edna's cottage might be cluttered, and it needed a few repairs, but it was in a prime position and Dee was sure it would fetch at least £500,000. 'It's a lovely idea but I'm afraid your cottage will be worth far more than I can afford,' she said.

'Let's get it valued and take it from there,' Edna suggested. 'If it was within your price range, would you be interested?'

'Definitely,' Dee told her.

'Then I'll contact an estate agent. It's easier if I give them your name and contact number as you're living there. If that's okay?'

'Of course. Thank you.'

Andi smiled as Edna finished the phone call. 'She told me earlier that she really wants you to have the cottage, she's so grateful to you and Babs for saving her life, and for looking after Snowy for her. She wants Snowy to stay in his own home.'

'That's very kind but I don't want her to lose out financially,' Dee said. 'Primrose Cottage must be worth a fortune.'

'It needs lots of work done on it,' Andi reminded her. 'That will be reflected in the price.' She tilted her head to one side. 'Would you be willing to do all that though? You'd probably have to clear it out too. Edna won't have room in the apartment for all her things. She said that Mabel will bring her down in a couple of weeks so that she can take back what she wants. The rest I'm sure she's hoping to leave.'

Dee thought about the quaint little cottage with its sea views. It's smaller than what she was used to, and was rather dated, but she loved it. She would be so happy to live there and be part of this community. She could take her time clearing it out and modernising it; she was happy to settle for Edna's furniture until she had time to replace it all. She didn't want to get her hopes up though.

'I wouldn't mind at all, but let's see,' she said.

It would be wonderful to live in the pretty cottage, and with Snowy too. Could it be possible that running away had turned out to be running towards her future?

45

The estate agent arrived the next morning. He walked around everywhere, making notes, and seemed to be taking a long time.

'It's very old-fashioned, as you must be aware. The bathroom needs updating, it needs central heating, and could do with new windows. I'll work out some figures and message you within the hour with what I think is a reasonable price,' he told her.

Dee waited eagerly for his message, trying to imagine herself living here. She walked around the cottage, assessing every room and what needed doing. The estate agent was right, the cottage did need a lot of money spent on it. Even if she could afford to buy Primrose Cottage, would she have enough funds for all the work it needed?

When the estate agent finally messaged Dee with the price she was delighted to see that she could afford it from her divorce settlement. They'd received Nigel's financial disclosure now and her solicitor had told her what figure to expect. It was enough to pay for the cottage but what about all the alterations she needed to make. Should she go for it or look for something cheaper?

She was still deep in thought when she went to meet Kenny

later that afternoon. Gordon had contacted Kenny to say that he'd thought about the affordable housing for locals scheme and it was something he was really interested in and wanted to discuss it with them further. They arranged the meeting for today as it was Dee's day off from the café this week. Gordon had wanted them to meet him at the site this time and asked them to wear sensible shoes. He greeted them wearing a hi-vis jacket, hard hat and boots, and gave them both a hard hat and hi-vis jacket to wear. 'Safety precautions,' he said.

The site was a hive of activity and a block of apartments had already been built but still needed decorating and appliances installed. 'This is the one Glenn will be living in,' Gordon said. 'Whilst he's caretaker the rent will be heavily subsided, but the flat is his for as long as he likes. The rest of this block will be affordable housing. Anyone who lives in Port Telwyn, or was born here and would like to move back, will be able to apply for one of these. There will be fifty homes.' He mentioned the rent and Dee and Kenny both gaped.

'That's very generous,' Kenny said.

They were both impressed as Gordon showed them around the site, pointing out where various things were going to be.

'It's going to be amazing,' Dee said.

'I'm glad you think so,' Gordon said with a smile.

As Kenny went off to look around the gardens, Gordon called Dee back. 'I wanted to talk to you alone. Keep this between ourselves but I'd also like to offer you one of the apartments at a discount, for old times' sake.' He mentioned a price that was definitely within her price range. 'It's not one of the affordable apartments for the locals so if you ever go on to sell the apartment there will be a clause that the discounted amount is to be repaid to me,' he said. He handed her his card. 'Think about it and call me if you're interested.'

Dee was gobsmacked. Two offers of a permanent home within a few days. What should she do? She loved Edna's cottage but it did need a lot done to it, whereas the apartments were modern and spacious, and Gordon had told her that one would be ready to move into within a month. Imagine living here, waking up to the beautiful sea view every morning.

Then she thought of Edna's cottage. It had so much character and was right in the centre of the village. She felt so at home there. And it was Snowy's home. She adored the little cat. Would they both be happy in an apartment?

She was genuinely torn.

'You've gone quiet,' Kenny said as they walked home.

She considered telling him about Gordon's offer but then that would be asking him to keep the secret too. Her mother had always said if you want to keep something a secret, then tell no one. Kenny had entrusted her with his secret, she remembered, when Gordon had first approached him offering to donate some money to the Artists' Studios.

What would the others make of Gordon's offer? Would they resent it?

'Look, I don't want to pressure you, if you don't want to talk about it, but if there is something on your mind and you'd like to offload, I promise you that it won't go any further.'

Dee bit her lip. She really would like a second opinion and she trusted Kenny. 'Gordon asked me to keep it between ourselves but I really would like someone to talk to.' She told Kenny about the offer of the apartment, and the repayment clause. 'It's a fantastic offer, and the apartments are beautiful...'

'Do I sense a "but"?'

'Edna is also selling up and staying with her sister in Brean. She's offered me first refusal on her cottage.'

Kenny thrust his hands in his pockets and whistled. 'Wow, two home offers!'

'I know! And now I don't know what to decide. The apartment will be ready in a few weeks. And Edna said that even if I don't want to buy the cottage, I can stay there until it's sold.' She shook her head. 'I really don't know what to do.'

Kenny turned and looked over at the sea. She followed his gaze and they both stood there thinking for a while. Then Kenny turned back to her. 'Dee, you have no one to answer to but yourself, so my advice is to choose whatever will make you most happy. Which home would you be happiest to wake up in, or snuggle up in on winter evenings? Which one does your heart lie in?'

Dee thought about her decision all evening. She walked all around the cottage, taking note of everything that needed to be done. It was a lot. Then again, it didn't need to be done all at once. She could take her time, do it bit by bit, turn Primrose Cottage into the home she wanted.

Meanwhile, the apartment had everything she could wish for and would have a wonderful view, but apart from putting paintings on the wall and furnishing it, she couldn't really give it a personal touch. There was the balcony and the sea view, but she wouldn't be in the centre of the town. There was no pretty front garden and backyard to fill with colourful plant pots.

She was considering phoning Babs to talk it over, when a text pinged in from her. She opened it up and saw a photo of Babs standing proudly beside a large white camper van.

> We've done it, we've bought a camper van!

Babs had messaged Dee a couple of weeks ago to say that

they'd decided to buy a motor caravan to travel around the UK and Europe in.

Dee immediately phoned her. 'It looks fantastic. When did you get it?'

'Today! I can't wait to show it to you. We're going to come and spend a weekend down in Port Telwyn soon. There's a caravan park on the outskirts. It will be so good to see you again.'

'That would be wonderful!' She couldn't wait to see her friend again.

'Now enough about me, what's happening with you? I feel like we haven't caught up for ages.' It had actually been a couple of weeks since they'd had a chat, although they had sent each other little texts.

'I was about to phone you actually. I wanted your advice...'

'Fire away.'

Dee told Babs about Edna giving her first offer on Primrose Cottage, and Gordon offering her a cut-price apartment. She'd kept Babs in the picture about the goings on with the harbour development. 'It's all top secret for now,' she said.

'Wow, that's brilliant. What are you going to do?'

'I don't know. The estate agent has valued the cottage and I can afford it – just. There's a lot to do here though, it drastically needs modernising and the garden is like a jungle.'

'That's not a problem, me and Geoff will help you. You know he's mad on gardening and DIY, and I'm up for a bit of painting. The main thing is, are you happy there?'

'Yes I am. It's so cosy. And I love living in the centre of Port Telwyn.'

'Can you imagine yourself living in a posh new apartment overlooking the sea? It sounds amazing, but is it you? It would probably be Nigel's ideal home. But is it yours? Listen to your heart, Dee. For once do what you want to do. Do what's best for you.'

Which is more or less what Kenny had said. Both of her friends telling her to follow her heart. The trouble is, that wasn't something Dee was used to doing. It felt strange to know that she could make her own decisions, live her life how she wanted.

Long after they'd finished talking, she sat in Edna's armchair, thinking. Then she heard a miaow. Snowy had come home and was perched on the windowsill, demanding to be let in. She went to the back door and opened it. The little cat miaowed, brushed himself against her legs then sauntered in. Dee went outside and sat in the garden, listening to the murmurs of life in the little town.

Suddenly she knew what decision to make. She didn't want a posh apartment. This little cottage was where her heart lay. She telephoned Edna immediately to let her know that she wanted to buy the cottage. Edna was over the moon. They both had wobbles in their voices by the time they'd finished talking.

Then she texted Kenny.

'I think you've made the right decision. Come to The Pirate's Head and let's celebrate,' he told her.

She glanced at the clock on the wall. It was just gone nine o'clock. Why not?

Her friends were all waiting when she arrived, a bottle of fizz in the middle of the table. 'We're celebrating you and Glenn both having new homes,' Andi told her.

Glenn actually smiled at her. 'Sammi and I are temporarily moving into the mobile home on the development tomorrow. Sammi's over the moon. Gordon has showed us the flat he'll be renting to us, it's brilliant and the garden is a decent size, and walking distance to the village and school. It will be ready in a few weeks. And I'll be getting a full time wage. I can't thank you and Kenny enough.'

Kenny and Dee exchanged a smile. 'It was Dee's idea, she was the one who talked Gordon around,' Kenny said.

They all raised their glasses, now containing champagne. 'To Dee.'

Dee felt her face flush. It was so good to feel accepted.

The talk then turned to the Artists' Studios, which would be opening soon. There was going to be a grand opening ceremony and a local celebrity was coming to cut the ribbon.

Everything was working out perfectly.

'Fancy a walk along the beach?' Kenny asked as they left. 'I think Toffee's too restless to go to bed yet.' He'd brought his beloved dog out with him.

Dee nodded. She didn't feel like going home just yet, she didn't want the evening to end. She felt so happy.

'Maybe I'll actually get myself a dog once the cottage is officially mine,' she said. She really enjoyed walking Betsy. 'I'm sure Snowy would soon get used to it, she's very laid-back when people bring dogs into the café.'

'They're good company too,' Kenny agreed. 'I wouldn't be without Toffee.'

They walked along the beach in the moonlight, then somehow Kenny's hand found hers and she left it there, enjoying the feeling of her hand being held. Something she hadn't experienced for a long time. Nigel had been demonstrative in the early years, but that had faded over time and it had been some years since they'd been intimate, never mind holding hands.

The crescent moon was shining over the glistening sea, its reflection floating in the still waters. 'How beautiful it all looks,' Dee murmured.

'Like you, with the moonlight shining on your face,' Kenny said softly. 'I'm so glad we reconnected again, Dee, and that you're going to stay down here.'

It was too dark to see his eyes, but she knew that they were looking into hers and her heart did a flutter. She didn't, couldn't possibly, have feelings for Kenny... Could she? Then his fingers were caressing her cheek, and his head was lowering towards hers, and before she knew it, they were kissing under the moon- light and Kenny had his arms wrapped around her and she didn't want him to let her go.

'I've been wanting to do that for a long time, but I was scared of getting too close to you in case you went back to Nigel or moved away again. It's taken me a long time to fall for someone else.' He paused, placed his finger under her chin and titled it upwards so he could look into her eyes. 'This is where you let me down gently if you don't feel the same way and I promise you there will be no hard feelings or awkwardness. We will carry on being friends and never mention it again, if that's what you want.'

But it wasn't what she wanted. She wanted him to kiss her, caress her. She longed to feel loved, desired again but her mouth wouldn't say the words. She simply stood there, looking at him, trying to say what she felt with her eyes.

'Do you want to come back to mine for a nightcap?' His voice was thick, soft.

She wanted to, but should she? What if she went back with him and ended up in bed with him, then they both woke up in the morning and decided it was a mistake? Or one of them did.

Just do it, she told herself, seize life with both hands.

She stepped up on her tiptoes and kissed him. 'I'd love to,' she said when they both finally broke the kiss.

47

Dee yawned, stretched, then slowly opened her eyes. She felt achy but alive. Who knew that making love could be so... wonderful? She thought back to Andi's comments that 'men all basically did sex the same'. How wrong she was!

Kenny stirred beside her. She leant over and kissed him on the forehead and he snaked an arm around her neck without opening his eyes, gently pulling her towards him, and kissing her soundly. 'Fancy a replay?' he murmured.

Just then Toffee started barking downstairs.

'I think Toffee might have something to say about that,' Dee replied. 'He sounds like he wants to go out.' She glanced at the clock. 'Goodness it's gone ten!'

Kenny opened his eyes then and a slow smile formed on his lips. 'I'll let Toffee out and make us a cuppa, then...?'

His eyes asked the question and she smiled slowly back. 'That sounds like a plan, but right now I need the bathroom.'

'Feel free. There's fresh towels in the cupboard, if you fancy a shower when you're in there.'

She did. She went to the loo then got a surprisingly soft

towel out of the cupboard, hung it on the towel rail by the shower cubicle and stepped inside. As she soaped the suds into her body she closed her eyes imagining Kenny's hands, and tongue, caressing her body last night. Yes, she definitely did want a replay.

She wrapped the towel around herself and padded back into the bedroom as her phone rang. It was Babs. What had happened? She thought in panic, pressing the green button to answer.

'Put the kettle on, we'll be there in ten minutes,' Babs said.

'You're coming to Port Telwyn?' Dee stammered, unable to hide the shock in her voice!

'Yes, we came down to surprise you. I wanted to show you the new camper van and congratulate you on making an offer on Edna's cottage. We left early so we can make a day of it.'

Sugar! Babs and Geoff were on their way to see her! She had to get home quickly!

She was hastily pulling on her clothes when Kenny came back with a tray containing their breakfast.

'Wow! Was last night so bad that you can't wait to get away?' he asked, his eyes twinkling.

'Babs and Geoff are on their way to visit, they will be at Primrose Cottage in a few minutes. I have to get home.'

Kenny placed the tray on the bedside table and sat on the edge of the bed. 'Why not tell them to come here?'

She stared at him. 'What?'

'You don't have to hide our relationship, Dee, especially from your friends.'

He was right, she didn't. And Babs would be pleased for her, she knew she would.

'I'm wearing yesterday's clothes and no make-up,' she remembered.

He kissed her on the nose. 'And you look beautiful.'

She thought of how Nigel had always made her feel inadequate if she wasn't wearing full make-up and dressed immaculately. How different Kenny was. She picked up her phone and texted:

> I'm actually at Kenny's. You're welcome to pop around but you'll have to take us as you find us.

She added Kenny's location. Babs texted right back:

> Hooray!

48

SIX MONTHS LATER

Dee read the letter slowly. That was it then, the divorce would soon be finalised. To her surprise, Nigel had been eager to settle and get the divorce through as soon as possible. She would have enough money to buy Edna's cottage with £50,000 left over, which would cover all the things she wanted to do to the cottage and leave her quite a bit spare. She could probably have fought for more, as her solicitor had pointed out she'd worked unpaid for Nigel for years and helped him build up his business. Nigel still had most of his pension and stocks and shares, but she was happy with what she'd got. She loved this cottage, and living in Port Telwyn. She'd made a wonderful life here. And she had more than enough money to live on as she was working regularly in Moira's Café. Moira had come back to the café now her daughter was better but she had asked Dee to stay on part time, which Dee was happy to agree to.

Loki, Dee's rescue dog, barked at her and Dee patted the little tri-coloured cockapoo's head. 'Yes, it's time for our walk, come on.' She took down the lead from the hook where she kept it and fastened it onto Loki's collar. Then she set off down to the beach. It was out of season now, so Loki could be let off her lead and run free. She really enjoyed that, running in and out of the waves, barking with happiness. Dee no longer walked Betsy because the Slaters' son had bought one of the affordable housing apartments in the new development and he and his wife and children now lived down here. The Slaters were so happy. They popped into the café now and again to say hello and catch up with Dee.

A paper bag floated towards her as they walked along and Dee put it into the rubbish bag she always carried with her when she took Loki for a walk along the beach. They still had regular beach clean-up days, so there wasn't that much litter about, but there was always someone who couldn't be bothered to walk to the nearest bin, and sometimes the sea brought litter ashore.

She heard a shout and turned to see Glenn and Sammi, walking across the sand towards her. She waved to them.

'We've been collecting shells,' Sammi said, showing Dee her bucketful of assorted shells. 'I'm going to wash them and make a treasure box with them.'

Dee smiled. 'Another craftswoman in the making here,' she said to Glenn.

He thrust his hands in his pockets. 'I never did thank you properly for, you know, what you did. Getting me that job and home.'

'It was Gordon's idea.'

'Only because you told him about me, about how hard it is to get reasonably priced accommodation around here. We all owe you, you and Kenny.'

'You don't owe me anything. I'm so grateful how you've all made me welcome and part of the community.'

Glenn nodded. 'Aye, you're one of us now.'

They carried on walking down the beach and Dee and Loki walked over to the new development. So many of the apartments were occupied now, although there were still some to be completed. In a couple of years, it would all be open, new shops, restaurants, leisure facilities. Babs and Geoff had visited again a few weeks ago and they'd been amazed at how the new development was progressing.

'To think you could have lived in one of those posh apartments,' Geoff had said as he gazed at them.

She was glad she'd turned it down though. She was happy in Primrose Cottage, happier than she ever thought she could be. She was happy with Kenny too. He was a gentle soul who gave her love but respected her need for time alone, as she respected his. He was working at the studio this morning, finishing a painting he'd been commissioned to do. They spent a lot of time together but they'd both agreed to keep their own homes, their own personal space. For now anyway.

Babs and Geoff were currently in Wales. They'd taken to spending whole weeks away in their camper van. And they both seemed happier than they had ever been. She was so pleased for them.

Annabel had let it out of the bag that Nigel was going to remarry. To the woman he'd been cheating on her with in Portugal. Apparently he'd been having an affair with her for some time. That's why he'd cooperated with the divorce and settled so quickly. Dee wasn't bothered. She felt sorry for the woman. Or maybe Nigel would treat her better than he did Dee, maybe he really did love her.

'Dad wants Hallie to be bridesmaid, Mum,' Annabel had said, worried that her mother would be upset.

'Of course he does, dear, she's his granddaughter. I don't mind! I have everything I want here.'

Annabel had been surprised and relieved, but it was true. Dee turned back from the development and, calling Loki to her, put her on the lead and set off into the village, stopping off at the Artists' Studios that were buzzing with life. There were twenty units and each one was filled with an artist. Such a variety of crafts. She stopped at the one Kenny was working in, watching him add the final touch to a sunset.

'It's beautiful,' she said in awe. She never lost her admiration for his skill with a brush.

'Thank you.' He stood up, turned to her, wrapped his arm around her shoulders and pulled her in for a kiss. 'There's still one studio space left if you want it.'

She'd started doing her paper crafts again, spending the winter evenings creating collage pictures, paper flowers, beads, a variety of jewellery. Kenny told her they were incredible and tried to encourage her to take some to craft fairs but she wasn't ready yet.

She thought about working here, having her work on display for people to come and look at. She listened to the buzz of the place, the lively atmosphere. Could she really be one of them?

'Try it for six months. What have you got to lose?' Kenny suggested.

She nodded. 'Okay, I will.'

His face broke into a beaming smile. 'Good for you!' Another hug, then he picked up his jacket. 'How about we go for some lunch. I'm starving.'

'Me too,' she said.

Hand in hand they walked down the hill with Loki to The Pirate's Head to meet their friends.

Life had never been so good, Dee thought happily. She glanced at Kenny, he looked almost wistful.

'Penny for them,' she asked.

'I wish I could freeze time. Keep everything like this for ever. I don't want anything to change,' he said.

She kissed his cheek. 'Change isn't always a bad thing. I had to run away, just to find my way home,' she reminded him.

He touched her cheek tenderly. 'You're right there.'

ACKNOWLEDGEMENTS

I am so delighted to be working with my former editor Isobel Akenhead again, and to be writing for the fantastic Boldwood Books. Isobel supported me when I changed genre from writing romance to psychological thrillers, and I am thrilled that she is once again by my side, cheering me on, when I try my hand at writing a golden years novel. Thank you, Iso, for all your support, advice and input.

It takes a whole team to turn a manuscript into a book, including editors, proofreaders, cover designers, sales and marketing people, so a huge thanks to everyone at Boldwood Books for their input. Thanks also to the bloggers, readers and other authors who support me, share my posts, review my books and host me on their blogs. I appreciate you all. Also thanks to the members of the Savvy Writer's Snug and the Boldwood Authors Facebook groups for their support, encouragement and advice.

Finally, but not least, a massive thanks to my husband, Dave, and my family and friends who all support me so much. I love you all.

ABOUT THE AUTHOR

Karen King is the internationally bestselling author of romance, psychological thrillers and women's fiction.

Sign up to Karen King's mailing list for news, competitions and updates on future books.

Visit Karen's website: www.karenkingauthor.com

Follow Karen on social media here:

Boldwood

Boldwood Books is an award-winning fiction publishing company seeking out the best stories from around the world.

Find out more at www.boldwoodbooks.com

Join our reader community for brilliant books, competitions and offers!

Follow us

@BoldwoodBooks

@TheBoldBookClub

Sign up to our weekly deals newsletter

https://bit.ly/BoldwoodBNewsletter

Printed in Dunstable, United Kingdom